Praise for the works o

T0248947

Happiness is a Shade of Blue

Di Pierro maintains the insightful pathos from her first novel with ease as she delves deeper into the disharmony of love. She creates characters who are fully human with their ticks and shortcomings. Characters who we agonize with and about depending on the moment in the storyline. *Happiness is a Shade of Blue* masterfully demonstrates the weightiness of love in all its manifestations. This two-book series is one which I will return to in the future to lose myself in both the writing and the story.

-Della B., *NetGalley*

Just like the first book, *The Lines of Happiness*, the sequel is just as emotional. It tells a story of grief, love, building relationships and moving on. It's a very moving story with bouts of laughter. You'll laugh, but you will also cry. Highly recommend the next instalment, *Happiness is a Shade of Blue*. I really hope we will see more of these characters.

-Jo R., *NetGalley*

The Lines of Happiness

The Lines of Happiness is a beautiful but poignant tale that speaks of loss, bravery in the arduous seasons of healing and a lasting encounter with love when it's least unexpected.

-Nutmeg, *NetGalley*

Lush and poignant are the two words which come immediately to mind to describe this debut novel. The writing itself is lush, luxurious, and brimming with wonderful, exquisite language, images, rural landscapes and rural life, horses and emotional depth. A real little gem of a book lovingly edited and polished. The story is poignant with loss, trauma, grief and coming to terms with it...The author doesn't succumb to the quick and easy "solutions" and stays away from the temptation of "love heals all."

-Henrietta, *NetGalley*

The characters make this tale something special. Both the main and secondary characters are well-developed. I became quite invested in Lo and Gloria especially. They made the novel a must read for me. If you are into deeply serious, thought-provoking love stories, then pick up this book. You won't be disappointed.

-Betty H., *NetGalley*

I sank down into *The Lines of Happiness* and allowed myself to wallow in the fullness of the language. The story of grief, loss and discovering love in an unlikely place is exquisitely written. It reminds me of the elegance of Jane Rule's writing in her novel *Desert of the Heart*. Di Pierro must be blessed with a third eye as her novel speaks of life, grief and love in meaningful poignancy and perception.

Underneath it all, *The Lines of Happiness* is a haunting love story slowly evolving from the devastation bequeathed one family. It is not a typical romance novel encompassing endless activities and interactions between the main characters. *The Lines of Happiness* is a deep dive into our motivations and self-awareness as we fall in love.

Something I am sure most of us have forgotten over time. This is an essential reminder.

-Della B., *NetGalley*

Venetia Di Pierro wrote a beautiful story about loss, grief and finding love and hope when you're close to giving up.

-Anna S., *NetGalley*

The
LAST
WOMAN
I Kissed

VENETIA DI PIERRO

Other Bella Books by Venetia Di Pierro

The Lines of Happiness
Happiness is a Shade of Blue

About the Author

Venetia Di Pierro grew up in the city of Melbourne in Victoria, Australia. She is the author of *The Lines of Happiness*, *Happiness is a Shade of Blue* and *The Last Woman I Kissed*. She has a collection of four leaf clovers, can sense a rainbow before it appears and believes in the power of imagination.

\

The
LAST
WOMAN
I Kissed

VENETIA DI PIERRO

BELLA
BOOKS
2024

First Edition - 2024

Editor: Heather Flournoy
Cover Designer: Kayla Mancuso
Photo credit: Nick Walters (www.nickwalters.com.au)

ISBN: 978-1-64247-585-2

PUBLISHER'S NOTE

For Mum

CHAPTER ONE

Things were pretty good for Cilla. She had a job she enjoyed (librarian wasn't a title that spoke of intrigue or high stakes, but she was mostly happy), a girlfriend who doted on her (well, *doted* might be a strong word, but Georgina had bought her flowers on her birthday), and a house in Twine River (a town she liked). Her golden retriever was pretty special too, probably the best dog she'd ever met, if she were being honest. Yes, she was happy enough.

Wednesday mornings were Cilla's favorite at the library. It was preschool story hour and Apricot, the therapy dog, always came in to enjoy the story with the kids. The only downside was that Roger, Cilla's self-absorbed colleague, liked to hang around creating jobs for Cilla to do so he could play Romeo to long-suffering Penny, who brought Apricot in for the kids.

The library was warm, and Cilla had placed colorful cushions on the ground for the children to sit on. Posters of book jackets were on the walls and the white tables were still unbesmirched by sticky fingers and craft glue. There were already a few parents with young children looking at books or chatting in low voices by the children's corner. Cilla could not see, but could hear, excitable Henry, who usually spent story time rolling around the floor, distracting others or pulling books from the nearby shelves.

On the lawn outside, the sugar maples had begun their fall show: acid yellow, traffic-stopping orange, and lipstick crimson. The morning mist was weaving among their dark trunks and up into the foliage, reminding Cilla of the time she and Georgina had rowed out onto the lake in the mist and Cilla had almost capsized the boat, causing an argument. Cilla squinted at the trees. Perhaps it wasn't such a lovely memory after all.

Her reverie was cut short by Roger's arrival, his cooling dandelion tea in hand. He followed her gaze out of the window. "Reminds me of the curtains we had in the living room as a kid in the seventies. Awful colors."

Cilla remembered her own living room curtains in the seventies, and she opened her mouth to say something in defense of sugar maples in the fall but was cut short by Roger thrusting his mug at her as he stood erect in excitement and licked his fingertips to smooth his eyebrows. "Cilla, did you bring the other chair over by the coffee table?"

Cilla placed the mug on the circulation desk's counter and wiped the spilled dandelion tea from the front of her blue shirt with her sleeve. It had left a damp patch across her left breast. "Not yet. I thought you wanted me to finish organizing the on-holds."

"Never mind that. The children are arriving soon." Roger beamed as he caught sight of the object of his affection through the window. "Go get the chair."

Cilla noticed a poppy seed between his front teeth.

"Pricilla," Roger continued, his tone as condescending as it was directive. And Cilla let the poppy seed moment slide by. "Did that book about the mating procedures of various species come in? I thought perhaps you could display it on the coffee table so Penny has something to flick through while you're reading to the preschoolers. This isn't a criticism, but sometimes your reading pace is slow and the words drag out. All right for small children, I suppose, but not very engaging for the adults."

Cilla felt rising giggles at the idea of Penny being engaged by a book about animal reproduction and had to disguise it in a coughing fit. Roger's attention was on the doorway. "The chair!" he commanded as he breezed off to welcome Penny.

In fact, the book had come in, and Cilla and the junior librarian, Emma, had spent most of Tuesday afternoon howling with laughter about the various animalistic things that Roger was imagining with poor unsuspecting Penny. The baboons particularly resembled Roger with his near-together eyes and prominent nostrils, and they kept finding lines to read aloud then saying to one another in a serious tone, "A good old rogering." Cilla felt slightly bad laughing at Roger when her own sex life had faded and she could use a bit of sprucing up herself— perhaps shed a few pounds, get rid of the fluff on her upper lip, and finally get to the gray roots in her mousy brown hair. She would, this weekend. She would book the hairdresser and go for a jog. She was sure she had some tweezers somewhere. She felt the cool patch of dandelion tea on her shirt and felt less awful. It didn't mean she was going to drag a heavy upholstered chair over to the table, though. Roger wasn't even her boss.

Roger attempted to usher Penny and Apricot past the circulation desk where Cilla was standing, but Penny stopped to say hello. Cilla knew she wasn't supposed to give Apricot treats, but she did like to touch her soft woolly head and scratch underneath her chin. Penny's cherubic cheeks were pink, making her very blue eyes bluer. She was such a kind, benign woman that Cilla couldn't picture anyone having animalistic urges to baboon her, but Roger's hovering presence was evidence to the contrary.

"Can I get you a coffee?" Cilla asked.

"The chair!" Roger muttered from one side of his mouth, making eyes over Penny's shoulder.

Cilla, who knew that Roger only wanted the chair so he could cozy up to Penny in the seat next to her and talk over Cilla's story, pretended not to hear.

"No, thank you, Cilla. Sorry, Roger, I don't mean to be rude, but you're a little close and Apricot isn't sure how to interpret that."

"Right, right. The dog. Pricilla, if you would be so kind as to get the chair for Penny, as you were asked to."

"I prefer to be on the floor with the children. Thanks, Cilla. I'll go grab a cushion before they're covered in crumbs."

Thankfully, Roger's accusing look at Cilla was blocked by a patron coming to check out some books.

Cilla began her walk home that afternoon along Main Street, making vows to get up early in the morning and go for a jog before work. Georgina was always telling her how her health would improve if she joined the gym or did a juice cleanse. Cilla found the gym equipment confusing but she could probably drink juice for a day. The ground was still soggy from yesterday's rain, and fallen leaves littered the gutters. Cilla admired the front yards at the tail end of Main Street as she walked. Some people put so much effort into their gardens. She turned down Time Street, where her own house was in the middle of the strip looking like a child with a dirty face and overgrown bangs in comparison to some of its tidy counterparts. She should do some yard work. It was on her list. The light was falling from the sky in an orange pool, but on a whim, Cilla passed her own house and kept walking toward where the street curved around on itself and the lawns became wider and the houses farther back from the road. The last one on the block was Cilla's favorite: an original Queen Anne-style house called Hollyoaks. The house itself was pale gray with decorative white trim, bay windows, intersecting roof lines, and dark-gray patterned shingles. It was the unexpected asymmetrical lines and turrets that captured Cilla's imagination, and she liked the way the overgrown garden and mature trees only made it seem more mysterious. She wanted to get a closer look, but she'd never been brave enough to pass beyond the leaning picket fence. A light flicked on in the front ground-floor window, and Cilla tripped over the uneven ground on the road in her haste to retreat, saving herself with her hands and muddying the knee of her jeans. The only thing more intriguing than Hollyoaks was its owner, whom Cilla had never spoken to but seen around town, always looking like she had been transplanted from another era—the seventies perhaps, like Roger's parents' curtains, only a hundred times more glamorous with eclectic clothing, jangling jewelry, and long dark hair. Georgina said the woman rarely left her house because she was a drug addict, and Roger said she ate pigeons because she couldn't afford food and danced naked around the trees in the yard in fertility rituals. Cilla wasn't sure what the woman would want with a fertility ritual, but she supposed Roger was overly focused on matters of reproduction. As she stumbled away in the fading light, Cilla couldn't help giggling to herself at Roger's attempts that day to foist his book upon Penny. Much to Roger's dismay, the book had found its way into little Laura's hands, who would not relinquish it because it had a photo of a giraffe in it, and Laura's mother had checked it out of the library.

CHAPTER TWO

Cilla pushed the front door open and was met by a speeding furry object attempting to lick her face and headbutt her legs, all while being propelled by his own tail spinning circles like a helicopter blade.

"Benson!" Cilla patted his head with one hand and unwrapped her beige scarf with the other.

The golden retriever bowed up and down as he leaped, trying to hurry her along the hall to the kitchen where she might begin to cook and give him some scraps. She felt sorry for him being alone all day. She had asked Georgina if she would mind taking him for a walk if she was free, but his leash was still hanging on the coat rack, exactly where she had left it yesterday. Which reminded her—she had forgotten to check her phone. She followed Benson along the short hallway to the kitchen and turned the lights on. She was starving. Not even eating all the leftover cookies from story time had helped—now she just felt full of remorse and hunger. She opened the freezer and pulled out a microwave meal.

"Terrible, I know," she said to Benson, who wagged his tail encouragingly. Cilla put the meal in the microwave but could feel Benson's brown eyes tracking her every movement. "Come on, then. Get your ball."

Benson bounced off to get his chewed tennis ball and Cilla took him outside to play fetch back and forth until the chill against her skin had faded and her shoulder was tired. They went back inside, Cilla's fingers spread wide in anticipation of washing the dog slobber from them.

"Oh, geez!" She jumped as she entered the kitchen because Georgina was sitting at the round table, her phone in one hand, a bag of takeout on the table in front of her.

"You haven't responded to my messages," Georgina said by way of greeting.

"Oh, I think my phone is still on silent from work. Let me get it."

"There's no point now, I'm here." Georgina flicked her blue eyes to the ceiling and gave her head one shake. "Anyway, how was work?"

Cilla washed her hands at the sink, aware of Georgina pushing Benson away with her foot. "Good. Penny was there with Apricot."

Georgina looked at her properly, her eyes traveling over her muddied jeans and tea-stained shirt. "You look like you've been tilling the fields."

Georgina, on the other hand, looked fresh from a salon, her silvery blond hair perfectly bobbed, her face made up like she was going out for the evening.

Cilla looked down at her own disheveled appearance. "Roger splashed his tea on me, and I tripped over on my way home. I should go get changed."

Georgina was already looking back down at her phone. "You could have done that already. The food will get cold."

Cilla blinked at the frost in Georgina's tone and Georgina looked up, her face softening. "There's a chardonnay in the fridge. I thought white would suit the prawn pasta."

Cilla heard her father's voice in her head warning her never to eat seafood inland, but she knew she was being awful so she took some bowls from the cupboard and surreptitiously threw the microwave meal in the trash.

"How was your day?" Cilla asked, sitting down opposite Georgina and accepting the glass of wine she had poured.

Georgina clanked her glass against Cilla's. "Cheers. I sense a bidding war for the weird little house in Huesville, a tenant for eleven Main Street, and you know that ugly brick thing next to the church? Selling it."

"What do you mean?"

"The owners originally gave it to Michael to sell but he's had no traction, so I've got it."

"A good day, then?"

Georgina popped a prawn into her red-lipsticked mouth and looked off to the side as though thinking. "Yes."

Cilla chewed on a prawn and tried to decide whether it tasted funny. Georgina was churning through her food like it was a competition. She drained her wineglass and pointed at Cilla. "You have parsley in your teeth." Cilla tried to pick it out with a fingernail as Georgina continued, "Don't forget we have Vince's birthday drinks tomorrow night."

"Shit." Cilla found the piece of parsley with her tongue and loosened it.

"I knew you'd forget," Georgina said triumphantly, refilling her own wineglass. "Did you pick up the black dress from the cleaners?"

"The…" Cilla tried to remember a conversation about a dress and came up short. Benson thrust his whiskery face onto her lap, hoping for a prawn, but Cilla had hidden them under the remaining spaghetti in her bowl. "Was I supposed to pick up your dress from the cleaners?"

"Yours. Your dress. I thought you were going to put in a bit of effort for once. There are some events that require more than an old shirt and a pair of jeans. It's not that I care how you look, it's just that…don't you want to feel better about yourself?"

Cilla had to admit that she was letting their side down. Georgina always looked immaculate, even without trying. Cilla looked at the breakfast dishes by the sink and the wilted flower bouquet on the sill. She did walk around most of the time looking like a farmer during crop season. She repositioned her wineglass to cover an oil stain on the white tablecloth. "You're right. I might color my hair tonight."

Georgina beamed, showing very even white teeth. "You are beautiful when you make an effort. Everyone will be there, and I want to show you off."

Cilla had hoped that Georgina might stay and watch a romantic comedy, but Georgina left to put some fake tan on for tomorrow's drinks. Cilla had given up trying to fight her pale skin but thought it was probably time to wage war on her gray hairs. Luckily, she had a home color kit that was named "Caramel Café Deluxe," which sounded like a Starbucks beverage. She examined the tips of her pale-brown hair and hoped her natural color was somewhat deluxe and not mousey brown, as her mother used to call it. As she applied the mixture in the bathroom, careful not to splatter it over the old porcelain basin, she couldn't help but notice lines across her forehead that surely hadn't been there before. She blinked against the fumes from the color. It was lovely that Georgina wanted to show her off. It wasn't often that they went out together, and Cilla was always slightly awestruck to be around such a beautiful woman. They had planned to move in together, but after two years of promises Cilla had let the idea go. She did get the bed to herself most nights, which was poor consolation, and Benson was an excellent electric blanket when she was lonely, which was far more often than she liked to admit. Georgina had said that it was important to keep a little mystery in the relationship, but sometimes Cilla wasn't sure where mystery ended and loneliness began.

CHAPTER THREE

Cilla had slept in, leaving the jog a casualty in the morning rush. It had put her off-balance for the day, and she didn't notice she had a splodge of brown on her forehead from the hair dye until she saw her reflection in the bathroom mirror at work. She rubbed at it with a paper towel and some hand soap, but it stayed stubbornly present despite her efforts. Her hair had turned an alarming shade of rust that she hoped would fade after some vigorous shampooing.

In the lunchroom at midday, Emma peered through her thick glasses at Cilla's forehead. "It looks sort of like Italy backward."

Cilla tried to shift back away from Emma's warm breath on her cheek. "I don't want a geographically incorrect tattoo of Italy on my face."

"I could add a backward Sicily down the bottom. It would look better in a mirror." Emma flopped back into the chair and picked up her chicken salad sandwich. "Everyone likes pizza. And coffee. Did Italians invent coffee? I don't know."

"I promised Georgina I'd make an effort for the birthday. Is the mark really obvious?"

Emma moved her head from side to side. "You could wear a beret?"

"I don't have a beret. Plus, that would look stupid. I want to look like I'm worthy of being on Georgina's arm."

Emma made a face into the crumbs on her plate. "More like Georgina should be worthy of taking you out."

Cilla despondently spooned another blob of yogurt into her mouth. She was trying not to eat too much so she wouldn't be bloated. "She's lovely when you get to know her."

Emma raised her brows and scrunched her little nose up.

Roger's face popped around the doorframe like a disgruntled meerkat. "It's very busy, ladies. I need one of you out here now. Cilla!"

Cilla and Emma exchanged a sideways look and Cilla stood and threw the remainder of her yogurt into the trash under the watchful eye of Roger, who liked to ensure immediate compliance. There was a woman standing at the circulation desk looking around, presumably because Roger had left the area to get Cilla, and two teenagers on the computers. Roger observed that Cilla had noticed the woman at the desk and immediately moved away to straighten a book on a display shelf. Cilla smiled and took slow breaths as she scanned the woman's books. Roger could have his way in the library, but she wouldn't let him have his way with her emotions.

"I loved this book," Cilla said to the woman, pausing to admire the cover of the historical romance by Marena Orellebowl. "The ending is very satisfying." Getting to order any books she wanted was a perk of the job. She had ordered all of the Highgate Village mystery series for the library. She loved that the romance between the main characters carried throughout the books.

"I've only read the first one, but I loved it."

Cilla scanned the book and handed the woman the stack she was borrowing. "Apparently, the author writes them all by hand."

"So some poor soul has to type them out on the other end." The woman laughed.

Cilla watched the woman walk out. Her mood had elevated again. That's why she loved her job—she got to interact with people and talk about books all day. Roger was just a little fly caught in the folds of the curtains, slightly obscuring her view and making a buzzing sound.

* * *

Cilla arrived at Georgina's townhome at exactly six in the evening and rang the bell. It had started to gently rain and Cilla could feel her straightened carroty hair joyfully stretching itself, ready to kink. On the plus side, the fine mist of rain looked atmospheric in the streetlights. Cilla wrapped her raincoat tighter around herself as she waited. She hadn't managed a dress, but she had wriggled into her black pants and a sheer black shirt that highlighted the good bits and covered the rest. She was about to ring the bell again when the door opened and Georgina greeted her in a robe. She kissed Cilla, careful not to press against her and get damp from Cilla's jacket.

"You look nice, but you can't wear that old thing. Take my black wool one instead, if you can squeeze in." Georgina turned and marched through the entryway into the living room. "God." She took another look at her under the downlights. "What happened to your hair?"

Cilla smoothed a palm over her head. "The carton said caramel."

"More like pumpkin soup. Sit, I've poured you some bubbles. Something last night didn't agree with me. I think it is your wine glasses from that old sponge you use to wash the dishes."

"I…" Cilla trailed off as Georgina left the room. She blinked at the spot where Georgina had been and pictured the blue sponge on the sink at home. She supposed it was time to replace it, but she always rinsed it out and let it dry. Surely not. She picked up the glass of champagne and took a sniff. Georgina's crystal champagne flute didn't smell of anything except maybe dishwashing tablets. Cilla relaxed back against the cream leather couch and looked at the paintings of various famous cityscapes in blues and grays on the wall. Georgina was a talented artist. Cilla loved looking at the paintings because it reminded her of when she had first started dating Georgina and she had come home from work one day to find a long rectangular painting in Bubble Wrap on the doorstep. Inside the wrap was an oil painting of a Hawaiian beach at sunset. It still hung in Cilla's living room above the mantel even though it didn't particularly match the rest of the more bohemian decor. It was the most romantic gesture anyone had ever made toward Cilla. She smiled to herself thinking about it. Those days were alive in Cilla's mind, the way the world had seemed lit up and everything felt as though it had been sprinkled with sugar. She realized her glass was leaning in her hand and straightened it, quailing at the thought of spilling on the dove-gray carpet.

"It's after six," she called.

"We have plenty of time," Georgina called back, making Cilla roll her eyes at the memory of the three messages she had received on her cell phone telling her not to be late.

When Georgina walked into the room, dropping her lipstick into her silver clutch, Cilla forgot to be annoyed and was grateful to be in the presence of such a stunning woman. Georgina looked like she had stepped from old Hollywood; she had on a pale-blue dress that brought out the violet in her eyes and showed off her slender figure. Georgina snapped her purse shut.

"I think I've gone down a dress size. Everything I ate went straight through me today. You need to invest in a dishwashing machine, and a hairdresser. You can't cut corners on everything." She rubbed her lips together to smooth out her red lipstick.

"You look beautiful."

"Thanks. Or at least use really hot water and some new sponges." She reached for Cilla's glass and drained the rest of the champagne, then swept the glass off to the kitchen. "Or it could be your tea towels. Put them in a hot wash!"

"I think it was the prawns," Cilla called back.

Georgina entered the living room and laughed. "That was thirty-dollar spaghetti. It wasn't the prawns."

* * *

The Saint Nobody was an old grain store that had been repurposed as a bar. The exposed brick and warm lighting gave it a timeless feel, and the cocktail menu was the fanciest the town had seen. Actually, Cilla wasn't sure if old Milligan's Tavern on the other end of the street even had a cocktail menu. The Nobody, as it was known, was only a ten-minute stroll from Georgina's house, which was situated in the newer part of town, accessible to the main strip, but it was too cold and wet to walk, especially for Georgina's satin stilettos. For someone who loved the gym, Georgina didn't particularly like to walk.

"The most practical thing to do is to drop me at the front so the puddles don't ruin my shoes. Oh, there's Vince! Drop me here," Georgina said, already opening the door of Cilla's old Honda, suddenly oblivious to the wet pavement.

Cilla hastily stopped the car. It seemed Vince also wanted to be fashionably late to his own birthday. Vince had on a black tuxedo with gold finishes, a top hat, and a cane in his hand, which he spun in a circle, and did a little dance as Georgina approached. Vince liked to claim that he brought all the gays to the village, which was probably right—Georgina had followed him over. Cilla smiled to herself at the sight of Vince and Georgina already doing the foxtrot like Ginger Rogers and Fred Astaire. She didn't have time to see who else was in Vince's entourage because a car behind her was leaning on its horn.

"Okay, okay," she muttered, putting the wipers on as it started to drizzle again while she looked for a parking spot.

The windows of The Nobody were already opaque with condensation, and the long room was loud with competing chatter and jazz music as Cilla walked in and looked around for Georgina. A male waiter with a tray of sliders paused by her, and Cilla took two. The time for fighting her bloated stomach was officially up.

"Pricilla!"

Cilla turned toward the loud shriek to see Sam, whom she'd dated briefly before Georgina and who was intelligent and attractive but kissed like she was fishing for vital organs with her tongue. Sam was with her current partner, Lisa, who was from the city and, thankfully, not part of the small pool of local lesbians. Cilla had tried to gently guide Sam toward a less intrusive kissing style, but it hadn't worked. She smiled at Lisa, wondering if she'd had more luck. Cilla wanted to sit down, but instead they got drinks and stood by the bar. Cilla was conscious of wishing Vince a happy birthday, but she could see he was loudly holding court over a group of men at the other end of the bar. As Cilla's eyes traveled the room, they lit on an unexpected figure with long dark hair in the shadows of the fire escape. Was that the woman who lived at Hollyoaks? A tall man moved in front of Cilla's line of vision, and then Georgina came sailing through the crowd holding two glasses of sparkling. She passed one to Cilla, and Cilla hoped she had forgotten the story about Sam's organ-harvesting attempts because she was liable to make a public joke out of it.

"Hello, Sam, Lisa. I thought I'd come say hi before things get wild. You know what Vince is like. I keep expecting the floor to be cleared for a drag show, or a naked man to pop out of a cake."

Cilla grimaced at the thought of a naked man being anywhere near cake.

"Vince is finding a house for us. Sam's is too small for both of us," Lisa volunteered.

"You're moving here?" Cilla asked. Without meaning to, she was automatically doing mental mathematics trying to figure out how long Lisa and Sam had been together. About a quarter of the time she and Georgina had been together.

"Well." Sam held up Lisa's hand, displaying an engagement ring.

Georgina turned Lisa's hand sideways to make the diamond catch the light. "Oh, I love it. Oval cut is classic." She reached for Sam's hand. "Show me yours."

"Georgina," Sam joked. "Not now, I'm almost a married woman." But she obediently offered her hand.

Georgina laughed and gave Sam's plainer gold ring a once-over. "When's the wedding?"

"I think it'll just be something small for family and friends." Sam looked at Lisa for confirmation. "Probably in the spring?"

Lisa smiled, and Cilla noticed how she looked lit from within.

* * *

On the way home in the car, Georgina was tipsy. "I can't believe Sam and Lisa asked Vince to find a house for them."

"I'm still getting over the engagement part."

Georgina adjusted the heat in the car. "I can't imagine being tied down like that. If anyone was to get me down the aisle, I would want a bigger rock than what was on Lisa's finger." She yawned. "I wonder if Sam and Lisa would go for the ugly brick thing next to the church."

CHAPTER FOUR

Outside, the birds were crooning their best hits, and Cilla lay on her side watching Georgina's face softened by the filtered light through the curtains. Georgina's breathing was slow and her face had been gentled with sleep. Cilla wanted to kiss her forehead but she didn't want to disturb her. Last night, they had made wild love like they hadn't in months. What Georgina lacked in tenderness, she made up for in energetic enthusiasm. Cilla's stomach did a cartwheel thinking about it. Sometimes she felt like the luckiest woman in the world. She eased herself from the covers and climbed out of Georgina's Jacobean four-poster. Georgina's dress was lying on the floor, so Cilla draped it over the back of a red velvet chair and put Georgina's slippers on to go and make a cup of coffee.

Georgina had a fancy café-style coffee machine with fifteen different settings. As she listened to the milk frothing, she thought guiltily of Benson at home alone. He could get in and out through the doggy door that she had installed despite the security risk it posed having a Benson-sized hole in the house, but she still didn't like leaving him alone so much. She put some bread in the toaster and went to check if Georgina was awake and might like a coffee, but Georgina was already in the shower. As Cilla was finishing her coffee, Georgina came to join her dressed in black leggings and a zip-up black-and-pink long-sleeved top, her short hair pulled back into a tiny ponytail, wisps already escaping at her neck. The arctic blond of her hair always looked striking no matter what color she wore.

"Good morning, beautiful. I made you a coffee," Cilla said, smiling.

Georgina took the glass coffee cup Cilla slid her way across the table and took a sip, still standing. "Thanks. I'm going to the gym. I ate far too many of those mini quiches. Will you go for that run you keep talking about?"

Cilla dropped the last square of toast back on the table. "I could. I mean, Benson would probably love it."

"He would." Georgina took another sip of her coffee then tipped the remainder down the sink. "Come on, then. I want to make the nine a.m. HIIT class." She opened the fridge to get a cold bottle of water and Cilla pushed her chair back to go get dressed.

* * *

Opening the front door at home, Cilla expected Benson to fly at her in tail-wagging joy, but the house was silent. A cold tingle ran along her spine, and she dropped her purse on the side table in the hall and hurried to check the backyard. It was empty. She called his name and looked in every room even though she knew he wasn't there. He occasionally sulked with his back to her if she had been away too long, but he always greeted her. She went back out into the square yard with its one weeping cherry tree, which was leaving its russet foliage all over the soggy lawn, and looked around. There were no holes in the wooden fence. She walked along the side of the house and out to the front yard. Everything looked normal, and she would have noticed if the front gate was open when she came in. She reached into her phone to call Georgina to alert her of the situation, but Georgina's phone went straight to voice mail. She must already be in the class. Cilla went back inside to get her keys and call Emma, because although Emma was young, she always seemed to know what to do.

Emma answered sounding half-asleep.

Cilla's voice came out in a squeak. "Benson is missing. I think he's been dognapped."

Emma cleared her throat, and there were some muffled sounds and possible whispering before Emma spoke again. "I doubt he's been dognapped. He probably got out."

"No, I checked the fences for holes. There's no way for him to get out." Cilla paced back into the living room to have another look around.

"You're sure he's not in the house? Maybe he's asleep."

"I'm sure!"

"Could he have jumped over the fence?"

"No, I doubt it. Golden retrievers are a highly desirable breed, and he is an extremely cute one."

"Your fence isn't that high. I've seen him up on his hind legs at the gate looking for pets."

Cilla scurried back to the front door, looked out toward the street, and reassessed the fence height. "He's not very athletic."

There were more muffled sounds, and then Emma said, "Give me twenty minutes. I'll come help you look."

Cilla's brain moved from panic mode for a moment. "No, it sounds like I interrupted something. I'll be fine, thanks anyway."

"Call me later!" Emma said before Cilla hung up.

Cilla shut the front door and walked toward the hip-high wooden fence. The azalea bush did look suspiciously shaped on the side by the gate. She went to examine the scene more closely. There were muddy gray marks along the inner rail of the fence that could be paw prints. Cilla squatted down so her vision was in line with the ridge of the fence and looked at the house across the road, then from side to side. Hmm. There were trees and lampposts—Benson did like both those things. There was the house a few doors down with the Doberman who always barked at Benson—not such an attractant but still a possibility. She still wasn't ruling out theft. Something blue and shiny, nestled under the azalea foliage, caught her eye and she bent down for a closer look. It was Benson's tag with her phone number on it. She picked it up and rubbed her thumb across the engraved digits. It was cold and damp from the wet leaves. Benson was probably alone and scared. She stood up and pushed the latch on the fence. It was all her fault for leaving him alone so long.

* * *

The glow from last night's lovemaking had well and truly faded as Cilla walked the length of the street and back again calling Benson's name. James from number eighteen was leaving in his car, but he rolled down the window and said he would keep an eye out on his way to the store. Cilla continued around the block asking anyone she bumped into if they'd seen Benson, up the next street and on toward Main Street, thinking Benson may have stopped at the café looking for treats because she often gave him the bacon from her breakfast there on Sundays, but he was nowhere to be seen. Feeling sick to her stomach, Cilla walked to the end of the block. Overhead the clouds had gathered, signaling another bout of rain. The only house left was the Queen Anne, all the way back from the street. Cilla stopped at the gate, which was ajar, and looked toward the house. There was an oriental rug hanging from the railing on the strip of porch out the front. On an impulse, Cilla pushed the gate open wider and stepped onto the path leading to the front steps. She felt a drop of rain hit her forehead and she gratefully climbed the four steps to the porch. Along the porch there were plants in pots, and in the middle was a white wicker sofa with faded pink cushions and a matching table. On the table was an empty ceramic cup and a pair of glasses. There was the sound of barking and the scrabble of claws on floorboards. Over the top of the clatter came the sound of a woman's voice. "Oh, hush."

Cilla stepped back, unsure of what she might be greeted with, but as the door opened, she was almost knocked over by a delighted dog—almost certainly Benson—and a Jack Russell terrier with tan patches who was yapping fiercely.

"Oh, Benson!" Cilla felt tears catch in her eyes.

"Is that his name?"

Cilla looked up from rubbing Benson's head to see a woman wearing peach-colored cords and a red Japanese-patterned shirt with a sharp collar and pearl buttons. Her long dark hair had streaks of silver in it, and her gray eyes shone like she was amused. When she moved, her silver bangles jangled. Cilla's mouth opened but nothing came out. She recognized her as the woman she saw occasionally around town, but up close, she seemed so different.

"Did you steal my dog?"

The woman laughed. "The way this dog eats, I couldn't afford to."

Cilla frowned and tried to hold Benson still as she put his leash on. "He is a large dog. Come on, Benson. Let's go home where you have your own kibble."

Benson reluctantly followed Cilla, throwing mournful glances over his shoulder at his new friends. Cilla didn't look around and didn't dare let go of his collar until they were closer to home in case he embarrassed her by running back. As they walked, she gently scolded him. "You could have ended up in a pie like the pigeons. You need to stay home and wait for me." But as her panic subsided, she felt she had been rather rude to the poor pigeon eater of Hollyoaks.

CHAPTER FIVE

At home, Benson followed Cilla from room to room, letting her know he had suffered a deep trauma in her absence. Cilla took a fresh towel from the linen closet and went to the bathroom. He followed her to the door. "Oh, for pity's sake. Go lie in your bed. Bed!"

Benson gave her a wounded look and walked slowly off, pausing to take a discarded sock from the floor in his mouth.

As Cilla soaped herself, she went over her interaction with the resident of Hollyoaks with some perspective. She had arrived on her doorstep with bed-hair and vestiges of last night's makeup on her face, acting slightly deranged and accusing the poor woman of stealing her dog. Cilla turned the water off and stepped out of the shower. She dried herself and wiped the steam from the mirror. She thought of Georgina at the gym and felt a bit old and useless. The rain was drumming on the tin roof, telling her that now was not the time for a jog. She hadn't called Emma back yet, either. She watched herself as she lifted each arm to apply roll-on deodorant and realized her biceps had either melted away or were well covered in preparation for winter. She just didn't feel like herself anymore. When had this happened?

She dressed in her usual jeans and shirt combination with the navy-blue sweater her mother had knitted her ten years ago that now had a hole in the elbow. The house was old and drafty, and unless she had the heat on, it remained cold. Georgina complained about the insulation, but Georgina was always critiquing people's homes; it was her job.

Cilla went to make a pot of chai tea and give Benson some attention, but when she went to find him in his bed in the living room, he wasn't there. Cilla called his name, already feeling she knew what had happened. She did a perfunctory inspection of the house, then grabbed her keys and raincoat and dashed through the deluge to her car.

As she drove along the streets, her wipers going a hundred miles an hour, she rubbed her sleeve on the misted windows, hoping she might intercept Benson on his travels, but by the time she arrived at Hollyoaks, she hadn't seen him. She sat in the car for a minute, staring at the house and feeling foolish. The rain showed no signs of slowing, and it was testament to Benson's determination that he had even ventured out. She pulled her hood over her head and jumped out of the car, trying to avoid the puddles as she ran along the path to the house that loomed dour under the storm clouds. The oriental rug was gone from the railing, but the ceramic cup and glasses were still there. Cilla didn't bother to knock—she felt the barking was alarming enough. Sure enough, the door opened and she was greeted once again by the dogs, Benson's blond hair damp from his adventures.

The woman looked Cilla up and down. "I believe I have something that belongs to you."

"Yes, I'm sorry. I'll close up the doggy door. I had a shower and…sorry, my name's Cilla." Cilla offered her hand, and after a second the woman shook it. Her hand was warm and Cilla's was cold.

"Lucky."

"Oh." Cilla wasn't sure how to take that. "Yes, he could have been hit by a car or run off."

The woman smiled. "My name is Lucky. At least that's what everyone except my mother calls me." She glanced past Cilla. "Would you like to come in?"

"I wouldn't want to intrude. I feel I should apologize for earlier. I don't know what overcame me."

Benson followed the Jack Russell back inside. "You'd better come in and visit your dog in his new home."

Cilla followed her in through the entryway. It smelled of incense and old wood with a hint of wet dog. Cilla felt responsible for the fragrant undertone. The oriental rug was on the floor, and to the right was a staircase. There were doorways straight ahead and off to the left. On the walls were photographs, and on a side table was a bronze sculpture of a naked woman next to a green-and-red art deco lamp. Cilla wanted to take it all in, but there wasn't time as Lucky led her into the sitting room to the left which was equally ornate with photographs and paintings on the walls, bookshelves, patterned rugs on the floor, and large potted plants by the windows, which had heavy burgundy-colored drapes fastened back with cord. A beveled mirror over the crackling fireplace reflected the gray day outside.

"Let me take your jacket. Please, have a seat where you like."

"Thank you." Cilla slipped out of her wet jacket and pushed up one sleeve of her sweater so the hole in the elbow wouldn't show. Benson stared at her, wagging his plumy tail. She took a seat on a pale-blue couch because it was closest to where she was standing. The Jack Russell came to grin at her, so she stroked his smooth head. On the other side of the couch was a dark-blue armchair with a cream woolen blanket draped over one side. There were little white dog hairs clinging to the sofa fabric, but Cilla was used to it.

"Coffee?"

"Thank you."

"Or I have gin."

Cilla wasn't sure if she was joking. "It's only ten thirty."

Lucky waved her away. "Someone boring made up that rule. Milk, cream, sugar, or black?"

"Black, please."

"Hmm." Lucky raised an eyebrow and departed the room.

Cilla noted a lilt in Lucky's voice that had just a whisper of an accent she couldn't quite place, and something in her speech patterns hinted at perhaps an education abroad. She shrugged, intrigued, and turned to examine the name tag of the small dog that snuffled at her feet. "Hello, Peanut The Second."

Peanut The Second wiggled his bottom in response, then scampered off after his mistress.

When Lucky returned, she had two steaming mismatched teacups on a silver tray and a plate of chocolate chip cookies. She placed the tray on a side table and handed Cilla a pale blue cup and saucer with a rose pattern and gold around the rim.

Cilla accepted the cup and settled the saucer on her knee. "Thank you. This is an extraordinary house. I feel like I could spend all day just looking around this room and still not see everything."

Lucky shrugged and took a seat on the armchair. "She is a lovely old dame but very cluttered. I'm not good at throwing things away, they become like people to me. For instance, that owl's feather poking out of the ceramic jar over there." She pointed to a tea trolley shoved against a wall by the fireplace. "I found that on a beach in Wales with a woman I was backpacking with when we were young. I have no idea what an owl's feather was doing on a beach, but we used it as a magic wand for the rest of the trip. Anything we asked of it, it provided."

Cilla would have liked to take a closer look, but she was scared to touch anything. "Like, what kind of things?"

"Oh, rides, places, hot food, tickets to concerts."

"I wouldn't throw it out either. Does it still work?"

"Let's try." Lucky stood up, placed her cup on a side table, and went to retrieve the feather. She ran it through her fingers, and Cilla thought that she did look a bit like a sorceress with her long hair, expressive fingers, and high cheekbones. Lucky's fingers paused and she closed her eyes. "Oh, wise and magical feather, please find my glasses." She opened her gray eyes and flicked the plumy end of the feather through the air.

"There's a pair of reading glasses on the table outside," Cilla volunteered.

Lucky beamed, showing one crooked eyetooth. "Still works! Thank you, feather." She placed it back in the jar. "If you'll excuse me one moment, I'm going to get my glasses before I forget again."

When Lucky returned, she had her glasses resting on top of her head but was also carrying something black and limp, which she presented to Cilla. "I have something of yours."

Cilla accepted her wet sock between two fingers. "Oh, what a traitor. Benson is being like an awful teenager, shaming me every chance he gets."

Benson's eyes shifted toward her at the sound of his name but he didn't move from where he was stretched out in front of the fireplace with Peanut.

"Be thankful it wasn't underwear."

Cilla placed the sock on the floor beside her foot. "I'm sorry he's been bothering you. He must be crazy about Peanut because he's never done this before. He's usually too lazy to do anything except sleep when I'm not home." Another thought struck her. "Were you at Vince's birthday party?"

Lucky's nose twitched and her gaze moved toward the ceiling. "No." Her gaze settled back on Cilla, and she took a sip of coffee.

"Last night? I'm sure I saw you there, just for a second."

"Well, maybe I was, just for a second. Is he a good friend of yours?"

"Not really, more of an acquaintance. He's a bit like a hurricane. You get swept up and put back down."

"Hurricane Vince. Realtors are always pecking at me about selling this place. I think they are waiting for me to die or for the place to fall into such disrepair that I will have to sell, then they can subdivide. That blond woman is the worst. They remind me of vultures."

Cilla felt her cheeks begin to burn and she took a hasty sip to hide her embarrassment. For some reason she didn't want to claim Georgina in that moment. In fact, she felt very far from her own life sitting on Lucky's sofa.

A boom of thunder shook the house, and Cilla yelped. Peanut sprang up and Lucky laughed. "I love storms! Here, have a cookie. I feel like we should have had gin after all." She offered Cilla a cookie and Cilla placed it on the saucer. "So," Lucky continued. "How was the vulture party?"

"It was fun, I think. It's a lovely venue, and there was plenty of food."

Lucky arched a dark brow. "Unconvincing. You clearly don't work at Lester and Co."

"I'd make a terrible real estate agent. I'm not charismatic or persuasive at all."

Lucky took a bite of cookie and dropped a golden piece on the floor for Peanut, which piqued Benson's interest and he came closer to sit and stare at Cilla. Lucky put her hand over her mouth to cover her chewing. "Do you work at the library?"

Cilla was surprised. "Yes. I don't know if I've seen you there before."

"I'm not one for public spaces."

"I wouldn't venture out either if I lived here."

"Perhaps if there was better company, I might," Lucky said, and Cilla wasn't sure if she was referring to Cilla being better or worse company.

"What do you do when you're not in public spaces?"

Lightning split the sky, illuminating the room and Lucky's face in a flash of white. "Oh, you know. Take in stray dogs and misplace glasses." She felt for her glasses on top of her head as though to reassure herself they were where she had left them.

Cilla was none the wiser. She had endless questions for Lucky, but Lucky was evasive. She wanted to know by which name Lucky was known to her mother, and who painted the pictures on the walls, and who was in the photos. Some were clearly younger Lucky, with long, thick dark hair, freckles across her nose, and large gray eyes fringed with heavily mascaraed lashes, on a bike, waving from the passenger seat of a car packed with excited people, standing with fashionable men and women looking effortlessly cool. There was even a photo of Lucky holding a Jack Russell that could only be Peanut The First. No, Cilla supposed, there would be no reason for Lucky to hang out at the library. She finished her coffee and settled the cup back on the saucer, wondering how someone who used to be everywhere now preferred to be nowhere.

"Well, thank you for the coffee. I'm really sorry about Benson." She leaned forward and picked up the sock. "And this."

"You're welcome to stay until the rain eases."

Cilla stood up and cast a glance toward the window. "That may be next week. You'll be taking in lost dogs and lost women."

Lucky stood too. "It's been nice to have some company for a while anyhow."

"Perhaps we could take the dogs for a walk sometime? Benson would love it."

"Oh, yes, maybe. We'll see."

Cilla felt brushed off, but she called Benson. "Where should I put the cup?"

"Leave it, I'll tidy up later."

Cilla placed the cup on a side table and followed Lucky out. Lucky took her jacket from where it had been hanging in the hall. It was cold and heavy.

"Thank you. I will look into a side gate so he can't get out anymore. Goodbye, Peanut." She took Benson by the collar and turned before Lucky could respond, then dashed out into the rain.

CHAPTER SIX

"Did she seem like the type who would eat a pigeon?" Emma asked the next day as she scanned the library returns back into the system.

Cilla was leaning against a counter taking the scanned books and placing them onto a cart. Not really a two-person job, but a chance to talk. "Aren't pigeons a delicacy in some countries?"

Emma's hand paused over a Colleen Hoover book. "Where is she from?"

"No, no." Cilla waved her away. "She doesn't eat pigeons. She's really normal. Actually, I don't know what *normal* is, but she's cool and the house is amazing inside with all these interesting bits and pieces around. And, hang on—who were you with when I called yesterday?"

Emma smiled to herself. "Never mind."

Cilla snatched the scanner from her and held it out of reach. "Tell. Not Chris?"

Emma lunged for the scanner and grabbed it back. "Not Chris, he moved to 'far away,' remember? Pedro, the guy from the gym who hogs the rowing machine."

"The weird one who ignored you when you asked him when he would be finished?"

"Yes, only he's not as weird as I thought. Or maybe he is. Anyway, I think I'll have sex with him again. The rowing machine must have been doing something for him. He had stamina. Look out, here comes big ears."

Cilla straightened the stack of books on the cart as Roger came to investigate what all the chatter was about.

"Is *The Mating Style of Animal Species* back yet?"

Emma shook her head solemnly. "I haven't seen it, however it is an engrossing read, so it may be out for a while."

Roger looked at Emma with renewed interest. "Have you read it? Not that I condone reading on the job."

Emma picked up another book. "I couldn't help myself."

Cilla tried not to smirk, knowing that the comment was both to answer Roger and a nod to her own wit for Cilla's benefit.

"I felt the same way. Pricilla, go and find something to do."

Cilla opened her mouth to say something, but it wasn't worth it. She went to the kitchen to get the window cleaner so she could take her time wiping the glass and looking at the brilliant day outside. The deep blue of the sky and the golden hue of the leaves against the emerald green of the grass was like a postcard. Cilla's mind wandered to the events of the day before. She'd had such a lovely time, but something had stopped her from sharing it with Georgina. Cilla wiped the same patch of glass again. Why did her mind keep returning to Lucky? It had been an unusual situation, but if she was truthful, she didn't have many friends of her own anymore. She didn't even really see her family much. She sprayed some sticky fingerprints and stared through the bubbly drips of cleaner at a mushroom that had sprouted beneath a tree until she became aware of Roger's reflection in the glass. She pretended not to notice him and went back to wiping the window.

* * *

Locking the side gate seemed to be working, and Benson remained at home for the rest of the week. Cilla expected to feel relieved but instead felt a little disappointed. Benson had lost his mojo too. He lay in his bed with his head on his paws and ignored Cilla as she sat in her bed on Saturday morning scrolling through her phone with a coffee. He didn't even stir when two crows started to squark at each other on the lawn outside the window. Cilla put her phone down. She didn't know why she ever bothered looking at social media. The only thing she liked were the videos of animals doing cute or brave things which usually made her cry anyway. She was waiting for the next Highgate Village mystery to be released. At least, that was her excuse for scrolling on her phone in bed.

"Come here, Benson." Cilla tapped the covers and Benson's eyes swiveled toward her, raising his eyebrows. She tried again but he looked away. Cilla laughed. "Oh, come on, it's not that bad."

His attitude reminded her of when her sister, Deb, had developed a sudden crush at age fifteen on the boy in the year above at school who didn't know she was alive. She'd spent all her time in her bedroom doing breast exercises and curling her hair, only emerging for meals. It turned out she'd taken all of their mother's romance novels and crossed out the titles and written new ones over the top such as *The Wonderous Marriage of Keith Pottinger and Debra Davis* and *Keith Pottinger and Debra Davis Move to Hawaii!* Their mother had howled with laughter and displayed them on the bookcase, and when Deb saw them she had been so upset she ran away. Their father had scoured the streets in the car until he located Deb at the bus stop by the gas station, watching all the buses go by. He had been so furious that the next morning he had marched onto the school bus with Deb and told poor Keith Pottinger to leave Deb alone even though Keith had no idea what he was going on about. It was a mortifying experience for all involved, and Deb didn't look sideways at Keith again and took to walking the five blocks to school.

Cilla didn't suppose telling Peanut off would have the same effect.

"You can't live there, you know." Cilla pulled back the blankets and went to get ready to take Benson for a walk.

* * *

Benson toodled along, lifting his leg on the usual lampposts, but he drew the line at stirring the Doberman a few doors up or paying any mind to the cat sitting on the fence at the end of the block. He did, however, indulge passers-by who wanted to stroke his head, but it was with tolerance rather than pleasure.

The park had walking tracks that wound down to the river and a playground with a wooden fort and various slides. Children teemed about, climbing and shrieking, and joggers and cyclists carried on past the slower dogwalkers on the path. Benson usually loved poking around in the scrub beside the track or greeting other dogs, but today he sat down beside the path and looked stoically into the distance.

Cilla groaned. "Do I need to take you to the vet?"

The last word caused Benson to look at her and lick his lips, but he wasn't swayed. Cilla was starting to get fed up. "We are here now, we will do a lap." She walked forward and tugged at Benson's leash. He didn't move, so she pulled harder. He shuffled forward after her, and they proceeded to do a slow lap until they turned for home and Benson picked up his pace, looking every bit his old self. "Oh, all right. Do you want to see Peanut?" Benson looked up at her and stared. "Peanut?" Cilla said again. Benson bowed and began to hop up and down with his front paws.

As Cilla was tugged along the street toward Lucky's house, she didn't allow herself to think that Lucky may not want a visitor. Benson pushed the gate open with his head and Cilla had to stride to keep up with him. The front yard looked vaster in the sunshine. It was no wonder the grass was unmown—there was so much of it. A walnut tree stood in the middle of the left side like a huge yellow umbrella, and along the porch grew hydrangea bushes, their leaves fading and remaining flowers turning toward pink. Cilla let go of Benson's leash and let him bound ahead. The front door opened before he got there, and Lucky stood with one hand on the door handle, one holding a drink, her mouth open as Benson and Peanut almost collided near her legs. She looked helplessly at Cilla, who quickened her pace.

"Sorry to intrude, again. Benson is completely lovesick."

Lucky smiled and let the door shut. "I was coming to sit on the porch and enjoy the sunshine. I have to admit Peanut has been a bit gloomy too. Here." She thrust a green glass at Cilla. "I haven't taken a sip yet. I'll make myself another. You may as well come in."

Lucky's hair was coiled up at the back of her head and she had on a long black dress with flared sleeves and a pattern of purple doves all over it. Her feet were bare, and there was a fine gold chain around her ankle. When she turned to go back indoors, Cilla could see there was a yellow chrysanthemum in the center of her coiled hair.

"You must think I'm an alcoholic, drinking at this hour," Lucky said as she led Cilla along the hall to the back of the house. "It's not that I drink all the time, it's just that when I do drink, it always seems to be at some odd hour. My concept of time is all over the place."

The kitchen was large with an old-looking range to one side that had a vase of shedding roses sitting on a hot plate. In place of an island was a stained wooden table with a stack of old magazines, at least four dirty glasses, a glass jar of felt-tip markers, and a pile of soil-crusted flower bulbs. The sounds of scurrying and yapping could be heard from outside as Benson and Peanut raced around the perimeter of the house. The back door was leaded glass depicting red and green flower bouquets, and it opened onto the rear back porch.

Lucky began mixing another gin and tonic, and Cilla looked out of the back window at the spread of lawn with its one huge oak in the middle and various garden beds. There was nothing but uncleared land beyond the leaning picket fence.

Lucky dropped a wedge of lemon into her glass and followed Cilla's gaze. "I sometimes get deer in my yard, they trample the flowers. Shall we sit out front?"

"Sure. It's such a mild day." Cilla was pleased that she'd had a mind to wear a shirt without stains and a sweater without holes where there should be no holes. "I like your flower in your hair."

Lucky reached a hand to touch the chrysanthemum. "Flowers add an elegant touch to anything, even this old bird."

Cilla thought that Lucky wasn't old, but she really couldn't pick her for any age. She had a timeless look. There was something unique and compelling about Lucky, and Cilla was trying not to let it show.

They went to take a seat on the sofa on the front porch. There wasn't a breath of wind, and the occasional fluffy cloud sat in the sky like it would never leave.

"Have you always lived here?"

"No, this was my aunt's house. I have been here, there, and everywhere. I couldn't wait to get started in life and have adventures, so I left home at sixteen to racket around."

"Wow, that's young. I think I was just allowed to go to the mall by myself at that age."

"I didn't give my poor mother much choice."

Cilla took a sip of the gin even though she wasn't accustomed to morning drinks. It was mellow and slightly sweet, with a fresh tang from the lemon. "What made you settle here?"

"A nomadic lifestyle has an expiration date. Sleeping on sofas and in different hotels, night after night loses its appeal once the joints start to age. I'd had my fun and I'd seen my share of tragedy, so when my aunt asked me back here, I was ready to come. I knew I couldn't go and live with my mother in a cramped house. Our lives were too different and there was no way to bridge that gap. My aunt, Nora, she is a bit like me, the odd one out. People used to call her a witch too."

"They don't…people don't call you—"

Lucky laughed. "I know what people say about me."

"Is that why you avoid coming into town?"

The dogs came racing up the steps and flopped at their feet. Lucky reached down to pet Peanut. "People see what they want to see. It's not my job to shatter their illusions, but I don't want to spend my time where I'm not understood." She shrugged. "I'm making it sound deeper than it is. They're not my people, so I keep to myself."

"Then why did you stay here?" Cilla hoped she wasn't being too forthright.

"It's not just them. I find things confusing. My people are gone. Scattered, dead, dealing with their own things. I didn't want to start over again. Plus, I love this house and I have Peanut. I'm used to my own company now. It's simpler this way. The world moves so fast, don't you think?"

"I guess. What about your aunt?"

"She's no longer with us. I like to think she's still around, though, somewhere."

Cilla looked at the cobwebs in the corners of the roof. She could easily imagine a ghost inhabiting the house. "Sorry to hear that."

"Don't be. What about you? You're a slightly newer addition to the town, aren't you? I may not join crowds, but I am a keen observer."

"I live a few blocks that way." Cilla made an action like throwing her pointed finger toward her house. "I've been there for about five years." She still didn't want to mention Georgina after Lucky's previous comments about her, so she attempted to change the course of the conversation. "There's a night market tomorrow in Singing Falls." Cilla wasn't sure where that had bubbled up from. "I was thinking I might go, and if you're not doing anything?" She herself rarely did anything on a Sunday night, but perhaps it was the gin talking.

Lucky looked at Cilla for a long moment, and Cilla forgot to breathe. "At Singing Falls?"

"Well, not at the actual falls, but in the town."

"I don't drive."

"I could pick you up?"

Lucky seemed to weigh it up.

"It would be an adventure," Cilla said. She had thrown the invitation into the conversation from nowhere, but now that it was out there, she really wanted to go. "Hopefully not a confusing one."

Lucky laughed. "Why not? I think a market is within my realm of comprehension. Thank you, that would be fun."

Cilla let out a long exhale, relieved. She thought of her filthy car and knew what she would be doing that afternoon.

CHAPTER SEVEN

On Sunday evening, Cilla was in her bedroom, naked, pulling items from her closet and throwing them on the bed in dissatisfaction. The problem, she was beginning to realize, was less her clothes and more the fact that they were all fairly snug on her at the moment. Not that she had ever been a stick, but if she was honest, she had developed an attachment to apple pie. Perhaps with a generous serving of vanilla ice cream. Every evening.

Van Morrison's "Brown Eyed Girl" blared happily from the record player that took up a lot of space in the living room along with her stacks of records, but she couldn't bear to part with them.

The doorbell chimed, making Benson scramble up from the floor and run barking to investigate. The sound shocked Cilla, as though someone had caught sight of her naked body. She grabbed her discarded towel and wrapped it around her even though it was now cold and damp. What if it was a rapist and she gave them the wrong impression by coming to the door half naked? She reassured herself that the umbrella was there by the coat rack. Even if she couldn't stab them, she could open it in their face and give herself time to escape out the back door. She unlocked the door to the sight of Georgina dressed in blue jeans with black boots and a white angora sweater, holding a bottle of red.

"Just dropping in, Cill!"

Cilla's mouth popped open but she was momentarily lost for words. "But I'm going to the market, remember?"

"Oh, you mentioned something. Isn't it a night market? It's only five o'clock."

"Well, quarter past," Cilla said weakly. "I was getting dressed."

"I'd hope so." Georgina gave Cilla a kiss on the lips and moved past her. "I'll grab a couple of glasses. Just keep doing what you're doing. I have this lovely red that Vince gave me for helping him offload that pokey house behind the butcher. It's from a local vineyard."

Cilla stared after Georgina's receding form as she made for the kitchen. Benson looked up at Cilla as if to say *What the?* and Cilla remembered to shut the front door. There was no stopping the Georgina train once it was in motion. Cilla went back to her bedroom and wriggled into the first outfit she had tried on—her black jeans and red sweater. She found two socks that looked close enough in length and hue to pass as a pair and pulled them on. She had wanted to blow-dry her hair properly, but she went out to the kitchen to see what Georgina was doing.

"Hello, Santa!" Georgina said from where she was leaning against the kitchen bench, already sipping from a glass of wine.

Cilla could see her own red-sweatered reflection in the windowpane.

"Oh, don't look so cross. It was just a joke. You look lovely, as always. Here." Georgina offered Cilla a glass of wine.

Cilla accepted the glass but didn't take a sip. Red wine and minty-fresh mouth wasn't an appealing flavor. Van Morrison started on "Dancing in the Moonlight." She could feel Benson watching her anxiously, knowing she was about to go out. "I have to…" She made a face at Georgina, hoping the rest of the sentence would be implicit, but Benson's ears sagged forlornly anyway. She put down the glass and grabbed a dried dog treat from the packet on the fridge and let him take it from her hand.

Georgina watched her but didn't move. "I haven't been to the market in years. What do they have? Those little knickknack type of things that you put on all the flat surfaces?"

Cilla's eyes wandered to the wooden elephant collection being crowded by the stack of papers on top of the fridge. There was also a goblin with feathery hair sitting beside a small potted plant on the window ledge. And maybe a glass paperweight that used to be her grandmother's that was gathering dust on the microwave. To be fair, it would be better displayed on the desk in the study.

In a moment of inspiration, knowing Georgina didn't see the point of sentimental objects at all, Cilla said, "Yes, I thought I could get some gifts for Christmas." She realized as she said it that she would be ripe for another Santa comment, but Georgina wasn't to be deflected.

"It's only October. Maybe I'll come anyway. We could have some mulled wine, and I don't mind those hand-knitted scarves."

"You can't!" Cilla said.

Georgina's eyes snapped in surprise.

Cilla continued, "I might find something for you, a scarf or something. I have to get ready now."

Georgina went to the sink and tipped the rest of the wine from her glass down the drain. Cilla fought against the sinking feeling in her stomach. Georgina was like a wooden elephant herself—unyielding and unforgetting.

"No probs. I guess I'll see you when I see you." Georgina didn't meet her eyes, but she lifted herself to her full height.

"It's not a big deal. I mean, you can come if you want. I just thought that you don't like shopping and I planned on maybe getting a gift for you." Cilla inwardly cringed at her own words.

"I wouldn't bother. I have a lot going on tomorrow anyway. I have a seven a.m. Pilates class and then straight into viewings."

Cilla screwed the cap back on the wine. "Here, take it with you."

Georgina sniffed. "Keep it. It was for you."

"Thank you, that's very thoughtful."

Georgina brushed her hands over her jeans and cast an accusing look down at Benson. Cilla could see that a few fine white hairs had stuck to the top of Georgina's jeans, but she could also see that they were from Georgina's angora sweater.

"I'm not sure when I'll see you. I have a completely packed week," Georgina said, making her way to the hall.

"I'll make some time." Cilla went to hug Georgina but she pretended not to notice, and Cilla let her arm drop. She watched from the porch to make sure Georgina was safely in her car and then shut the door firmly and stood leaning against it for a moment. Instinctually she wanted to keep Lucky to herself, but it didn't feel good.

* * *

Cilla was ten minutes late, and Lucky was waiting at the gate in a long brown wool coat from which spilled the cream-colored silk frills of her shirt collar. On her head was a chocolate-colored beret.

Lucky leaned forward and Cilla rolled down the car window. "Where's Benson?"

Cilla wondered if it was a trick question. "At home, I hope."

"Oh, Peanut was all excited to have a gentleman caller. He's even wearing his bow tie. I told him to wait inside so he wouldn't get muddy."

"Benson would have loved that."

Lucky glanced back toward the house, its peaks silhouetted against the deepening sky. "Do we have time to get him?"

Cilla laughed. "A dog limousine service. Come on."

Lucky skipped over a puddle and made her way to the passenger door. "This is like a Bond mission," she said breathlessly as she bucked her seat belt. "How has your day been?"

"Good, sorry I'm late." She stopped short of saying she'd had an unexpected visitor. "My hair can be quite unruly if it's not treated to some severe heat therapy."

"Is that sort of like saying you can't go out because you're washing your hair?"

Cilla pulled out onto the road. "No, just trying to spare you being seen in public with a walking bottlebrush." Lucky laughed but didn't say anything, and Cilla wondered if she was worried about being seen in public at all. There wasn't time to fill the silence before Cilla pulled up at her own house. "Won't be long." She left the car idling so the heat would stay on and went inside to find Benson, who had already heard the car and was waiting at the door.

Cilla insisted on carrying Benson from the car up the path to Lucky's front door so he wouldn't track muddy paw prints through the house. He writhed in his excitement to get to Peanut, and she half dropped, half deposited him on the porch and brushed the dog hair from her black jacket. The dogs touched noses and wagged their tails and immediately took to their game of zooming along the hall.

"I hope they don't knock anything over," Cilla said.

"They haven't yet. Let's go."

They crept out and shut the door behind them like parents leaving their toddlers at daycare.

* * *

The market was held a block from the Singing Falls train station, which still ran a steam train for tourist purposes. Cilla parked at the car lot by the station and they walked toward the market with hands stuffed in pockets, avoiding the pools on the ground from yesterday's downpour. The night was clear and starry, reminding Cilla why she loved the countryside.

"I love the falls," Lucky said, breathing in the night air.

"I've never been," Cilla confessed.

Lucky's stride paused and she looked at Cilla. "You've never been?"

"It's on my list, but my list seems to grow faster than I can check it off."

"What else is on the list?"

"The rose festival in spring, the portrait competition at the gallery, umm…there's lots. How about you?"

"I haven't been to any of the wineries. I want to go to the summer fair—"

Cilla cut her off. "You've never been to the summer fair?"

"No. Does that mean we are even?"

Cilla shrugged. "Yeah, it's just such a huge thing here. The whole town stops. So that means you've never had Aunt Carol's secret spiced corn on the cob? I live for that every year."

"Never had it." Lucky brushed away a strand of hair that had stuck to her lip. "Crowds make me uneasy."

"Why is that?"

"Oh, look!" Lucky pointed toward the market with its strings of lights across the branches overhead. "It's so beautiful." She took an appreciative sniff. "It smells like pine and cinnamon."

Cilla took in a draft of air. It smelled of sweetness and excitement. "If this were a candle, I would buy it and burn it all the time." She looked over at Lucky, and the string lights were shining in Lucky's silvery eyes, turning them warm and golden. She knew Lucky had deflected from answering the question, but Cilla wasn't sure she should have asked it. Maybe another time. If there was another time. Cilla wanted to smooth over the moment. "I love candlelight. It makes everything seem more dramatic. So, what else is on your list of things to do or places to go?"

"Right now, the crepe truck?" Lucky laughed at herself and continued, "The cinnamon is a powerful force. What else is on your list of places to visit?"

Cilla thought of all the places she had meant to go to but never gotten around to. "Hmm. Well, the falls, the rose festival, the portrait competition…there's this high tea thing they do at the bakery on the first Sunday of the month." She thought of Georgina saying it was a literal recipe for a flabby gut. "I suppose it is indulgent."

"I love high tea. Everything is so dainty and cute. It reminds me of birthday parties as a kid. In London, my girlfriend and I were friends with a waiter at these tea rooms in a fancy hotel.

He'd sneak us in at the end of the seating. We'd be so hung over and stinking of cigarettes. I remember throwing up pink iced cakes right next to the toilet bowl once. Poor Alby got moved on not long after that."

Cilla was listening but her attention had snagged on the word *girlfriend*. She wasn't sure if Lucky meant female friend or girlfriend. She quickly chastised herself for having those thoughts. This was not a date. She had a girlfriend herself, and it was lovely to have a new friend. She was trying not to notice the childlike way Lucky observed the world, or the subtle elegance in her mannerisms.

"Sorry," Lucky said as they joined the line at the crepe truck. "That was an awful story to tell before we eat crepes."

"It takes more than that to affect my appetite."

The market was busy. Cilla looked across at a stall that sold local wines and thought of Georgina. It had been kind of her to bring the bottle of wine over. Then she looked at a stall that sold tiny porcelain animals and thought of how Georgina made fun of her "knickknacks." Sometimes keeping up with who she needed to be for Georgina was exhausting.

Lucky interrupted Cilla's thoughts. "What are you going to order?"

Cilla gazed up at the chalkboard as they moved up in the queue. "Strawberries and cream. You?"

"Banana and cinnamon. Their dastardly marketing strategy of pumping delicious odors into the crowd has worked on me."

The crepes came folded in a paper cone. There was no elegant way to eat them but Lucky didn't seem to mind. They wandered along and stopped to watch a man sketching a small girl's portrait and to listen to a woman playing a harp. Lucky tossed a coin into the woman's hat on the ground. Cilla looked down at the coin. It was an old dollar that caused Cilla to wonder if it was valuable. She wondered if she should say something but thought better of it. It wouldn't surprise her if Lucky was a coin collector. She seemed to love old things.

Lucky paused to listen to the music. "I wish I knew how to play the harp."

"Why don't you learn?" Cilla asked.

"Don't have a harp. I have a piano, but I can't play that either. I used to play the guitar a bit."

"Really? I used to play the piano."

Lucky balled up her empty paper cone and tossed it into a bin. "Why'd you stop?"

"What do you mean?"

"Well, you said you used to."

Cilla wiped her chin with a paper napkin. "My mom stopped forcing me to practice."

"Are you any good?"

"Doubt it." Cilla could see a stall up ahead that sold hand-knitted hats and scarves and throw rugs. "Can we look over here?"

Lucky tried on hats and Cilla concentrated on the scarves so she wouldn't have to notice how good Lucky looked in all of her selections. Lucky decided not to buy any of them as she said she had too many hats already, and Cilla found a dark-blue scarf with gray threading through it that she knew Georgina would like. There was a sign at the stall that said, *Every time you buy local, you wipe off a year of karmic debt.*

"I'd better get buying," Lucky said as they walked away.

Cilla hadn't had the foresight to bring a shopping bag, so she slung the scarf around her neck and hoped it wouldn't smell like crepe syrup.

Lucky indicated to a professional-looking stand with pale green and white banners. "Like eating a slice of pizza and biting into an olive stone."

Cilla knew what she meant. The stand stood out like a sore thumb among the craft stalls. There were aerial photos of land divided by thick yellow lines and pictures of smiling families standing in front of large newly built houses. Cilla saw a life-size photo of Vince grinning mid-handshake with an equally grinning man. She almost fainted with relief to see it was no one she knew operating the stand.

"Did you go to the rallies? Not that protesting did any good."

"I'm not the protesting type." Cilla was relieved as they moved on past the eyesore.

"No one wants miles of land ripped up to put new estates in. People buy in because they love the scenery and then they wreck it. There's no infrastructure, either. They promise schools and train lines and hospitals. That Georgina woman makes my skin crawl. She brought a basket of muffins over one day, as though oatmeal muffins would convince me to sell my property to her."

Cilla's back prickled hot and her cheeks burned. She wanted to say something but didn't know how. "Lucky, there's something—"

Lucky's attention was drawn to a secondhand bookstore. She picked up a copy of *Salem's Lot*. "Stephen King has written that many books that secondhand bookstores always seem to be at least thirty percent his books." She opened it up. "I've never actually read one. Have you?"

"Lots."

"Of course you have, you're a librarian. You've read everything. Is this one any good?"

"They're all good if you like Stephen King books."

"Will I get scared?"

"Hopefully."

Lucky turned the book over and read the back of the tattered jacket. "Is this like the Cap'n Crunch of the literary world?"

Cilla picked up a copy of *The Bell Jar*. "Wash it down with this."

"I probably have a copy of this in the shelves at home. My aunt refused to read anything that wasn't written by a woman." Lucky addressed the woman working at the stall. "I'll take these two, please." She handed over four dollar bills. As they wandered on, she said, "She was also a complete romance novel addict. She drank carrot and ginger juice every morning and smoked a cigar before bed."

"Good way to bookend the day."

"Do you ever think," Lucky said, pausing before continuing, "how at any given moment, someone is doing the same thing as you?"

"Walking at a market?"

"Anything. Lighting a fire, washing their hands…Right now, someone is licking an envelope somewhere in the world."

Cilla pictured a woman licking an envelope in a post office somewhere or in her car before going to a mailbox. "I've never thought about it."

Lucky's brows scrunched together. "I think about it a lot."

Cilla laughed, and Lucky began to laugh too. "I'm sure now I will be thinking about it too."

"It's quite comforting." Lucky stopped at a table covered with a white linen cloth and picked up a candle. She took a sniff, then held it out for Cilla. "Honeysuckle and wild jasmine."

Cilla breathed it in. "Smells like balmy nights." The moment for mentioning Georgina had passed, and Cilla was loath to sour this moment.

"Delicious," Lucky agreed. "I want one. Actually, you should have one too. It will remind us of summer when the trees are bare."

Cilla barely had time to protest before Lucky had paid for the two candles and handed her one. Cilla carried her candle and Lucky carried hers with the two books until they found a table with two chairs by the food trucks. Across the square of grass, a country band was working their way through a cover of a vaguely familiar pop song. Cilla and Lucky bought paella and sat in the pink and blue neon lights of a hot dog sign. Between mouthfuls of rice, Lucky read aloud random lines from *Salem's Lot*, and the expressions on her pink-bathed face were so genuine that Cilla couldn't help laughing. Cilla's hand hurt from carrying the candle and her face was cold, but she couldn't remember the last time she had felt so happy.

CHAPTER EIGHT

Cilla had been scanning returns into the system after story time and she was looking forward to making a coffee, but she was aware of Roger across the room performing tasks in Penny's line of sight with great flourishes. Penny was talking to Henry's mother as Henry stood relatively still for the first time in the past hour, playing with the allowing Apricot's ears, fashioning them into a hat above her head, then pressing them back down to her cheeks. Cilla had put aside a book that had been defaced and was waiting for the right moment to show Roger. Now was not the moment. Roger was running out of books to align on shelves and cushions to tidy away one by one.

Emma came to stand beside Cilla and narrated in a breathy voice, "The male of the species displays his brown-vested acrylic, hoping to attract the ideal mate."

Cilla picked up the thread. "The female of the species senses genetic discord in the approaching male and chooses not to respond."

"The male perseveres. Look how he puts on a splendid display of strength, single-handedly adjusting the angle of the couch. Will it arouse her attention?"

"It seems not. She is focused on tending to the young."

Penny glanced toward them with an alarmed look and Cilla had to choke back a giggle. Thankfully, a father arrived with his little girl to check out some books. Emma picked up the stack of returns to rehome on their shelves.

Cilla read the title of the book aloud. "*Hands Are Not For Hitting.*" She looked up at the father, who grimaced.

"We may need to read this one a few times." The little girl gazed up at her father with an angelic face. "When her sister comes near her toys, she moves faster than a Lamborghini."

Cilla smiled. "I have a sister. Sometimes I feel like giving her a smack."

The father smiled back. "I'll let you know if the book works any wonders."

Cilla waved goodbye to the little girl, and when she looked back toward the story corner, Roger was making a beeline for her.

"Pricilla!" he hissed. "I need—Oh, there it is!" He snatched up *The Mating Style of Animal Species* that Cilla had put aside. Before Cilla could say anything, he marched back toward Penny, who was gathering her things to leave.

Cilla watched as he proudly showed Penny the cover. Penny was blinking at it with a slack expression on her face. After a moment, she tentatively took the book and was escorted toward the circulation desk where Cilla was standing.

"Don't worry about scanning this one through, Pricilla. We trust Penny."

Penny's lips were pursed, but she offered the book to Cilla anyway. "I, ah…"

"No, no. It's my pleasure." Roger pushed Penny's hand back.

"Thank you." Penny's face had gone red.

"You don't have to take it," Cilla said. "I mean, if you've got a lot of books on your list already."

"I do, but..."

Roger intervened. "You're such an animal lover, Pen. I'm sure it will be particularly fascinating."

Cilla knew that Roger thought it was the ultimate crime to let someone borrow a book without entering it into the system. Penny still looked uncertain but was persuaded to take the book. Cilla said goodbye and shot a look at Emma, who had paused with a stack of books in her arms to watch the exchange. She raised her eyebrows at Cilla, and Cilla couldn't wait to tell her that someone had drawn giant penises on the rhinos on the first page.

* * *

Cilla checked her cell phone after work. On the screen were two messages. The first was from Georgina saying she was held up at the office and would have to cancel dinner. The second was a message from Cilla's friend Will, whom she had only seen once since she'd moved. The message read, *Big news! I'm a dad!* with an accompanying image. It was funny how hours became days which became weeks, months, years. They always picked up where they left off, but she felt she hadn't been an attentive friend lately. She clicked on the message to see the photo. It was a picture of a tiny pug sitting in an upturned fedora. Cilla smiled to herself, thinking sometimes time didn't change a thing and sent back a recent picture of Benson wearing socks on his paws with the text, *Welcome to the club.*

Cilla didn't mind that Georgina had canceled dinner—she was happy to put her sweatpants on and take Benson for a walk. As she walked toward the park, the sun was catching the treetops like they were alight and blurring the rooflines in a blaze of orange and red. Cilla had wanted to give Georgina the scarf at dinner, but she would wait until Georgina was free over the weekend.

At the park, Cilla let Benson off the leash and he cavorted off into the shrubbery to chase down some smells. Cilla walked on, knowing Benson would catch up with her when he had finished snuffling around. Her phone beeped in her jacket pocket, and when she looked at the screen, her heart leapt gladly. It was a text from Lucky: *The old cemetery in Singing Falls.* Cilla smiled and wrote back, *Add it to the list.*

She stopped to touch the smooth bark on a birch trunk. She had to keep reminding herself that Lucky was out of bounds and then she felt bad for even thinking of Lucky that way, but when another text came through saying, *Gin Rummy?* Cilla texted back, *Have you been at the gin again?*

Cilla stared at her phone, waiting for a reply, but after a minute nothing had come through and Benson was standing in the middle of the path staring at her. She put her phone back in her pocket wondering if she had offended Lucky and then wondering how many women at that exact moment were wondering the same thing about someone they cared for. Up ahead she could see the old man with his gray poodle shuffling along toward her. She couldn't remember his name and they had spoken too many times to ask again. He always wanted to chat for fifteen minutes and she usually indulged him because she felt that he was lonely, but today she didn't have it in her. She waved at him and cut across the grass to her left and headed toward the bridge over the river that took her out toward the trails that she generally avoided after sunset.

Benson gleefully aimed toward the bank of the river. "Don't even think about it," Cilla called, and Benson's trajectory arced back toward her.

As she walked along the path toward the first exit point, her phone beeped again. It was a photo of a card deck and a glass of gin arranged on a table. Cilla smiled and typed back, *Is that a game of solitaire?*

After a few seconds, a message came back through: *I hope not.*

* * *

Lucky's living room seemed to offer new things to look at every time. Cilla wasn't sure if that gong had always been in the corner or if she hadn't noticed it before. The fire crackled in the grate, casting flickering light over Lucky's face and hands. Benson and Peanut had spread themselves out on the rug in front of the fire.

"You know," Lucky said, dealing the cards. "I forgot how nice it is to have company."

Cilla took the cards that Lucky had dealt and fanned them out in her hand. She began to reorder them. "Why have you left it so long between drinks, so to speak? You seem very social to me."

Lucky picked up a red ballpoint pen and drew a line down the middle of the notepad on the table. "I am social, but I had to learn to be alone and I quite like it. I'm not really alone. I have Peanut."

"Dogs are great, but they aren't people. The market wasn't so bad, was it?" Cilla watched Lucky write down their names on either side at the top of the notepad. Something about seeing her name written beside Lucky's in Lucky's curly script thrilled her.

"It was fun. You go first."

Cilla looked back at her cards. "Oh, right." She took a card from the pile and discarded a four of spades. "But did it feel fine to you?"

"It is easier walking with someone than on my own." Lucky examined the cards in her hands before selecting one to place on the pile. "When I was young I didn't really care that much what people said, even though I was brought up in an environment where reputation was everything and a man's word was king."

"It's easy to say it doesn't matter but we are all hardwired to want acceptance."

Lucky picked up her glass, and the ice cubes clinked together in a tune that matched the silvery clashing of her bangles. "If someone says something about you loud enough and long enough, more people start to believe it and then it hardens into a type of fact. My friends turned their backs on me and it hardened me for a long time, being misunderstood that way." She took a sip and then shrugged. "I'm fortunate to have this house. It's my sanctuary away from the world. I don't know where the time goes. But here we are. Your turn."

Cilla looked back down at her cards and picked up a mystery card from the stack, then discarded a two of diamonds. "What type of things were said about you?"

Lucky looked at Cilla, her eyes moving from Cilla's eyes to her lips and back again as though weighing whether she could trust her. Cilla felt heat rush to the spots where Lucky's gaze landed, and she had to look away toward anything other than Lucky's eyes. After a few seconds, Lucky's gaze shifted back down to the fan of cards in her hand and Cilla could function again. "It was a long time ago. You're right, I shouldn't let it get to me."

"I don't know how anyone could think badly of you at all."

Lucky cleared her throat and placed the cards face down on the table. "My drink needs refreshing." She stood up and took Cilla's glass from the table even though it was still three-quarters full.

Cilla watched Lucky hastily leave the room, her slender figure like a shadow weaving through the jumble of furniture. She thought over the last sentence she had spoken aloud. But what did she know about Lucky, really? Snippets here and there.

It was several minutes before Lucky returned with the two glasses. The fire gave off a loud popping sound, making Cilla jump.

Lucky sat down and picked her cards up. "Whose turn was it?"

"Yours. I hope I didn't offend you before."

Lucky smiled, but it wasn't altogether convincing. "Don't be silly. It takes more than that to offend me. I'm a bit rusty on the conversation front. I have a feeling that you need a seven of hearts, but I'm going to throw it anyway."

Cilla watched Lucky place the card on the pile. "How do you know if I need that? I barely know if I need that. Are you a mind reader?" Cilla would believe it. Despite all the false rumors, there was something witchlike or otherworldly about Lucky.

"I used to do a lot of traveling. After many a night spent at a train station or on a long bus ride, I learnt to carry a deck of cards with me."

"All right, Miss Card Shark, you got me." Cilla picked up the seven of hearts and threw down a queen of spades. They both laughed.

Cilla took a sip of her drink and watched Lucky deliberate over her next move.

"I'm going to knock," Lucky announced, placing a card face down on the discard pile.

"Do I have to show you my cards?"

Lucky raised her arched brows. "That's exactly what you have to do."

Cilla dutifully laid her cards face up on the table. "I don't think I'm very good at this."

Lucky leaned forward to assess them. "Actually, you're better, or worse, than you think you are because you could have gone Gin."

"Oh." Cilla turned her mouth down at the corners. "So do I win or lose?"

"Let's call it even."

Cilla plucked a card from the pile and looked at it without revealing it to Lucky. "What card am I holding?"

Lucky squinted at her. "Two of hearts."

Cilla was impressed. She turned the card around. "Three of hearts. That was pretty good."

"You know what they say about me. To be fair, I'm only half witch."

"What's the other half?"

"Gin and chocolate cake?"

Cilla laughed. "I'm probably seventy percent apple pie at the moment. Five percent ice cream."

Lucky picked the cards up and began sorting them so they were all facing the same way. "Actually, I do have a magic tree."

Cilla took another sip and got a lemon seed. She thought about spitting it back into her glass but swallowed it instead. "What magic does it do?"

"Do you believe in magic?"

Cilla contemplated the question but couldn't draw a conclusion. "Undecided. Will the tree convince me?"

"The tree is only as powerful as you believe it is."

"What does it do?"

"Come have a look first."

They both stood, and the dogs jumped to their feet too. Cilla followed Lucky's route across the room and along the hall. Lucky didn't turn the light on in the kitchen, but the waxing moon illuminated the room enough to navigate to the back door that led out to the darkened porch. Outside, the air was cool and the smell of soil and damp foliage was all around. The dogs went off with noses down to sniff through the grass. Overhead, the stars were like holes for the light to get through. The plants shone silvery under the lunar glow and the oak tree rose large and mysterious against the sky.

"There she is," Lucky said, halting her stride to gaze at the tree.

Cilla was slightly awed by its expansive arms and weathered trunk. They crunched over the fallen leaves to stand beneath it. Its scent reminded Cilla of the tin her mother kept the baking spices in growing up. The remaining leaves seemed to whisper above them.

"What does the magic tree do?" Cilla asked.

"It's unpredictable, but if you stand here at a full moon, strange things are liable to happen."

Cilla peered up through the gaps in the branches and a tingle ran along her spine. "Is it full tonight?"

Lucky grinned and a moonbeam caught her teeth. "Almost." She tipped her head back to look up into the rustling leaves. "Can you feel that?"

Cilla's pulse was thudding so hard being in close proximity to Lucky. She wasn't sure if it was magic or adrenaline, but she was tingling all over like her body was vibrating at a high frequency. She nodded. "I feel something."

Lucky looked at her. "It's the tree."

As lovely as the tree was, Cilla thought, it was probably more that Lucky was so close that she could feel the radiant heat from her body. She felt Lucky's cool fingers find her own, which sent a zing up her arm. Nope, definitely not the tree. Cilla tried to take a deep breath, but it felt like the air was skimming the surface of her lungs. Who needed breath right now anyway? She could probably survive on this feeling alone. It was rising in her, swelling her heart as she looked into Lucky's eyes, a current running between them. Somehow Cilla's hand had found Lucky's waist and Lucky's hand was on the back of Cilla's neck, and it felt like the ground had opened and she was tumbling through Lucky's eyes into the best kiss of her life. Lucky's lips were soft and she tasted of gin and lemon. Time slowed and Cilla lost herself in the unexpected pleasure of the kiss. Until her phone rang in her pocket.

CHAPTER NINE

And just like that, the spell was broken.

Cilla pulled back. "I'm sorry!"

The phone continued to ring, and she pulled it from her pocket, seeing the name *Georgina* flick across the screen before a missed call notification popped up.

Lucky glanced down at the phone, but Cilla couldn't tell by her expression if she had seen the name or not.

"No, I'm sorry," Lucky said. "I shouldn't have launched on you like that. I got caught up in the moment."

Cilla flicked the phone to silent as she placed it back in her pocket. "You didn't launch at me. I kissed you back. I like you, I just…" The good feeling was being replaced by a heavy feeling in her stomach. "I should go. Thank you for a fun evening."

"Don't feel you have to run off, but believe me, I understand." Lucky waved her hands in front of her face. "Let's just pretend it never happened. It's been a long time between kisses, and I don't know what overcame me. Let's forget it."

"Good idea." Cilla laughed in a way that sounded false to her own ears. She was fairly sure—in fact, she was entirely positive—that she would never be able to forget it. "I should go."

They called the dogs and walked back into the house, the slight distance between them growing awkward. Thoughts were leaping through Cilla's mind like jumping fish from a river. That kiss was amazing and she didn't want it to stop, but she had a girlfriend. Still, being with Lucky felt so different from being with Georgina. She just needed to be by herself to process what had happened.

Lucky walked her all the way through to the front door, and when she opened it for Cilla, she didn't look her in the eye. Cilla didn't want to leave things on a sour note. She drew Lucky into a hug and whispered, "Thank you. That tree really is magical."

Lucky laughed. "I'm glad you agree. Sorry again. Too much gin for me. Do you feel okay to drive?"

"Yes, absolutely." Cilla busied herself with Benson's leash so she wouldn't have to look back up, then coaxed him along to the car. She could sympathize with his unwillingness to leave.

At home, Cilla couldn't sit still. She felt like her body was a shaken soda bottle full of excitement with a splash of guilt and a chaser of confusion, and that at any moment the lid might pop off. It was giving her a different angle on her relationship with Georgina. Georgina didn't make her feel like she was walking on air, but that wasn't fair. They had been together for a long time. Relationships got stale; that was completely normal. But a little voice inside her said she felt calm and happy around Lucky. She was free to be herself.

She took a deep breath. She was getting way ahead of the situation. It was one kiss. Half a kiss, really. Almost a peck on the lips, and Lucky had immediately retracted it. The feeling of kissing Lucky rushed back, and she felt her heart expand with a painful joy. She had run off on poor Lucky but she didn't know what to tell her. She took her phone out and saw two missed call notifications from Georgina and a text message. The message said that Georgina had escaped the office earlier than expected and did Cilla want her to grab takeout on the way through. Cilla hastily typed back a message that she had eaten. She hoped Georgina hadn't already bought the food or she would be annoyed. Georgina didn't respond immediately, and Cilla's fingers itched to message Lucky but she knew she shouldn't. She needed to get some control over herself first. Benson watched her stand up from the sofa and pace over to the record player, flick through the stack of records on the shelf without picking one, then go sit back down. She wanted to cry and she wanted to laugh and she wasn't sure what she wanted but it didn't feel right.

"You know what?" she said to Benson, wondering as she said it whether she was drunk from the gin. "I'm going to go for that jog."

Benson looked at her uncomprehendingly. Clearly the word *jog* was not in his doggy vocabulary. He followed her from the room with hesitant excitement as he could see she was moving purposely to do something. She pulled on sweats and her running shoes and got her keys and Benson's leash. She didn't allow herself any time to think about it, just headed out at a brisk walk along the street in the opposite direction from Lucky's, and when she reached the end of her street, she began to jog. All her parts felt a bit jiggly, but it wasn't so bad, really. Benson lolloped along beside her until she got to the park and let him off leash. Her pace wasn't much faster than a walk but she was jogging, carefully scanning the evening ground lest she should trip. Past the water fountain, past the playground. It was hard work focusing on keeping her legs going, and her lungs weren't too pleased either. Her mind slid to Lucky. *Nope, back you come. Breathe in, breathe out.* She headed along by the river and had to drop back to a walk. She hadn't made it very far, so she walked for thirty seconds then took up a running stride again, squinting into the dark, her pace hastened by the fear of murderers in the bushes. Benson scooted around sniffing at trees and patches of grass. She startled as someone rounded the path, but it was just a man walking his dog. Cilla puffed a greeting as they passed, aware that her face must resemble the inside of a watermelon. She should stop seeing Lucky at all. Should she tell Georgina that she had been hanging out with Lucky? No, that was a terrible idea. Should she tell Lucky that Georgina was her girlfriend? She thought back to Lucky's comments about Georgina. Ugh, also a terrible idea. This was like that game "Would You Rather?" that she and her sister had played as kids. Would you rather eat raw turnip or give yourself five papercuts? Would you rather run through the graveyard at night or tell Charles Donnard that you think he's hot? Neither! She didn't want to do any of those things, and she hadn't. She'd quit the game when it got too intense and told Deb that she didn't want to play anymore. She slowed to a walk and tried to catch her breath. She needed to quit something. She did like to play things safe, and she and Georgina had been together a long time. Lucky was just a friend. She needed to draw a line in the sand. She took a long haul of air and began to jog for home, grateful to leave the black night-shapes of the park.

Back home, her muscles were tight and she was proud of herself—about the jog, at least. The feeling of Lucky's lips on hers appeared in her mind, accompanied by a thrill, and she pushed it aside. She checked her phone and there was another call from Georgina. She hit call, and when Georgina finally answered she could hear chatter and music in the background.

"Georgina?"

"Cilla, I'm at The Nobody. It's too loud in here."

"I've already eaten, sorry."

"What?" Georgina yelled above the background noise, then, "The cabernet."

"What?" Cilla asked, pressing the phone to her ear.

"Not you. I can't hear you, Cill. The tile guy is starting tomorrow. I'll have to stay at your house for a few days."

"What?"

"They had a cancellation and can slot me in early."

"You're staying at my house?"

"To do the tiling. The man is coming to do both the bathrooms tomorrow. I can't hear you. I'll call you later."

The line went dead, and Cilla stared at her phone for a moment. For years she had dreamt of living with Georgina, but

Georgina rarely stayed over and usually only if she was drunk and Cilla was driving. In fact, the only time Georgina had stayed two nights in a row was when her hot water system blew and the plumber couldn't get there until after the weekend. Cilla's house was old and drafty. It didn't have the modern conveniences that Georgina's had, and Cilla knew that. She looked around at the disheveled room and realized she would have to tidy up and change her sheets and make sure the shower was clean and the basin was free of toothpaste smudges. She didn't feel like cleaning now. She felt like resting her legs that were unaccustomed to any pace faster than a walk, but she went to get the vacuum. She passed the photo of her and Georgina at a brewery in Oregon. It was only a few years ago, but Cilla looked so much younger and fitter and, well, happier. Her face was glowing and her eyes were lit up by a smile. Georgina looked unchanged. It made Cilla feel like crying. She wiped the dust from the glass with her sleeve. Something had happened but she wasn't sure how she had gone from one-half of a happy couple who liked to do things together to someone who was about to do an anxiety-clean because she was worried her girlfriend wouldn't stay again if everything wasn't perfect.

CHAPTER TEN

"Wouldn't it make more sense to do one bathroom and then the other so you can use one?" Cilla asked the next evening.

"Under normal circumstances, yes, but Silas gets so booked out. It's only because I know him intimately through work—well, professionally intimate—that he agreed to do mine at all. The fact that he had this cancellation and it's such a small window means he can come in and tile both rooms and then be done. I can't have anyone else touch it, you know I'm a perfectionist. It's the artist in me. I feel down if I'm surrounded by unattractive things." Georgina's gaze fell on the water ring on the coffee table.

Cilla looked around the living room. Georgina had a way of making her see things with fresh eyes. It was good for her. She found it too easy to ignore a dent in the wall for so long that she no longer saw it. She'd been meaning to clean the walls, and now that she looked, there were some fingerprints by the light switch. "At least it will be done quickly, and it'll be fun spending more time together."

"Yes, that's why I like using tradespeople who are overbooked. You know they are popular for a reason, and they will get the job done quickly."

"Aren't you worried that he'll do a rushed job?"

Georgina picked her feet up from the floor and tucked them underneath her on the sofa as Benson walked in. "If he does, he'll be staying to fix any imperfections or I'll let every new homeowner know not to use him."

Cilla would usually let that kind of comment slide by, but she felt unsettled. "That would ruin his business."

Georgina's laugh was hollow. "I don't care. All he has to do is tile a bathroom properly. That's what I'm paying him for."

Cilla turned her attention back to the movie. She had wanted to watch a romance with Georgina and now that's what they were doing. She should have felt happy, but there was a nagging sensation in her chest that she needed to talk to Lucky and set things right, but she couldn't with Georgina there and she didn't dare risk texting Lucky in case she responded and Georgina saw it. It was for the best anyway. She needed to have some space to get her feelings in check. She really loved being friends with Lucky and she had been happy to have a friend. Nothing had changed. She had kissed women before and gone back to being friends. On the screen, the sexual tension was building and the romantic in Cilla wanted them to tumble into bed. With a sudden bolt she realized that Lucky was the last woman she had kissed. She looked over at Georgina, who was staring at the television, and knew that she didn't want anyone else to erase the feeling of Lucky's lips. Not even her beautiful girlfriend who was sitting right beside her, just where Cilla had always wanted her. Cilla suddenly longed for Lucky's warm smile with its crooked tooth and her forgetful habits. Her wild hair and eccentric ideas.

"How come you said you would stay and never did?"

Georgina turned to look at her. "What? I even brought my pillow."

"Yes, but I mean so many times before. At the start, we would go away on vacation together and I would stay over and you would always talk about how you wanted to get a place together. But it was just talk."

"I'm literally here. I have an incredibly demanding job, you know. I can't just snap my fingers and make things happen. Besides, it feels like you're not really on the same page as me. I thought we were both into taking care of ourselves. I like the restaurant culture and doing things, not just staying home all the time or walking the dog." She turned back to the movie. "For someone who apparently wants me to stay, you're not making me feel very welcome."

Cilla's cheeks burned with shame. There wasn't much she could say to any of that. She had put on weight and she had been spending a lot of time at home, and now that Georgina was here, she had started an argument. "Sorry, I didn't mean it like that. It's just that…don't you feel our relationship has changed over the years?"

"No. It's fine. See, this is why we couldn't live together. One night and you're getting upset over nothing."

Cilla didn't bother responding. Maybe the on-screen couple shouldn't tumble into bed after all. "You know what, I think I'll turn in."

Georgina looked over at her with surprise. "You were the one who wanted to watch this."

"I know, sorry. I think jogging is taking it out of me. My fitness isn't very good."

"I could have watched *Real Housewives* after all."

Cilla stood up and shook her leg to vanquish pins and needles. "You could have. Are you coming to bed too?"

Georgina stared up at her. "Let me know when you're done in the bathroom. I need to do my facial rejuvenation routine."

Cilla escaped to the bathroom and contemplated sending a text to Lucky, but Lucky hadn't texted her either and it would be awful if Lucky responded while Georgina was peering over her shoulder. Cilla knew that she would make a terrible spy. Leading a double life just wasn't for her. She needed to tell Georgina that she and Lucky were friends.

Cilla awoke to the sensation of the mattress dipping as Georgina rolled out of bed to get to the early gym class. It wasn't even daylight yet. She must have fallen asleep before having the conversation about Lucky. She turned to say good morning, but Georgina had already left the room. Cilla reached for her phone, but there was nothing from Lucky. She pretended to be asleep until Georgina left, then she stared miserably into the dark for five minutes, having circular thoughts that seemed like a whirlpool sucking the joy out of the day. Benson came to stare at her, his wagging tail thumping rhythmically against the chair in the corner until she had to smile.

"Do you want to go for a run?"

The rhythmic tail thumping picked up tempo, and Cilla found that the idea of a jog was somewhat alluring. It must have been the endorphins. She hadn't always been so resistant to exercise. As a child, she had played softball and ran track. She'd never been good at long distance, but she could sprint all right. As she pulled on her running shoes, she reminded herself that it was all mind over matter. Think like an athlete.

That mindset was more difficult to maintain out on the street as her breasts bounced and her stomach jiggled, but she liked the way her thoughts were preoccupied with her body's demands instead of what felt like plumbing the depths of her being with a broken flashlight. As she jogged along the path at the park, the sun was beginning to rise, giving birth to a new day. Everything sparkled golden and dewy. She made it farther along the track before she needed to slow to a walk to catch her breath.

"I'm doing it, Benson! I'm a runner!"

Benson grinned at her, his pink tongue flapping happily from the side of his mouth. Suddenly, his attention was drawn to something. Cilla followed his gaze to the part of the trail that opened to the back streets, and trotting along the path was a Jack Russell terrier. Her heart lurched and Benson bounded forward, but at the same time they realized it wasn't Peanut at all but a different dog with longer legs and a narrower body. Walking along behind was a couple holding hands.

"Benson!" Cilla called a little too harshly, taking off at a jog again. She smiled at the couple as she passed, and they returned the gesture.

By the time she returned home, she had sweat filming her skin and her face was like a red Christmas bauble. Benson went to have a drink and flopped down on the kitchen tiles where it was coolest. Georgina's overnight bag was on the chair in the bedroom but there was no sign of Georgina. The bag was pale-pink leather with rose gold buttons and zipper accents. It was new, or at least so well preserved that it looked new, and was a clear mismatch to Cilla's antique bureau and chair with the worn fabric, home to Cilla's discarded sweater and jeans. Cilla made the bed, which didn't take long as she wasn't one for throw pillows or decorative bedspreads, and got ready for work. She told herself not to check her phone but did anyway. It was still early. Did she think that Lucky would message her at seven in the morning?

CHAPTER ELEVEN

Emma had been listening intently, her burrito paused on the way to her mouth, dribbling sauce toward her wrist until Cilla could no longer take it and wiped it with a napkin. Emma put the burrito back on her plate and took the napkin from Cilla. "Thanks. I can't believe you didn't tell me earlier."

"There was nothing to tell."

It was thirty minutes before happy hour half-price margaritas, and the restaurant had yet to fill up. It hadn't taken much arm-twisting to get Emma to agree to an early dinner after work. "You kissed a woman under a magic tree and now you are reassessing your life? That's something."

Cilla picked up a piece of lettuce that had fallen onto her plate and popped it into her mouth. "I'm not reassessing my life."

"Well." Emma picked her burrito back up and took a large bite, talking through her mouthful. "Maybe you should be."

Cilla was beginning to regret pouring her troubles out to Emma, but once she had started, the floodgates opened.

"Anyway, there's nothing I can do about it. It's probably for the best that Lucky hasn't messaged me." Cilla thought for a moment. "Do you think she's okay? I mean, she is on her own, and if she fell off a ladder no one would know." As she said it out loud, she knew she was being ridiculous.

"Have you called her?"

"No! You've got sauce on your top."

Emma looked down at her paisley shirt and scooped at the sauce with her thumb. "That's why I wear patterns. Pricilla, my misguided friend, allow me to speak plainly, please. I see you have a phone there. Right there, on the table beside your meal—a new thing for you who usually can't find her phone, might I add—and presumably you have Lucky's number?" Cilla nodded. "Pick up your phone and call her. Arrange a time to see her. Talk to her and be clear about what you want."

Cilla glanced down at her phone. "Be clear about what I want?"

"Exactly."

Cilla knew that was the trouble. What did she want? "Is this one of those conversations where you guide me into making my own realizations?"

Emma dropped the last bit of burrito onto her plate and leaned back against the chair. She sighed. "Cilla, I am just killing time until happy hour."

"What if what I want is too hard and I'll never get it?"

"Then you can spend your life with what you sort of want just so you don't ever have to take a chance."

"You're a different generation," Cilla said because Emma was making an uncomfortable amount of sense.

"The generation that knows we are allowed to choose freedom and happiness over tradition?"

"Security?"

Emma raised her eyebrows and reached for a toothpick. "I've got a bean skin in my back teeth."

Cilla felt like she did too. Metaphorically, at least.

A waiter came to take their empty plates, and Emma touched his sleeve. "Excuse me, can happy hour start a few minutes early?"

The waiter looked like summoning an answer while both hands were occupied with dirty plates might be beyond him. "Um, happy hour hasn't started."

"Please? We work at the library and my friend is having an existential crisis that involves some serious life decisions that would be best formed under the influence of alcohol."

The waiter transferred both plates to one hand and picked up the soiled napkin. "Either pay full price for your life decisions or wait eleven minutes."

"Can we at least please get some more water?"

"Hydration station is over there. Go for it."

Emma watched him depart. "I don't know why we come here."

"Two-dollar Taco Tuesdays and happy hour margaritas."

"Well, it's not Tuesday."

"Do you really think I should call her?"

"If it will stop you from glancing at your phone every three minutes, then yes. What's the big deal? You half kissed. She kissed you, whatever."

"Should I tell Georgina?"

"You know how I feel about Georgina. Same way I feel about waiting eleven minutes for a drink when the drink is right there and there is a pointless void of time between me and it."

"Emma, I will buy you a drink."

"That's not the point."

Cilla picked up her phone and it lit up with its screen saver of Benson wearing socks. "Can I be friends with Lucky and be Georgina's girlfriend?"

Emma let the question hang, and Cilla knew that if she had to ask the question, she probably had the answer.

After a moment, Emma said, "You can if you're open with both of them. It's not really a big deal."

Cilla thought that Emma didn't know Georgina at all. It would be a big deal, and if she was truthful, she was scared it might be for Lucky too, but she also knew that she had to be honest about who she was. "Okay, I'll call her, even if it's just to fill in time until the drinks. Is it too noisy in here?"

"Just call her!"

Cilla scrolled through her recent contacts to Lucky's name and hit call. The phone rang and rang until it went to voice mail. She hung up and put the phone down. "She didn't answer."

"That was anticlimactic."

"See, she probably hates me now."

"Yeah, she kissed you because she hates you. How many minutes now?"

"For pity's sake, just let me buy you a drink."

Emma checked the time on her phone. "No, we are so close."

Cilla's phone trilled with the message tone and they both snapped their attention to the screen, but it was Georgina asking when Cilla would be done.

"I'll ask her if she wants to meet us here?"

"Lucky?"

"No, that was Georgina."

"Oh. Sure."

Cilla typed out the message and one came flying back saying that Cilla could meet her at The Nobody instead because Vince was buying after-work drinks. Cilla declined.

"That's okay, she's going to The Nobody for drinks with the office."

"Do you see your life with Georgina, night after night, day after day? Is she the person who has your back?"

"You make her sound like an easy chair."

"If I was to get married, I'd want it to be to someone who I feel excited to go home to. Someone who I know supports me no matter what and has my best interests at the forefront of their mind."

"We're not getting married."

"You know what I mean."

"I thought you were going to the hydration station."

Emma stared at her. "Yeah, okay, I'm finished. We can talk about the man I am definitely not going to marry but will definitely have sex with at least three times this week."

"Pedro the gym equipment hog?"

"Pedro with the nice arms and creative endurance." Emma picked up the water carafe and gave Cilla a meaningful look before she sauntered off to get a refill.

Cilla wasn't sure whether to be pleased that Emma was making her face her dilemmas head-on or annoyed at herself that rather than making things easier, she had made them clearer but harder.

Emma returned with the water and looked at her phone. "Two minutes left. I'm going to walk slowly to the bar and hope I'm served by someone with a more flexible approach to service. Do you want one or two drinks?"

"Just one."

"You don't need to play it safe in the beverage department too."

Cilla shook her head. "Just go get your drink. I'm a middle-aged woman. Safety is my ecstasy."

Three cocktails and a few of Emma's outrageous sexcapades later, Cilla wobbled toward home. It was a mild night with the whisper of a breeze through the drying leaves. Somewhere up above an owl hooted, and Cilla noticed that the moon was full or perhaps one degree past full. She thought of standing under the tree with Lucky, the magical feeling of being with someone who made her heart sing, and instead of opening the gate of her own dark house, she continued on toward Lucky's. It seemed every time she saw Lucky's house it emitted a different feeling. This evening it seemed watchful and bleak. There were no lights on, nor signs of movement, and Cilla almost didn't go up the path, but Emma's words were ringing in her ears. If Lucky never wanted to speak to her again, then so be it. She'd tried. The long grass brushed her legs and a puddle on the broken pavers caught the moon's reflection. Cilla climbed the steps to the front porch but there was no barking. To her right, on the table, moonlight glinted from a pair of discarded glasses. Cilla shivered but proceeded to the door and used the brass knocker to announce her arrival. She waited but there was no sign of movement, so she knocked again, more assertively. When that didn't produce any reaction, she went to the window and peered into the darkness. Maybe Lucky really had fallen from a ladder and was lying on the ground. She called her name and waited, but there was nothing. Surely Peanut would be there too, unless Lucky had fallen on top of him and squashed him, or maybe he had fainted from dehydration because his water bowl was empty. She went to the table and picked up the glasses and unfolded the arms. She put them on her own face in an attempt to view the world through Lucky' eyes. Everything just felt a bit off-center, which was pretty much how she felt after three margaritas anyway. Where would Lucky go without her glasses? She walked down the steps and around the side of the house feeling like she was walking on the moon. The tree stood vast and noble like a cathedral, emitting a magnetic energy that drew Cilla forward. The rustling of its leaves seemed to be speaking a language Cilla couldn't quite understand, but she felt that it was trying to tell her something.

"Where's Lucky?" Cilla asked, then she looked over her shoulder even though she knew no one was there.

There was a swishing coming from the foliage at the side of the property, and two glowing eyes peered at her. Before she knew what she was doing, she'd turned and begun to run back the way she'd come. She didn't stop running until she was back out on the street. She looked back at the house and had the feeling that it was laughing at her. It was a weeknight. How had she let herself have three cocktails?

CHAPTER TWELVE

Georgina opened the door before Cilla had time to finish unlocking it. Benson wagged his tail in delight, but Georgina said, "Where have you been?"

"At the Mexican place with Emma."

Georgina blinked at her, seeming large and blurry. She was still wearing her navy-blue business suit and had the ruthless whiff of realtor on her.

"When did you start wearing glasses all the time?"

Cilla touched the arm of the glasses and whipped them off. "I forgot I was wearing them." She stooped to pat Benson, and Georgina stood aside to let her pass.

"How many drinks have you had? You've got little dry leaves on your pants. You didn't fall over again, did you?"

Cilla continued through to the kitchen and poured herself a glass of water and put Lucky's glasses on top of the fridge where they wouldn't get broken. "Too many drinks. How was The Nobody?"

"Good, except all I've eaten are these breaded fried olive things." Georgina wrenched the fridge door open, wobbling the objects on top including Lucky's glasses.

Cilla watched them shaking, her mind still half with Lucky.

"I might have to eat one of those horrible frozen meals you like." Georgina pulled out a carton and examined the label. "Supercharged lentil and wholegrain bowl." She held it up for Cilla to see. "The packaging tastes better than the meal, no doubt."

Cilla smiled. She knew that usually she would have laughed, but a fiery sensation was growing in her chest, bringing a realization with a flash of clarity. *It's not meant to be this hard.* "Georgina."

Georgina had turned back to the freezer and was pulling out another meal. "Really, some eggs might do me instead. Is this lasagna edible?"

"Georgina."

She turned around with the expectant expression of one who was used to being singled out for compliments. "I'm only joking."

Cilla looked at Georgina's symmetrical face with its pointy chin and brows that made her appear sophisticated and elegant even when she didn't act it. "I think we should break up."

Georgina stood there, the lasagna in her hand like someone had pressed pause. Her dark lashes flicked up and down a few times and her mouth opened to say something but nothing came out.

Cilla felt shocked herself. "We can still be friends."

Georgina turned and put the lasagna back in the freezer and shut the door, causing a cloud of frost to billow. "You want to break up?"

Cilla clutched her own elbows. "I don't know. That sort of came from nowhere."

"I'm literally in your kitchen, depending on you for shelter for the night, and you're going to drop this on me?"

"Sorry, I didn't plan it."

Standing in Cilla's homely kitchen in her dark-blue suit, Georgina looked as out of place as her overnight bag did on

Cilla's old chair. A set expression crept across her face and she drew herself up taller. "What are we even breaking up from? It's not like you ever meet me at the level I need."

"You do need someone on your level who wants to be a power couple with you and do the things you like to. We're just too different."

Georgina made a huffing sound from her nostrils and looked toward the window. "I feel like the person I met is not you. The reality of you is a complete misrepresentation of the way you portrayed yourself to be." She returned her gaze to Cilla and her eyes traveled up and down. "You know what? This is the first thing you've done in years that resembles the girl I met. You've become as insipid as a tea bag drying in the trash. Don't call me, and don't bother begging like last time." She snatched up her purse from where it was sitting on the bench and brushed past Cilla, stopping in the doorway to say, "The only reason I didn't do it myself is because I was worried that you'd have nothing else to live for."

Benson hid under the table and Cilla watched with a panicked feeling as Georgina left the room, listening to the sounds of her collecting her belongings. Georgina's travel mug adorned with her company logo was still on the drying rack. The front door slammed, and Cilla took the mug and dropped it into the trash, right on top of the microwave dinner packages and a used tea bag from Georgina's mint detox tea. Cilla stood looking at it for a moment. She remembered Georgina telling her that she was the prettiest woman she'd ever met. She let the trash lid close. And, begging? How many times had Georgina humiliated her? Still, part of her felt she'd just done something terrible that she couldn't undo.

CHAPTER THIRTEEN

Cilla struggled through the work week even though every morning she lay in bed staring at the ceiling and debating whether or not to call in sick. She did have a headache from crying, but she couldn't bring herself to do it. Karma would probably swiftly deal her a real, unimaginably horrible illness with pustules and green snot. Instead, she allowed herself six minutes of ceiling-viewing—there were some cobwebs she needed to attend to—then she dragged herself out of bed and sadly jogged a lap of the park and back with Benson, who was also sad on account of his Peanut breakup. Cilla had left a voice message for Lucky asking if she was okay and letting her know she had her glasses, but she hadn't heard anything back. Cilla had moved on from the ladder story to Lucky being called away to tend to a long-lost uncle who was dying richly and demandingly in the Caribbean. Georgina had always insisted they send Christmas cards to Cilla's wealthy grandfather who lived in Boston, even though he never sent one back. Cilla remembered him as demanding and overbearing, so she could sympathize with Lucky if that was the case. Or maybe an old flame had called from London and Lucky had thrown her glasses to the wind, knowing she could exist on the seductive touch of her lover alone. Eventually, Cilla decided that Lucky probably just didn't want to see her because she was boring and as insipid as an old tea bag.

"You'd think Peanut would at least have the decency to call you," Cilla said to Benson on Saturday morning after they'd returned from their jog. Benson raised his eyebrows and looked at her forlornly. Peanut was a touchy subject.

The scarf that Cilla had bought for Georgina was hanging over the back of the chair where Georgina's overnight bag had been. Cilla was sick of noticing it and being reminded of her. She shoved it into her closet behind the shoeboxes on the bottom shelf and laid the photo frame down on her bureau so she wouldn't have to see the photo of her and Georgina looking like life was a dessert they were about to dive into. Then she turned down the photo of them with Benson as a puppy. He looked like a fluffy ball of cuteness, but unfortunately Georgina looked equally beautiful, and Cilla did not need to be reminded.

Her friend Will had sent her another photo of his pug, Bowser, this time with a link to its Instagram page. Cilla browsed the images and showed Benson a video of Bowser wearing a dinosaur costume, but Benson was unmoved.

"He's cute but he's no Peanut, is he, Benson?"

Instead of messaging Will back, Cilla decided to call him. She spent an hour on the phone, which turned into a bitch session about all the nasty things Georgina had said to Cilla.

"Did she go home and sleep at her own place where she would have to smell the tile glue or whatever it's called?" Will asked.

"I don't know what she did. They aren't tiling the bedroom, so I'm sure she managed."

"Does she have a mirror on the ceiling over the bed so she can watch herself having sex?"

Cilla blushed, but she laughed. "No! But she does have a self-portrait she painted on the bedroom wall." She felt bad for talking about Georgina, but it was such a relief to let it out.

"I'm picturing one of those glamour photos with the pink feather boa and strings of pearls. *Toddlers & Tiaras* vibes."

"She's not that bad." There was still a part of Cilla that felt the need to defend Georgina. "It's a painting and it's more abstract than that."

"Have you seen Picasso's *Woman Pissing*?"

Cilla started to giggle. "Stop it. Okay, you've made me see the funny side. We can leave her alone now."

"It's those arched eyebrows. She has that wicked stepmother look and it reminds me too much of my father's third wife. When are you coming to stay? I miss you."

At those words, Cilla's levity dropped a notch. It had been so long since anyone had missed her. Somehow, she was the one who had done all the missing: Georgina; her family, who were far away; her friends, whom she rarely spoke to anymore; and now Lucky, who had disappeared without a word. "Thanks, Will. Let's organize something."

"Is that what you say every two years until we are too decrepit to operate heavy machinery?"

"I'll make sure we are in the same old folks' home together. We can share a room and I'll let you put photos on the wall of Jason Momoa."

"I will have moved on by then. My crushes are short and sharp."

"Short and sharp. I'm moving on too. Georgina who?"

"That's the way, Tea Bag."

"You can't call me Tea Bag."

"I'll call you Tea Bag until you come and visit. Bowser loves meeting new friends."

After she hung up, she did feel lighter. She cleaned out her closet, then took the broom and attacked the cobwebs she had been staring at every morning. After that, she weeded the front yard and pruned the rose bushes. She needed to buy groceries, but she was nervous about bumping into Georgina. No doubt Georgina would be someplace more entertaining than the grocery store after dinner, so Cilla would just have to wait. There were plenty of chores to do. As Cilla continued on her home makeover, she contemplated what she did for fun. She used to love photography and dancing and hiking. She thought about Lucky's question about playing the piano. She had loved playing the piano too. Anything to do with music. She wondered at how weak she had been to let Georgina sweep into her life and blow away her own true self until she didn't know who she was anymore except a mirror for Georgina. It wasn't Georgina's fault, it was hers for allowing it. In the garden shed, Cilla found a box of the photos she used to take before digital cameras were around. She had loved capturing nature, and there were occasional portraits of people. There was a lovely one of her sister, Deb, in the kitchen at home with their mother. She put it aside to send to her parents. She felt she hadn't been much of a daughter lately either.

The day passed, and before she knew it the sun was setting and a chill had crept into the air. Cilla went inside to shower and throw her earth-crusted clothes onto the dirty laundry pile. She had ruthlessly culled half her closet in an attempt to be less insipid, but now all she wanted to do was put on her worn-out jeans and T-shirt. Too bad. They were gone. She had no chicken for Benson, and he was staring at her as though he hadn't eaten in days despite the kibble in his bowl. Cilla contemplated serving him a microwave lasagna and then decided that would add insult to injury.

"I know, I'm being silly. It doesn't matter if Georgina is permanently camped out at the grocery store, I have to live my life." She was going to see her at some point. "You're coming with me, though, for protection."

Benson was only too happy to oblige, and he wagged his tail and stood for her to clip his leash on. Together, they set off fearlessly for the store.

Cilla's fears were unfounded. Whatever Georgina was doing, it didn't involve staking out the grocery store. If Cilla hazarded a guess, it would be the gym or The Nobody, two places Cilla was happy to give a wide berth. She was feeling strong. Things were fine, she was fine. At home, she gave Benson his dinner but she couldn't bring herself to eat any microwave food. She needed to start eating better. Lucky's glasses glinted down at her from the top of the fridge. Despite her full day, she didn't feel tired in the least. She should walk the glasses back and leave them where she had found them. She ran her fingers along the frames and over the arms, then put them on again. It made her feel like she was in an altered state and a little bit closer to Lucky. She would return the glasses and forget everyone. She was here for herself, no one else. Sometimes it seemed that Benson could read her mind, and he went to stand in the doorway as though to hurry her along. They ventured out again, this time heading toward Lucky's. Cilla's stride was purposeful, and she kept her head down, pushing straight through the gate and up the path to Lucky's. Benson strained at the leash, making whimpering noises, ecstatic to be in Peanut territory. He bounded up the porch stairs ahead of Cilla, straight to the door. Cilla went to put the glasses back where she'd first found them on the table. She heard yapping coming from inside the house, and the door opened. Cilla jumped back from the table like she'd been caught red-handed, and Lucky's face peered around the corner.

"Cilla?"

"I didn't expect to see you."

Lucky looked just as surprised to see her. She opened the door wider for Cilla to come in. Benson had already invited himself in with Peanut.

Lucky led Cilla into the front living room where a fire was jumping in the grate. Cilla hadn't even noticed the smoke from the chimney, she had been on such a mission, but now that she was inside she could smell the comforting wood smoke. She tried to ignore the pull to look around at all the lovely old paintings and photos.

"Please, sit. Gin?"

"Not for me, thank you." Cilla took a seat in the same spot she had sat in the first time she had been in the room, only this time she perched on the edge, unsure how the conversation would go. "I accidentally picked up your glasses the other day. I came looking for you and I tried calling, I shouldn't have taken them...well, I didn't mean to."

"I hope you don't mind if I have a glass of gin. Sometimes it helps ground me." Cilla shook her head and Lucky continued, "I was looking for the glasses. I thought I'd put them somewhere strange."

"Sorry, that was my fault. I came to say hello but you weren't here, and I didn't realize I still had your glasses until I got home."

"It's Saturday today?"

Cilla nodded. She supposed the days of the week would blur when there wasn't a job or regular routine to mark the passage of time. "You didn't fall off a ladder, did you?"

"No, I get called away from time to time." Lucky took a sip of her drink, and the ice cubes jangled against the glass.

Cilla waited for Lucky to elaborate but that was all she said. Perhaps she had a secret relationship she didn't want anyone to know about. The thought made Cilla feel jealous, but she worked to keep her face neutral. Or was there a secret job? She stood up. "I'm sorry I took your glasses and I'm glad you're okay."

Lucky smiled up at her. "I made a wish on the feather that I would find them, and then you showed up."

Cilla laughed awkwardly and clutched her elbows. "I guess I'll see you around."

The smile slipped from Lucky's face. "You're welcome to stay."

"Thank you, maybe some other time. Benson!"

Benson looked up at her from where he was rolling on the rug in front of the fireplace with Peanut, and Lucky stood too. Cilla called Benson again and he rolled onto his stomach, alert to what she would say next.

"Really, Cilla, you don't have to go."

"It's dinnertime. I didn't realize you would be back or I wouldn't have dropped in unannounced."

Lucky reached to touch Cilla's arm. "If this is about the other night, it's no reason to go. I promise I can contain myself!" She clearly said it as a joke, but she looked strained.

"Honestly, Lucky, that's the furthest thing from my mind. I wasn't planning on staying, but we can plan something another day."

Lucky's brow furrowed and she dropped her hand to her side. "Sure."

Cilla called Benson again and made her way to the front door, then stood back against the coatrack to allow Lucky to let her out. On the wall was a black-and-white photo of a young woman in front of the house, but the house had a hedge wrapped around the porch railing. The woman wore a blouse and skirt in an indistinguishable pale shade. She was tall and slender but most of her face was obscured by the shade from her hat.

"Cilla."

"Uh-huh?"

Lucky's silvery eyes fixed on her, and it seemed there was the weight of knowledge behind them. "Never mind."

Cilla looked at her a moment longer, and it felt like Lucky was begging Cilla to intuit something but Cilla couldn't read the meaning. Lucky dropped her eyes and Cilla turned for the door. "Bye."

The previous times that Cilla had walked the streets back home with a joyful spring in her step after spending time with Lucky seemed to mock her now. She wondered if the trust and closeness she had felt with Lucky was just a projection and it wasn't reciprocated at all. Benson dragged his paws beside her, wafting an aura of resentful teenager. It had been a huge and confusing week, but Cilla felt like she had made some type of emotional breakthrough—she just wasn't sure where she had broken through to. Even though she was no longer with Georgina, there were residual feelings, and if she was honest with herself, she did feel hurt that Lucky had gone away and ignored her calls and then wouldn't talk to her about it. She thought back to the heaviness behind Lucky's eyes, but she didn't understand what it meant and she was getting tired of worrying about everyone's hidden intentions.

"I'm going to be a basic bitch," she said to Benson as they rounded the corner for home. "I'm not sure what that means, but it feels simple. Less worrying about anyone other than myself, and you. I'll still worry about you, not that you cause me any worry. Maybe more than usual lately. Crushes can do that, I know."

She felt a sense of accomplishment as she approached the tidy garden which no longer had foliage hanging over the street or weeds along the path. Usually by now she would be on the sofa watching television or reading a book, but she just felt pleasantly aware that she had been active all day. She had a quick shot of panic as she realized that she hadn't checked her phone in hours and Georgina might have been trying to call, but then she remembered she didn't have to worry about it anymore, and for the first time she felt calm instead of sad.

CHAPTER FOURTEEN

Cilla noticed an uptick in communication from friends she hadn't heard from in a while. Suddenly, Sam was texting her to come over for dinner and other people she hadn't spoken to for months were checking in. Cilla answered but didn't bite. She knew that somehow news of the breakup had spread and people probably wanted to know if Georgina was back on the market. Cilla was aware that when it came to marketing, whether it was property or herself, Georgina needed no assistance, so she declined the invitations. On Monday, she put her phone on silent and left it in a bedside drawer. It was liberating not to worry about anyone.

By Thursday afternoon, Cilla had changed her tune. She had been doing so well but then she had seen Georgina sitting at an outdoor table at the café attached to the bookstore, and seated across from her was an incredibly attractive dark-haired woman who looked vaguely familiar but Cilla couldn't place. They looked relaxed, a shared cheese board between them, and Georgina was smiling as she spoke. Cilla had stopped in her tracks on the way to the grocery store and pivoted before she was in Georgina's line of sight, then scurried home without buying anything. At home, she had burst into tears, remembering the times that Georgina's generous spirit had shone through and all the sweet things she had said. By Friday morning, she felt she had made a grave mistake.

"You don't miss her," Emma said as she scanned the emails that had accumulated in the library inbox overnight. "You're still adjusting, and your Georgina addiction is telling you it's time for a hit." She looked over her shoulder at Cilla, who was sorting the returns that had come in. "By the way, apparently we have inherited eighty million pounds from a business magnate in Spain. The money has been fully recovered by the United Nations fund recovery committee, so we have their assurance that our bond fee will be returned in full."

Cilla took a disinfectant wipe and cleaned some crusted cereal from the cover of a children's book. "They should know librarians can't afford a bond fee."

"Plus, I'm sure there's some type of currency conversion involved. Reply or delete?"

"Delete." Cilla ran the wipe over a thriller, not wanting to know why the cover was sticky. She wondered if Lucky had read the Stephen King book.

"May as well, because we've also won five hundred million in a super jackpot. Actually, there's an email from a local author wanting to do a book launch."

Cilla threw the wipe in the trash. "Who is it?"

Emma turned around to address Cilla. "Helen Bowers."

"Local?" Cilla hadn't heard of any local authors by that name. "What has she written?"

"Historical romance. Says here she has just moved to the area and is keen to get to know some people and do a reading of her new book."

Cilla stacked the returns onto a cart. "I'm fine with it as long as she wants to provide snacks. Wait and see what Roger says because an evening would probably work better. Just flag the email and we can respond later."

"You know, Cilla…" There was a sly tone to Emma's voice that made Cilla feel Emma wanted something from her.

"Yes, Emma?"

"I think you should Google Lucky."

Cilla laughed. "What for?"

"To figure out what her deep, dark secret is."

"I'm not Googling her."

Emma was already opening a browser window. "What's her last name?"

Cilla sent her mind back through the conversations she'd had with Lucky, and she had to admit to herself that she didn't even know Lucky's name. "Not sure."

"Is Lucky a nickname, or her actual name?"

"I'm not Googling her!"

"I know, I am."

Cilla spun the cart around and left the service area to go put the books away. Thankfully, a woman approached Emma with items to check out and Cilla could busy herself with other tasks. But by late morning, Emma still hadn't forgotten, and as Cilla was inputting cataloguing data into the computer system, she said, "I know what you have to do."

"About what?" Cilla felt she already knew what.

"You need to find the historical sale records for the house."

Cilla sighed. "What for?"

"Because I've tried looking her up and there's not enough to go on, even for a world-class Internet investigator like myself."

"I wouldn't even know how to do that."

"You know who would?"

Cilla's mind was momentarily blank until local realtor Georgina popped into her head. "No!"

"Not even if she was right over there?"

Cilla frowned. "Over…" Her words caught in her throat and a cold sensation permeated her body. Georgina was walking through the entrance dressed in a gray power suit, and hot on her heels was the brunette woman from the café. There wasn't even time to run and hide. All Cilla could think was, *I'm not ready for this!* She busied herself with the computer screen. She had lost her train of thought, so she just typed random numbers into the field box to make herself look busy. Title? Cilla typed in "Ground swallows up librarian" and hit enter even though she knew she would have to go back and delete it later. From the edge of her awareness, she could see Georgina and her friend approaching at a businesslike clip.

"Hello, Emma," Georgina said, ignoring Cilla. "I wanted to bring in our newest journalist and novelist and introduce her. This is Helen Bowers. She's just bought that lovely little place beside the church."

Cilla's mouth almost popped open. Lovely place? Georgina had referred to it as ugly last time. Cilla knew Georgina was a great salesperson.

"Welcome, Helen," Emma said.

Cilla didn't know what to do. It was so awkward. She was right there, but as Georgina hadn't acknowledged her, she felt she couldn't bust into the conversation.

Helen reached out a hand toward Emma. "Thank you, Emma. This town is adorable. I can't wait to move in."

"Helen is staying with me for a few days," Georgina announced, most likely for Cilla's benefit. "We just wanted to do an in-person visit because Helen is launching a new book and she emailed about organizing a meet and greet."

Cilla was about to make herself scarce when Emma said, "Helen, this is Pricilla Davis. She's the coordinator here."

Cilla could feel a flush creep along her neck and cheeks, and she pretended she had been so absorbed in the cataloging that she was noticing the group for the first time. "Hello, yes, that's me."

Helen was intelligent-looking with a slender face, pale brown skin, and shoulder-length hair. Cilla wanted to dislike her but she looked too friendly. Helen extended a hand again, wafting a floral scent, and Cilla shook it. She had lovely cool skin. "Hi, Pricilla. Sorry to barge in, I just thought you're probably swamped by emails, and I wanted to organize a few things while I'm here and before I get snowed under with moving. Georgina said you were all so lovely here. Pricilla, have I seen you jogging in the mornings at the park?"

Cilla felt her blush intensify at the thought of anyone witnessing her puffing along. "Possibly." She felt she had to do the right thing and greet Georgina. "Hi, Georgina."

Georgina smiled, showing her very white teeth. Her phone rang in her purse and she fished it out and mouthed, "Client." Cilla felt a mixture of relief and disappointment as Georgina turned and walked farther away for privacy. It was hard to know how to behave, but having Georgina look her in the eye and mouth "Client" in the exact way she used to when they were a couple made Cilla's heart constrict.

"Always on the clock." Helen smiled, and Cilla thought, *Right, you are fucking. That took all of thirty seconds.* Then she felt ashamed of herself and pushed the thought away.

Emma quickly picked up the conversation. "It'll either be Roger or myself who will work with you on the event, as I'm assuming you'll want to do it in the evening? Usually the author supplies some little nibbles and drinks, although sometimes we have some wine here." She dropped her voice. "It's not very good." Her voice picked up again. "The deli on the main strip will do platters for you depending on budget. We can put some posters up on the bulletin board if you want to send us a file, and we can post the event on the library social media channels. There's an online booking system for free events so we know how many to attend, but it's all straightforward. Did you have a date in mind?" Emma clicked open the calendar on the computer she had been using.

"A couple of weeks?"

Emma looked up and Cilla paused in scrolling through the catalogue items.

"I'm excited to time it with the new book's release. I have a decent social media following of people from around the country, and I'm sure people will show up, even here."

In her peripheral vision, Cilla saw Georgina talking into the phone, idly picking up a book on the recommended display shelf, turning it over to scan the cover, then putting it back. Cilla was about to make an escape to the lunchroom, but an elderly man approached the circulation desk looking for assistance with the

Internet on the community computers. Cilla didn't need to be asked twice. She led him over to a workstation to help him log in. Once he had logged in, he knew how to browse the Internet but Cilla ensured his unsolicited tutorial was in-depth.

"I think I'm okay now, thank you," he said once he was on a page about fighter jets.

"No, no, it's fine," Cilla said, glancing over her shoulder to see if Georgina was still there. "Let me show you how to do an advanced search."

"I'll only forget it," he said good-naturedly, peering at the screen through his reading glasses. "Yes, this is the right page. Thank you. It's just that my grandson liked my model planes, and I thought I could print this page out for him so he can look it up at home. They live in Tulsa, so I don't see as much of them."

"It'll be easier to send him a link than to print anything. Do you have an email address for him?"

The man peered up at her. "Oh, I don't know if he has his own one. My daughter works at an architectural firm there. They do a lot of infrastructure work."

Cilla was watching Georgina in the window reflection. She looked like she was getting ready to leave. Yes, Helen was saying thank you and glancing Cilla's way. "How old is your grandson?"

"Seven."

"Lovely age."

"Perhaps you might help me print this information?"

Cilla heard Emma saying goodbye and watched Georgina and Helen cross the room until the reflection lost sight of them. Relief flooded her body. "Sure. I might even have an envelope for you. I'll check."

When Cilla returned to the circulation desk, Emma was laughing. "What on Earth were you cataloguing?"

"Oh." Cilla looked at the screen and had to laugh at herself. "Please delete 'Oh God make it stop' and 'Ground swallows up librarian.'"

"What about 'Helen's the one with a sex mirror on her ceiling'?"

Cilla grimaced. "May be an ebook sensation but, yes, delete." She groaned. "I'm sorry. I should be over it."

"I hope someone writes that book, I kind of want to read it now." Emma highlighted the entry and hit delete. "Don't they say it takes half the length of a relationship to get over it?"

"What? You're telling me it'll take years?"

"Nah, I think you're well on your way. But listen, I did ask Georgina about historical property records, and she said you can look them up online."

"You didn't mention Hollyoaks did you?"

Emma rolled her eyes. "I'm not an idiot."

"Good."

"But I do think you're being one about Lucky."

"Wow, tell me how you really feel."

Emma smiled. "I always do."

"I'm going to make a coffee, do you want one?"

"You're overreacting. Just because Georgina played you like a badly tuned violin, doesn't mean Lucky is a player. You're writing off the friendship over something small. At least discuss it first."

Cilla stared at her a moment. "That's no to a coffee, then."

"No, it's a yes to a coffee."

"I really don't like you. Find that gentleman an envelope for this printout, will you?"

Cilla dropped a sheaf of papers onto the desk and went to make coffee in the little kitchen. She thought about what Emma had said. There was nothing she could do about it now anyway. Her phone was still in the drawer at home.

Emma's words were still ringing in her ears as she walked home from work. Had she written Lucky off unfairly? When she opened the door at home, Benson greeted her with his furry enthusiasm, but he had been generally flat too. Every day was starting to feel the same. Wake up, jog, work, home, putter around, sleep, repeat. "Some days we go to the store," Cilla said out loud as she hung up her jacket. Benson cocked his head at her. "You're all right, of course. I'm socially incompetent and as insipid as a tea bag." She was almost ready to laugh about the tea bag comparison but there was still some sting to it. She went to her room, retrieved her phone form its hidey-hole, and turned it on. Thank goodness it was the screensaver of Benson in his socks instead of Georgina and Cilla at the beach. Instantly, messages started to ping onto the screen. Cilla felt a rush in her chest as she saw Lucky's name pop up. There were several messages from her sent a couple of days apart.

Hi Cilla, how are things? Keen to have a chat if you're free.

Have you seen the moon? It's like a glowing wheel of Camembert. Just think, right now, someone is looking up at the moon and eating camembert.

Hi Cilla, I hope everything's ok. Your phone is going straight to voice mail. You haven't been climbing ladders, have you?

Call me! I'm worried!

Cilla stared at her phone for a moment. The prideful part of her said that Lucky had disappeared without speaking to her so she could have a taste of her own medicine, but the reasonable part of her really missed Lucky and knew that she was a good person who didn't owe Cilla anything. The last message had been sent yesterday. A warm relief crept over her that made her want to cry. She felt like since her relationship with Georgina, she was so anxious that people didn't mean what they said or that people were liable to lose complete interest in her and wander off. The number of times that Georgina had played hot and cold with her, and she had allowed her to come back when she was ready. Cilla didn't know what was normal anymore. She thought of what Emma had said about discussing things before writing the friendship off. It was sad that she had to get life advice from a person half her age. She took Benson's leash from where it was hanging on the coat rack and Benson immediately began to bounce around, huffing happily. She didn't want to say the P word in case Peanut wasn't there, but as soon as they closed the gate behind them and started heading down the street in the direction of Hollyoaks, Benson began pulling Cilla along like he was a fluffy tugboat. It was easier to run along with him.

Cilla slowed the tugboat to a power walk as they approached the property. It looked different again. Instead of menacing, the windows glowed warmly, as inviting as melted butter on bread fresh from the oven. Cilla let Benson lead the way up the path, immediately enveloped by the autumnal scent of decaying leaves and damp grass, combined with the spicy scent that reminded Cilla of nutmeg and cinnamon. Benson announced their presence with a yap at the door, and Cilla stood nervously on the top step leading to the porch, unsure of the reception she would receive. The glasses were no longer on the table. There was the sound of Peanut's barking, and Cilla let go of the leash before her arm was popped out of its socket. The door swung open and Peanut bounced out. Lucky's silhouette was backlit in the doorway. The dogs bounded out onto the porch, almost knocking Cilla over. Cilla grabbed the porch railing for support as Benson rebounded from her leg.

"Right now, there's someone in the world knocking on a front door," Cilla said.

"Cilla!" Lucky said. "Come in. I should imagine there are lots."

"Thank you."

Lucky held the door for Cilla and Cilla tried not touch Lucky as she sidled into the entrance, but she caught a breath of the bouquet of scents that were unique to Lucky and felt her knees wobble. She chastised herself. She was too old to let attractive women wobble her knees. Or was she? Her hands suddenly itched to grab Lucky, and she felt like her energy field was being teased by Lucky's.

Lucky closed the door behind them. "Where would you like to sit?"

"Wherever. I interrupted you."

"You've interrupted nothing at all. I was writing something in the kitchen while I was cooking soup and polishing some silver."

"That's a lot of things at once," Cilla said, feeling the awkwardness beginning to melt away. "I don't think I've ever polished silver."

"We can remedy that." Lucky led Cilla through to the kitchen, which was warm from the open oven and pleasantly steamy with the smell of something on the stove. On the kitchen table, the Stephen King book was lying open, face down, its already cracked spine curling further, and cutlery was spread out on a tea towel. Lucky picked up a notebook and pen from the table and placed it on top of the fridge.

"See, this is what happens. I polish a few pieces and get sidetracked and so I never have a full set of polished silverware and then I think, what does it matter? No one ever comes to use it anyway. So I put it away again in a hodgepodge of dull and sparkling. I can't even claim a method to my madness because I just grab whatever is closest."

"How about I polish while you finish the soup?"

"Oh, the soup!" Lucky went to lift the lid of the pot. "I was going to add some chicken. Never mind. Sit anywhere you like."

Cilla pulled out a wooden chair and sat facing the stove and picked up a polishing cloth. Lucky stirred the soup and replaced the lid, then came to sit opposite Cilla. They both began to speak at the same time. Lucky stopped. "You go first."

"I was only saying that my phone has been in a drawer at home. I didn't mean to ignore you."

The expression on Lucky's face was unreadable, and Cilla got the impression that Lucky was assessing something. After a beat, Lucky said, "Why was it in a drawer?"

Yikes. That was a good question. Cilla picked up a spoon and rubbed the cloth over its stained face, like a speckled moon. Cilla wanted to avoid answering but she felt that was a surefire way to resolve nothing. She thought of Georgina. Telling Lucky about the breakup would involve admitting she had a relationship in the first place, and it was too far gone. She knew she would have to do it at some stage, but it felt like they were just building a friendship bridge over troubled waters again. She was aware of Lucky waiting for an answer, but she was resisting letting her feelings for Lucky show. Her upside-down reflection stared back at her in the spoon, mirroring the confusion of her inner world. She placed the spoon on the tea towel, and when she looked up she caught sight of a list that was fixed to the fridge with a magnet. It read:

Old cemetery
Rose festival (spring)
Summer fair
Portrait prize
Library

Lucky cocked her head to the side. "You don't have to tell me."

Library? Suddenly Cilla wanted to tell her. "Lucky, I like you. I really like you! I was sick of looking at my phone and never seeing your name come up."

A slow smile crept across Lucky's smooth lips and she bit down over it, looking like a small girl despite the gray through her hair. Cilla wanted to take her face in her hands and kiss her. Then, just as suddenly as it arrived, the smile fell and Lucky was nervously chewing her lip. "Cilla, there's something I should tell you, but I think I will have to show you first."

"Okay."

"Will you come outside to the tree?" Lucky seemed to remember what had happened under the tree last time and she looked away. "Not...not for that."

Cilla had to admit that she was disappointed. The more she looked at Lucky, the more she wanted "that," but obviously Lucky regretted their kiss. So what? Cilla had told Lucky that she liked her, and Lucky didn't like her back. Not in that way. Cilla hadn't expected her to. It didn't hurt that much. She stood up and Lucky looked relieved. She motioned toward the back door. "I once knew this girl who would make these handmade books full of her thoughts and then eat them page by page. Weird, huh?"

Cilla laughed, but she wasn't sure if it was a joke. She thought of the notepad Lucky had hastily shoved on top of the fridge. "One way to eat your words."

Lucky turned the gas burner off and they went out into the cool evening air. "It was deep and messed-up but very self-contained."

"Did she let anyone read the books first?"

"Her thoughts weren't that interesting."

Cilla thought about her own dull habits and embarrassingly recurring thoughts of Lucky. "I would have thought someone who ate volumes of their own musings would have interesting ideas."

"Let's just say I found them hard to digest."

Cilla laughed, drawing in a waft of night. "Can you smell that?"

Lucky sniffed the air. "I don't know, is it bad or good?"

Cilla stared at the tree shimmering under the light of a million stars. "Good. Like pumpkin spice." She had to pause to admire the tree from a distance first. "The tree reminds me of a creature. A gentle giant."

Lucky stopped beside her. "I'm glad you feel it too. It's like the spirit of nature. At once a castle and an old wise man and a lighthouse. It's impossible to feel anything other than awe and enchantment under this tree."

Cilla felt the same magnetic pull drawing her toward its gnarled trunk. Beside her, Lucky removed her shoes and tossed them onto the ground. Cilla laughed. "What are you doing?"

"Grounding. I love the feeling of the earth under my feet."

Cilla's nose scrunched up. "Isn't it cold?"

"It's lovely and squishy."

Lucky was staring at Cilla with her eyes lit up and her face aglow. Cilla was momentarily lost as Lucky's eyes were fixed on hers. She didn't want to break the spell of feeling Lucky's excitement focused on her, but she bent forward to pull her own shoes and socks off. She shoved her socks inside her sneakers and Lucky offered her hand. Cilla took it and it felt warm and dry and it made Cilla inordinately happy. As they ran across the lawn, Cilla felt the cool softness of the grass tangling at her toes and the damp earth beneath, but it was wonderful. In her haze of happiness, she marveled at how it was all perspective. She had never found running barefoot through the garden a blissful experience before, but now the sky had cracked open into an infinite velvety cosmos that she could feel in her being as though her very atoms were humming the same melody as that of the stars, and the air wasn't nothing, it was full of information and energies that had always been there but she'd never really noticed before. There was nothing separating the atoms that made up Cilla from the atoms that made up the sky.

"Wait!" Lucky stopped abruptly, pulling Cilla to a halt beside her just before the open arms of the tree. She swung Cilla so they were facing each other. "I'm sorry. Let me just say that now, because I do like you. I really like you too, and I did like you from the moment I met you." Cilla's heart sang, and although the words rang true, she scarcely dared believe them. "But," Lucky continued, and Cilla braced herself. There was always a *but*. "If anything happens between us, I will only hurt you." Cilla began to protest and Lucky shook her head. "No, Cilla. I would never intentionally hurt you, but I will end up leaving you and…" She looked down at Cilla's hand held in her own. "Maybe I'm weak, but I really want to kiss you again and I don't want to stop there. I want to touch you right now and feel your skin…"

She trailed off, and Cilla's heart thudded in anticipation of what else Lucky wanted to do. Lucky's eyes were alive with desire and sadness. With Cilla's free hand, she pushed a tendril of hair from Lucky's face, and then they were sizing each other's intentions, eyes-mouth, eyes-mouth, until Cilla's hand moved to the back of Lucky's neck and their lips met. Lucky's mouth was hesitant at first, their lips gently testing one another, and Lucky mumbled, "I'm sorry," and like a dam breaking they were kissing, falling into each other and grabbing at each other. Lucky's hands crept up under Cilla's shirt, and Cilla didn't even care that she had on her old sports bra.

She found the smooth skin of Lucky's stomach, and Cilla's fingers brushed over her navel, feeling the knot of her belly button, an intimate relic of her birth, a mystery to them both. Cilla's nipples jumped to attention as Lucky's fingers swept over them, and Cilla felt like she was on the edge of losing her mind if she didn't somehow have Lucky's entire body and being inside of her. Her hands moved to Lucky's breasts—no bra—her palms lightly brushing over the soft skin and hard nipples. She pulled Lucky's shirt up and then they were stumbling backward under

the tree until somehow they were on the ground and Cilla
was on top of Lucky and Lucky was pulling Cilla's shirt over
her head. Sensations were flying through Cilla like comets,
sensations she had never felt before in her whole life, and she
tried not to squash Lucky as she kissed her jaw and neck and
she heard Lucky gasp as her lips found her taut nipple. Lucky's
fingers were in Cilla's hair and Cilla's hands were wrapped
around Lucky's waist. She found Lucky's lips again and rolled
so they were both on the ground, then said, "I don't want to
squash you."

"You're not, I love it. I can't get enough of you." Lucky's
fingers made their way into the waist of Cilla's jeans. She
breathed into Cilla's ear. "You need to stop me. I can't stop
myself."

"Oh, my God." Cilla squirmed as Lucky's fingers crept
between her legs. "I don't want you to stop."

Overhead, a slight breeze ruffled the remaining leaves,
and somehow Cilla's jeans were undone and Lucky's skirt had
become a belt, and Cilla had never wanted to elicit pleasure from
another person in the same way she wanted to tease every moan
from Lucky right now. It felt like being in a waking dream, where
everything was so perfect that she didn't trust it was true. Like
a dim light at the back of a building, Lucky's comments about
leaving her flickered, but nothing could eclipse the feeling she
was having as Lucky's fingers moved inside of her and the smell
of spiced cinnamon and nutmeg and Lucky's skin and the stars
overhead burst into a firework of bliss that was at once physical
and psychological and like nothing she had known.

Lucky lay half on top of her, her head resting in the nook of
Cilla's neck, and slowly the roots of the tree and the acorns on
the ground made themselves known to Cilla. She shivered, and
Lucky's hand moved to lie flat, its fingers splayed, over Cilla's
heart as though that would keep her safe from the cold. And in a
strange way, it did. Cilla wanted to tell Lucky that she loved her
but she knew it was ridiculous. She didn't know her.

"Was that what you wanted to show me?"

"No. That was what I have been trying not to do." Lucky's voice vibrated into Cilla's chest, and Cilla felt Lucky's cheek pull back in a smile.

Cilla kissed her forehead and marveled that right now she was allowed to do that. She was allowed to touch beautiful, free-spirited Lucky, and hold her, and let those intimate things that she had been holding in spill out. "Do you still want to show me something?"

"Not anymore. I'm afraid that you'll see for yourself, but I'm trying not to think about it for as long as possible. Just don't let me go."

"Are you going to get up and sprint off?" Cilla asked, but Lucky didn't laugh.

The memory of Georgina popped into Cilla's mind. She already felt like a lifetime ago, like a clay model of a real person. Cilla had been worshipping at the altar of a statue when the saint had been standing in front of her with open arms all along.

Lucky raised her head from Cilla's shoulder. "Can you hear that?"

Cilla halted her breath to listen. She exhaled. "Just the sound of leaves. Oh, maybe there is a car in the distance. Why?"

"No reason."

Cilla frowned to herself, but she didn't want to ruin the moment.

"Is your back sore? The ground is all bumpy."

Cilla had to admit it was. "I think there is an acorn lodged where no one wants a tree."

Lucky sat up and reached to help Cilla sit up. "I need a gin, like, now."

Cilla buttoned her jeans and Lucky stood and adjusted her skirt. Cilla snuck a glance up at her standing as beautiful and encompassing as the Statue of Liberty. A queen of wands. In the dark of evening, Lucky looked half in this world, half in the next.

"Cilla, I don't think I'm going to make it."

"Make it where?" Cilla stood up and dusted her jeans off.

"To get a gin! Dammit, why don't I grow lemons out here? Even a lime tree. No forethought whatsoever. I never did have."

Cilla stumbled over a tree root as she tried to keep up with Lucky, who had taken off like she'd heard the start gun for the one-hundred-meter sprint. Cilla's knee hit the ground and she cursed herself for being clumsy, but truth be told, she still felt out of body. She rubbed her knee and looked up for Lucky, but Lucky was gone, only her shoes remained. Cilla halted in amazement and searched the shadows. "Lucky!" Her voice carried loud and alien across the lawn. Something rustled in the bushes, but she couldn't see Lucky anywhere. Cilla couldn't understand why Lucky needed gin so badly. She stared toward the illuminated kitchen windows. Suddenly, it fell into place. Lucky had a drinking problem. Cilla ran her mind over the idea but it still seemed ill-fitting, like a puzzle missing some pieces. She picked up her own shoes and reached the half-open back door and went inside, ready to ask Lucky directly, but Lucky wasn't there.

CHAPTER FIFTEEN

The kitchen was still cozy with the fog of soup. Cilla spun a circle as though Lucky might jump out from inside a cabinet. "Lucky?" At the sound of her voice, there was the clicking of dog paws on the floorboards as Benson came in to see what the yelling was about.

"Where's Peanut?" Cilla asked Benson.

The gin was still on the bench next to a bowl of lemon wedges. Cilla called Lucky's name again and walked into the hall and stuck her head in the living room. The fire was dying in the grate and there was no one there. Cilla's bewilderment was giving way to a mild panic. She felt like she was missing something obvious, but what was there to miss? Lucky had been right in front of her one moment and vanished the next. Had she done something to offend her? It had seemed like Lucky was into it. Cilla sent her mind back over the events of the evening. She didn't think she had forced Lucky to do anything and she knew she could occasionally put her foot in her mouth, but she couldn't recall saying anything that could upset her. Benson went to the foot of the staircase and Cilla stared up the banister toward the mysterious rooms above. She felt that going up the stairs uninvited would be an invasion of privacy, but Benson had no such qualms. He bounded up the blue-carpeted stairs. Cilla paused to touch her fingertips to the blue and gold wallpaper with its foliate pattern of oak leaves and acorns that was echoed in the woodwork of the staircase. She climbed two steps and paused to listen. There was no sound except for the tinkling of Benson's tag and his movements up the stairs. Part of Cilla knew that Lucky wasn't upstairs, but she had to check every corner before she would allow her mind to sink into the strangeness of it all.

Upstairs there was a central landing room with an original fireplace with dark-blue tiling and a mottled mirror. A small desk had been placed in front of tall windows that looked out over the front yard, and on it sat piles of papers. The rest of the room housed two occasional chairs, a sofa, and a coffee table that looked out of place in the Victorian house, like a relic from the seventies. To the left and the right were more rooms, and a door that was ajar to a staircase, presumably to an attic. Cilla crept into the one on the right. Something moved and she jumped, but it was her own reflection in the mirror of an antique wardrobe. There were cardboard boxes piled in a corner, and although there was a bed against one wall, it didn't have the feel of a primary bedroom. Cilla wandered over to the window and looked out across the backyard, afforded a view of the tree and the garden beds with their fading fall colors turned gray by the moonlight. Cilla stared at the tree and marveled that as recently as five minutes ago, she and Lucky had been wrapped around each other beneath its branches. It felt surreal now that events had rapidly changed like a cartoon flip-book, moving the images to create a sequence of actions.

"Lucky?" Cilla called, her voice cracking. Her throat felt dry and her body felt out of sync with her mind.

The primary bedroom was large and opened up onto a small porch. The corner of the room was rounded with elongated windows, following the shape of the turret that Cilla had only ever seen from the outside. There were white window seats with lacy cushions, and beside the windows were tall bookshelves. The bed was against a wall which was papered in an off-white and cream pattern of daisies and roses. This felt like Lucky's room, with the red-and-pink covers hastily thrown over the sheets and a side table that bore a lamp with a lopsided cream shade and a half-filled glass of water. There were Lucky's horn-rimmed glasses folded on top of an old hardback copy of *Vintage Season* with a fabric cover and metallic lettering on the spine that looked like it probably came from the collection of books on the shelves. Despite the strangeness of it all, Cilla was drawn to the bookshelves, so timeless and beautiful with their dull-colored spines. She ran her finger along the rough fabrics and shiny papery covers. "*Black Beauty*," she breathed. "*Wuthering Heights*." Benson charged into the room and skidded to a halt beside her.

"Where's Peanut?"

Benson barked once, imploring her to tell him the answer.

Cilla glanced uneasily toward the landing. It was like a trapdoor had opened up and swallowed the residents of the house. She glanced around the room as though it might contain clues. On the cream walls were paintings of natural landscapes: fields, rivers, forest glens populated with wildflowers. They looked old-fashioned and intricate and very different from Georgina's bold interpretations. On top of a walnut bureau was a framed photo of a little girl with long dark hair, very dark lashes, and a dusting of freckles across her nose. The photo was faded sepia but the dreamy look in the girl's eyes gave her away as Lucky. Without warning, Benson spun around and shot toward the doorway. Cilla's heart bounced up into her throat, and she felt like she was about to choke on the breath. She exited the room, hurrying as quietly as she could back down the stairs behind Benson. She expected to see Lucky standing in the kitchen, but it was still empty. Even the steam from the soup had vaporized itself into extinction. Benson was looking up at her as if to say, "What next?" Cilla didn't have the answers either, so she sat down at the table and picked up the polishing cloth, hoping that Lucky would return in time to forget to finish the set again.

Cilla had no such luck. She had polished all the silver, put the soup away in the fridge so it wouldn't spoil, and washed all the dishes. Three attempted phone calls and a text message later, Cilla was starting to wonder if she was part of some elaborate ruse to get an unpaid housecleaning service. She scribbled a note asking Lucky to let her know that she was okay and dragged Benson out the front, shutting the door on the house but taking its strangeness with her.

She drove home with a knot in her stomach. Lucky had warned her that she would only leave her, but boy, was that quick. Maybe she should have checked the house for a basement or cellar. There could be unstable ladders in the cellar! The thought almost made her turn around, but she could hear Emma's voice in her ear telling her to go home and let the situation sort itself out.

"Just my luck, Benson," she said as she opened the front gate to her cottage. "I finally get lucky and then I don't." Usually she could make herself laugh, but the joke fell short. She remembered Emma telling her that historical records could be found online. She retrieved her reading glasses from beside her bed, went to the living room, and opened up her laptop, unsure what she was looking for but sure that there had to be a missing piece to the strange events. In the yellow lamplight she searched the street address and that brought up other recently sold properties and building plans (ugh!).

As she reached to secure her hair in a bun, she caught a whiff of Lucky's floral perfume on her sleeve and died a slow death of pleasure-pain at the memory of her arms full of Lucky. It made Cilla think that it didn't matter what age you were, the feeling of wanting something so much and getting it was exactly the same. So was the utter despair of having it snatched away. And hovering somewhere in between the two was a bit like having your brain as the ice in a martini shaker, your heart the speared olive.

She stared at the search bar on the screen. Lucky didn't even really know what social media was, let alone have any accounts. She got temporarily sidetracked looking at the land parcels for sale in the area designated for development just outside of town. They were promising schools and playgrounds, and offices and supermarkets, and buses that went directly to the train station and short commute times to the city that weren't that short if you wanted to spend any time at all with your head on a pillow. There were photos of happy children on bicycles and people walking shaggy dogs, sipping lattes, and laughing for the joy of being in fresh country air that was about to become less fresh—in Cilla's opinion, anyway. The small agency Vince and Georgina worked for had adopted an if-you-can't-beat-'em-join-'em philosophy and sold out to the developers, the developers savvy enough to keep the old-town charm of the office so no one really noticed the change, like a sleight of hand. Cilla knew the town was divided over it. Some were welcoming an injection of fresh money and facilities to the area, and some dreaded the disruption to peace and quiet. It was all too close for comfort. She hoped Lucky would stand her ground. If they couldn't get the land behind Hollyoaks, they would at least have a buffer from the creep of the promised new town.

None of this helped explain Lucky's disappearance, though. If she was that scared of a relationship that she had immediately run away, it was curiously at odds with her behavior less than a minute prior. Despite her reading glasses, Cilla's vision was blurring from staring at the screen so intently. Maybe she was looking at it through the wrong metaphorical lens. She typed in "disappearing Lucky," which brought up something about a magician and a cocktail, then she tried "disappearing Twine River," and the browser suggested "disappearance Twine River," which produced a brief list of links to the disappearance of Eleanora Bromwell.

Cilla clicked the top one, and it took her to an article from seven years ago that was brushing the dust off a missing persons case from 1943. Cilla blinked her eyes and squinted at the black-and-white photo of a young woman posed with her chin resting on a loosely clenched hand, her gaze off to the side of the camera. Her dark hair was parted to one side, its softly restrained waves ending in gleaming curls. Despite the languid pose, her eyes had a fire that looked fit to burn a hole in the atmosphere. Something tugged at Cilla like mud sucking at the feet of trespassers in a murky pond. The angles of the face were all Lucky, even the blaze in the eyes. Cilla thought back to the photo hanging on the wall of the woman in the skirt outside the house. Her throat was dry, and her eyes wanted to flick faster over the words of the article than her brain could process what she was reading.

Vanished Without a Trace

Eleanora Bromwell has sunk to the bottom of history with barely a ripple. The young woman's disappearance in 1943 was seen as suspect, however investigations were stymied due to the timeline of the case. It took two weeks for Dudley Bromwell to report his wife missing. The case was treated as suspicious, but despite extensive searches of the area, no trace of Eleanora was found, no suspects identified, no charges laid. Eleanora was reportedly a quiet woman and had only been married for two years. Prior to that she lived at the family acreage on the fringes of Twine River. She was described by townsfolk as a recluse who did not regularly attend church services and was seen only infrequently in town. Although foul play could not be ruled out, no body was ever found and rumors have always swirled around the town as to Eleanora's whereabouts, dead or alive. Despite town gossip, no witnesses have come forward, and even if someone held the missing key, their secrets may have been buried along with the case. Dudley never publicly commented and later remarried, producing one son who died at twenty-one months.

Cilla read the article again, slower this time, trying to take it all in. Then she clicked through the links, but the few amateur sleuth theories merely said the same thing, the information rearranged. All had the same black-and-white photo of Eleanora.

Cilla bookmarked the first article to go back to. There was a thread to what was happening with Lucky—she could feel it tenuous and spidery, too weak to pull on, but it was there. The likeness in the photo…could it be Aunt Nora? It had to be. And there was the part about the recluse by herself in the house. It sounded similar to Lucky. But where would Lucky have gone with Peanut? She didn't even have a car. Benson lay flopped at her feet. She leaned forward and petted his head, and he looked up at her with his eyes showing their whites. Cilla switched off the computer and checked her phone—even though it was right beside her and she hadn't heard it make a sound—then she stared at the wall feeling uneasy. It was too weird and embarrassing to share with Emma.

CHAPTER SIXTEEN

Cilla primed the display shelves with *Meg and Mog* and *Goosebumps* books to keep with the Halloween theme at the library.

"Here, add this one," Emma said, dumping *Pet Sematary* on the top shelf so it knocked over *The Witches*.

Cilla saw Stephen King's name boldly emblazoned across the cover and, as soon as Emma had turned around, took the book and returned it to the shelf. She had done enough promotion for that man lately and she did not need to think about Lucky any more than she already was. Which was just about every waking minute. A day and a half of silence from Lucky's end and Cilla had been deliberating whether to call the police. She didn't know if she should be worried or offended or both. She felt the same way about sex with Lucky. How could she have done that and how could she have not? Everything was up for exhausting mental debate.

She had always loved Halloween; the pumpkin spice lattes, backyard bonfires, and the houses all done up with their cutesy horror. The excitement of the kids' activities at the library, where even Roger got into the spirit and put on his same *Phantom of the Opera* costume every year that he thought made him look like a dashing rogue but most kids thought was a toothless vampire. And the candy. It was almost mandatory to eat chocolate this time of year. On the plus side of Lucky's disappearing act and the breakup drama with Georgina, Cilla had been steering clear of apple pie and ice cream, and jogging was now part of her daily routine. She was by no means 1980s Jane Fonda, but she felt energetic, and more comfortable in her jeans.

"Here," Emma said, making Cilla jump as she appeared beside her, shoving a staple gun toward her hand. "Go put these paper jack-o'-lanterns on the bulletin boards. You're so lovesick you look like you need a puke bag."

Cilla realized she had been staring right through the display shelf into her own imagination that had been presenting all types of horror stories: Lucky hurt, Lucky hating her, Peanut abandoned alone in the big house with no food or water. It was fertile ground for Halloween tales—broken legs, broken hearts. "I think I need to check Lucky's cellar," Cilla shout-whispered, snatching the staple gun.

Emma gently took Cilla's elbow. "What's going on?"

Cilla glanced around, taking stock of the activity in the room. Thankfully, it was quiet, and Roger had disappeared into the kitchen to make a pot of his dandelion tea that would sit by the counter like a putrid diffuser. "You'll think I'm crazy."

"I already do. Come on, let's put these jack-o'-lanterns up." Emma tugged Cilla by the elbow to the bulletin board by the entrance. She held up a leering orange face with its spout of green stem-curls, its features drawn on by an ambitious preschooler. "Fire away!"

Cilla banged a staple into its chin and stem. It felt good. "I was at Lucky's, we did it, and then she disappeared." She fired off another round into the next pumpkin head that Emma held up.

"Wait, there's a lot to unpack in that little bag. By 'did it,' do you mean you had sex?"

Cilla nodded and couldn't help a smile poking through. Emma held another jack-o'-lantern to the next corner of the board. Its purple eyebrows were so large that Cilla had to spear one with a staple like a ring. The artist had signed in large uneven letters on one cheek, "HENRY." Figured.

"I feel like I blinked and missed something," Emma said. "You were moping about Georgina, you half kissed Lucky, and then you panicked and didn't speak to her."

Cilla opened her mouth to protest but a woman approached and said, "Excuse me. Can you recommend spooky stories for a seven-year-old boy that aren't too scary? Gross is okay, but nothing nightmarish."

"Sure." Emma handed Cilla the remaining artwork, giving her a look that said, "To be continued."

Cilla finished decorating the bulletin board, letting a particularly hideous orange face cover Helen Bowers's author photo on the flyer about her upcoming reading. As she walked back to return the staple gun to the cupboard where they locked the office supplies, she could see Emma was now deep in conversation with a different woman by the biography section. It wasn't until Cilla made herself a coffee in the kitchen that Emma found her and stood just inside the doorway, glancing back over her shoulder to make sure someone hadn't started a book fire in a corner, then peppered Cilla with questions.

"Was the sex good?"

"Magical. So in my body but also out-of-body experience. I can't even describe—"

"What do you mean, disappeared?" Emma whispered after another glance back toward the library floor.

"We were walking back toward the house—"

"Wait, you were outside?"

"Yes."

"Okay, continue."

Cilla drew breath. "We were walking back toward the house, and I tripped and looked up and Lucky was gone."

"Gone how?"

"As in vanished into thin air."

Emma took a step farther into the room and crossed her arms. She squinted at Cilla. "Explain."

Cilla blew on her coffee, then took a sip and set the cup back down. She was running the moment back through her mind for the hundredth time. She had heard that each time you remember something, you are remembering the previous time you remembered it, and slowly it became distorted. Sometimes it made her not want to remember happy things for fear of losing them. After a moment where she could almost feel Emma salivating in anticipation, she said, "I really can't. That's exactly how it was. She was ahead of me walking back toward the house, and I stumbled and looked up and she was no longer there. Neither was Peanut. I looked around the yard and then went inside and looked around, and then I hung around for about another half an hour or so and left. Oh, and when I got home, I thought of what you said about historical records and thought it might give me a clue, but instead I found articles about a woman who vanished from the area who looks similar to Lucky and her aunt."

Emma backed up toward the door and said, "Shit. There's an old man waiting at the desk. Anyway, do you mean, like, the woman was abducted?"

"It's a mystery. You can look it up. Do you want me to go and assist the man?"

"No, stay there. This conversation is going into overtime. I'm going to help that dude, and after work we are going to get to the bottom of the disappearing witch."

"She's not a…" Cilla let her words trail as Emma spun on her heel, off to do some work. "Witch," she muttered to herself. Or was she? No, that was silly. Witches weren't real. Well, maybe they existed in Barbados or somewhere exotic where people believed in that stuff and knew what they were doing. Not here in Twine River, where property developers and real estate agents were carving magic from the earth one red-lined parcel of land at a time, and the butcher was Tom McCreedy, who knew everyone's name, and there was a police station and post office down the road from the school. No magic in that. She glanced out of the kitchen door right at a cutout of a witch on a broomstick that was hanging from the ceiling. Its one yellow eye seemed to be staring right at Cilla, its gap-toothed grin all for her. No, beautiful Lucky was no witch. Witches weren't known for vanishing anyway.

CHAPTER SEVENTEEN

Cilla wasn't sure how she had let Emma talk her into driving her past Lucky's. Just the sight of the front gates made Cilla ache with a longing that had sprung up from a depth she didn't know she possessed. Witch or not, Lucky had bewitched her.

"If a witch lives anywhere, it's here," Emma said, mouth agape. "I have always loved this place, though. It reminds me of a picture storybook. When we were kids, we used to dare each other to go up to the door, but we were always too chicken to go past the gate."

"Do you remember Lucky?"

"Not really. That's what made it weird. No one ever saw her. I still can't believe you've, like, been in here, let alone…you know."

Cilla could barely believe it herself. It seemed like a dream. "We were around the back and walking toward the back steps and then, poof, gone." Cilla mimed an explosion with her hands.

"In a cloud of smoke like that?"

"No, just nothing. What do you make of it?"

Emma pursed her lips, her eyes running all over the dark house like mice up a cabinet. "She has to be in there somewhere. She went into the house or the woods. She can't have gone far. She freaked out about it because she's not used to being around people, and she just did the most intimate thing you can do with a person, and she hightailed it. Say what you will, she is a bit odd."

"Look, you could be right that I'm not very good at all that stuff. Maybe she was that unimpressed that she left." Cilla thought of Georgina giving her forthright instructions in bed so it felt like a choreographed dance and reflected that it had felt natural and different with Lucky, then felt a squelch of embarrassment and pushed the thought away. "That's plausible, but it was the speed it happened that shocked me. Also, she seemed happy afterward."

"Could you have hit your head when you fell?"

"It was just a little stumble. My head didn't touch the ground." She didn't want to tell Emma the part where Lucky had said she would eventually leave her because it made her seem like an utter idiot for sleeping with her anyway.

"Do you want to knock on the door? I can wait here in the car."

The house had an unoccupied feeling to it. There were no lights on, and it seemed lifeless like a store after hours. "There's no one home, I can tell." She opened the door anyway because her conscience was still niggling at her that she would be responsible if Lucky was lying in a basement or on a cold cellar floor. As she opened the gate and walked up the path, she was conscious of Emma watching her but also alert for any movements at the windows or barking at the door. There were none. She knocked on the weatherboard beside the door and called out Lucky's name. Nothing. She tried the door but found it locked. She should have ensured she could get back in when she left the other day, but she hadn't thought about it. Plus, that was stalking. She knocked harder and yelled, but there was nothing. She turned around and raised her hands in a gesture for Emma's benefit and began the walk back along the path to the car.

"So weird," Emma said as Cilla got back in. "You know what I think? I think you should come back tomorrow night. Halloween. The magic portal."

Cilla scoffed, but after she dropped Emma home, the idea was still pinging around her head. Halloween, when the veil to the spirit realm was thinnest and magic wove itself around the material world like vapor from a cauldron. Cilla had done a séance one Halloween with her sister and friends in middle school and scared herself so badly that she had never meddled in the dark arts again. Despite that, she had never been scared by the idea of ghosts or spirits, but Emma was right—it was weird. A weird problem needed a weird solution.

* * *

The library was abuzz on Halloween. Kids dressed up as skeletons and devils and witches, Harry Potters, superheroes, and Disney princesses. Cilla had on her spotted dog onesie that she wore every year that made her look like a giant furry fool, but the kids loved it. Roger, as usual, had on his confusing *Phantom of the Opera* outfit, and Emma was dressed as a carrot with an orange unitard and a green sprout of leaves on her head. For the children's benefit, whenever one spoke to her, she would jam her arms by her side and her legs together so she looked more carroty, but one boy still asked her if she was a crayon. Penny had brought in Apricot, who was dressed as a hot dog with a fabric mustard-drizzled wiener in a bun on her back. Penny herself was dressed as a hot dog vendor with a white hat, red apron, and a cardboard tray hanging around her neck that said "Hotdogs $2" across the front. Cilla and Emma had filled black plastic cups with candy as a post-story-time treat, and there was a craft activity laid out on the table to make spiders with pom-pom bodies, googly eyes, and pipe-cleaner legs. Cilla fussed around the table making sure the glitter glue and spider parts were in easy reach. Emma was putting a candy cup at each spot. She pinched a black cat from a candy cup and bit its head off.

"Tonight's the night, huh?"

Cilla stuck her lower lip out and nodded nonchalantly even though she had been thinking of little else. "Guess so." She reached to intercept a toddler trying to get a head start on a candy cup. "Not yet. Story time first." She moved the cup out of reach, and the boy's mother picked him up and gave Cilla a sour look like she was a serpent with forbidden fruit. Cilla resisted the urge to pluck out a green jelly snake and eat it. She hadn't done so well with the forbidden fruit last time herself. She turned to Emma in time to see her reach for a chocolate frog. "Leave the cups alone, there'll be none left. Come on, I've got more under the counter."

They walked back to the circulation desk where Roger was dramatically hurling his cape across his face, trying to get Penny's attention. *The Mating Style of Animal Species* was in the returns pile, so Penny must have brought it back despite not checking it out in the first place. Cilla reached a furry paw dangerously close to Roger's Phantom crotch to retrieve her candy stash from below the counter and held the bowl out to Emma.

"No, thank you, Pricilla," Roger proclaimed loud enough for Penny to hear, even though Cilla hadn't offered him any. "I'm watching my waistline."

Emma took a chocolate frog and Cilla popped a jelly eyeball into her mouth so she wouldn't have to smell the dandelion tea stagnating in Roger's cup. Then she fished two more out and held them over her own eyes and turned toward Emma. She heard Emma snort and removed the candy eyes in time to see Georgina standing on the other side of the desk, blinking incomprehension.

"Pricilla, your lady is here," Roger said unnecessarily.

Cilla didn't bother to correct him, just watched her own fluffy paws place the eyeballs down onto the keyboard of the computer. To her right she was conscious of Emma melting into the background like chocolate caught between warm buttocks and a couch cushion, and to her left, Roger puffing out the chest of his Phantom jacket, readying to dazzle Georgina with a cape-sweep.

"Cilla, I've brought over a box of Helen's latest novel for you to display in the lead-up to the reading. There's a rolled-up poster too. Best put it up now so the edges don't curl."

"Madam, I can take that from you," Roger said in his most Phantomly bass, throwing his cape for effect. He walked around to take the box from Georgina.

Cilla wasn't sure why Georgina had brought the box over. She rarely did anything for anyone. Maybe they were in the early stages of a relationship where Georgina was portraying a character in a romance novel just like in Helen's books. Cilla tried not to mind, but she still did a bit.

Georgina passed Roger the box and smoothed the front of her gray suit jacket. "There are a couple of items of yours at my place. Would you like me to drop them on your doorstep tomorrow?"

"Okay, thank you. I have a few things of yours too. I can do the same if you'd like." Cilla felt like crawling into a kennel somewhere to hide. She pulled the floppy-eared hood down.

Georgina smirked. "That's for the best. I've just been so busy with the renovations and work and everything else that's going on."

"Are the bathrooms done?" Cilla regretted the words as soon as they left her mouth. It would only remind Georgina of Cilla throwing her out at the worst time.

Georgina sniffed and ran her eyes along Cilla's fluffy torso. "An age ago."

Cilla could read between the lines there. "That's good." She didn't know what else to say, but Georgina was still standing there looking at her.

"Have you lost weight?" Georgina asked, tilting her head to the side and looking at Cilla's face.

"No, I..." Cilla raised a paw to cover her mouth, feeling self-conscious.

"Hmm." Georgina's brow furrowed as though she was considering something, then shrugged one shoulder. "I've put an information pack in with the books so you know what to do with them if anyone wants to purchase one ahead of the event.

I've been giving Helen some business advice. You know what writers are like, all about the passion."

That wasn't Cilla's experience but she figured Georgina just wanted to highlight Helen's passionate side. "Roger can take care of it."

"All right, Snoop Dogg, enjoy your spook-fest." Georgina raised her arched brows that were like perfect strokes of a sepia calligraphy brush.

"Take care." Cilla watched Georgina leave, feeling like her heart had swollen itself to the point of bursting then jump-started itself again.

Emma returned and flipped Cilla's hood back on. "Don't sweat it, Snoop Dogg. She's just turned up like an evil spirit at Halloween to rub your nose in the Helen thing. Don't buy in to it."

Cilla nodded. Georgina and Helen did make an impressive couple. She didn't want to be with Georgina, but that didn't mean she wanted to bear witness to Georgina's happily-ever-after moment. Instead, she longed for Lucky's interesting, genuine conversation that was at once no-nonsense and totally out there. She and Emma picked up an eyeball each and threw them back like shots, chewing and staring at the automatic doors sliding back against Georgina's trail of Dior perfume.

CHAPTER EIGHTEEN

Cilla had changed out of the dog costume. As much as she and Lucky both loved dogs, she didn't want to be one for more than eight hours a year. The evening was mild and the sun was a golden residue across the blackening hills. The usually quiet streets were transformed with a carnival of trick-or-treaters, and it seemed there were more people on the streets than populated the town. Cilla walked among them, cloaked in the appearance of a mother or aunt, moving along Time Street with a herd of zombies, pirates, and ghosts, Benson snuffling along beside her in his bow tie because Cilla hadn't gotten his full tuxedo from the shed.

A block over, she could see Hollyoaks rising up to meet the stars, and up there in the turret, a light burned. Cilla's pulse came roaring through her ears to push at her temples. She was almost certain that light hadn't been on yesterday or the day before. Unless she hadn't noticed. Benson began to lean into his collar and Cilla's step quickened, trying to dodge around a tiny policewoman with a skewed hat with a pregnant mother in tow. The gate to Hollyoaks was still latched, and a snail-pocked paper tongue hung from the wooden mailbox indicating no one had collected the mail in days. Cilla unlatched the gate, almost snagging her finger as Benson pushed his way onto the property. Cilla let go of his leash, knowing he was heading in one direction only—right up the path and to that door. As she tried to close the gate behind her, the pregnant mother and mini cop pushed it open wider, followed by two teenage boys in band T-shirts and Doc Martens who looked like they'd come as themselves but possibly not. Cilla had no right to tell them they couldn't be there and she tried no such thing, merely led the way up to the porch and knocked on the door, an ever-growing gaggle of ghouls behind her. She waited, but it was hard to hear over the rustling of children unwrapping candy and little voices with big questions and patient parents with measured answers. After a minute where the policewoman had dropped her candy through a gap in the porch slats and started to cry, Cilla heard the sound of barking, and the door opened. Lucky pushed open the screen door, and Benson and Peanut began to hurl themselves around in their little love dance. Lucky looked like a mug shot of herself, such was her surprise at finding eight people on her porch and more on her path.

"Trick or tre-eat!" sang a chorus.

From an angle, Cilla could see the teenagers elbowing each other at the sight of Lucky like they had scored the jackpot. She could imagine them telling their friends at school the next day that they had been up to the house and seen the witch.

"Oh, ah…" Lucky looked at the expectant faces. "Let me see if I have anything. Cilla, come in."

Cilla squeezed in past the screen door and let it close on the sobs of the baby policewoman. She wanted to get a good look at Lucky—she had so many questions—and was working at not resenting the children on the doorstep who were making the moment more terrifying than it already was. She stood by the brass statue of a naked woman, stuck between the noises of Lucky in the kitchen, the dogs rumbling along the hall, and the trick-or-treaters outside. There was that familiar smell of incense and polished wood mingled with Lucky's bouquet smell of wild honeysuckle. Lucky emerged with a handful of speckled owls' feathers and presented them to the stunned group on her doorstep. Baby policewoman's mother snatched her child's white-gloved hand out of the way before she could touch the feather, and the little girl started to wail again.

"Dirty, Avery, dirty," the mother said, squatting to awkwardly pick her up to the side of her baby bump.

The teenagers accepted a feather each and looked at each other and said, "Nice."

Once the crowd had dispersed, Lucky still had one remaining feather, which she turned and gave to Cilla. "Cilla, I am so sorry. Please come and sit down and let me explain."

On closer inspection, Lucky had bags under her eyes and she looked exhausted. Cilla twirled the feather between thumb and index finger. "Is this one magic?"

"You'll have to let me know."

As Cilla followed Lucky through to the kitchen, she reflected that after this evening, Lucky's reputation as resident witch had probably gained momentum among the younger generation. She took a seat at the table, and Lucky filled a kettle and set it on the stove.

"Firstly, I wanted to say thank you for polishing the silver and putting the soup in the fridge. That didn't go unnoticed."

Lucky seemed nervous, picking at a fingernail, an expression on her face like someone waiting on blood test results. Cilla noted a bottle of gin and a glass full of soggy lemon beside the sink looking out over the backyard. She was trying not to judge, but it wasn't great. She wondered if Lucky's explanation would involve a gin-fueled bender.

"You're welcome. I can't bear to see food go to waste." Although it probably did anyway. She should have put it in the freezer.

Lucky reached up to a cupboard overhead and retrieved two earthenware mugs with a blue-and-tan glaze. "Coffee? Tea?"

"A tea would be great, thank you. If I have a coffee now I'll be up all night."

"Black, mint, dandelion?"

Cilla grimaced at the mention of dandelion, immediately thinking of Roger. "Mint, please."

"Good choice. I'll have the same."

The doorbell chimed, and Peanut and Benson barreled along the hall like they'd heard a war cry. Lucky looked around. "I'm all out of owl feathers. Do you mind if I ignore them? I know it's awful, but I'm not prepared. I forgot all about trick-or-treaters."

"No problem." Cilla felt stiff and unsure what to say until she knew what had been going on. She was sick of putting her heart out there and having it bounced up and down.

"In fact, this is the first year in a long time that I have had trick-or-treaters." She looked toward the door. "Or should I find them something?"

"I'm sure they have plenty of candy. You're probably saving them a trip to the dentist."

"True." Lucky went to rummage around in the pantry, opening various jars before finding what she was looking for on the counter by the stovetop. She turned to Cilla. "Give me a second. I'll be back."

Lucky stepped out into the yard and was swallowed by darkness. The dogs continued to bark in the hall, and Cilla called Benson back. She eyed the door to the rear yard, unsure whether Lucky would return but, after a minute, she was back with a fistful of mint. This was no ordinary tea, but it seemed Lucky rarely did anything in an ordinary way.

Finally, they were seated at the corner of the long table, Cilla facing northeast and Lucky facing southeast. Cilla could tell because there was a gold compass on a chain lying on the table beside a bowl of lemons.

Cilla cleared her throat. "Are you okay? I've been worried."

There was resignation in Lucky's gray eyes, like two pebbles sinking to the bottom of a still lake. "Yes, you would have been, and I feel bad. This is why I stay away from people. It's all too hard."

Cilla felt exasperated. "But you didn't. Stay away from me, I mean."

Lucky straightened the chain of the compass and ran a finger along it. "No, no I didn't. I tried to. It may not look like I do, but I really care for you."

Cilla flinched inside. Georgina often said she "cared" for her on purpose, just to avoid saying she loved her because she knew Cilla wanted to hear it. She felt like crying because she could see she was repeating some weird cycle but in a different way, like she hadn't learned the lesson set for her by the universe or God or whoever was out there pulling the strings. "It's been bothering me on a few levels. Why, how, and what did I do?"

"Nothing, you're amazing. You're the prima ballerina on my stage of life. A solo act, really." Lucky sighed. "I avoid talking about certain things because traditionally it hasn't worked for me. People think I'm crazy, as you know—well, crazier. A little bit of crazy is necessary, but I've learnt that people don't respond well to different."

"Lucky, I'm not here to judge you or gossip or whatever else you're scared of." Cilla glanced at the lemons sitting like a slurp of sunshine on a rainy day. "Is it alcohol? My uncle was a changed man after he did this chewing gum therapy thing. Stone-cold sober to this day."

The corners of Lucky's mouth lifted, south and west. "The symptom but not the cause. I will tell you because I owe you an explanation, and you can do with it what you will." Lucky took a sip of tea and looked to see what the dogs were doing—which was lying in between the kitchen and the front door, ready for whatever provided the next call to action. "But before I begin, I need to know if you believe in magic, or at least if you would be willing to look beyond your own beliefs."

CHAPTER NINETEEN

Cilla looked down at the owl feather on the table beside her cup. She wondered if she actually did believe in magic or not. "Believe?" She tried to picture the owl's feather granting her every wish. "No," she had to admit. "Believe is too strong a word."

"Are you open to believing, or at least nonbelieving?"

"Belief implies utter faith, and I have more doubt than I do faith."

"Ah." Lucky picked up the compass, moving it back and forth to watch the hand flutter. "That's where people go wrong. Faith comes first, then the magic happens."

"Can you tell me anyway?"

"I can."

Cilla was wondering which end of the crazy scale Lucky's jittery needle pointed to, mild or nutcase. When she had agreed that the tree outside was magic, it was because she had felt it, but sitting in Lucky's kitchen with the distant sound of teenagers hollering over the Hallmark magic outside, it was hard to find that feeling. She chewed on a piece of mint that had found its way into the tea and waited for Lucky to give her something that could pull the faith up from her insides and make it shine through.

"When I was a kid, I realized I could do something that other kids weren't doing, and it got me in a lot of hot water, so it taught me to be secretive and that people couldn't be trusted. As I have gotten older, something changed, and it seems the control I had over the situation isn't there anymore."

"What could you do?"

Lucky took a deep breath, opened her mouth to say something, shut it again, then took another breath and came up short again. She tipped her head to one side. "Okay, this situation is stressful enough that I am trying not to eat a lemon or swig that gin, because I see that you think I need to do something called chewing gum therapy but all I'm trying to do is stay grounded and open up about something that I have hidden for years."

Cilla stood up and went to get the gin bottle from the sink, unscrewed it, and took a sip, then placed it on the table between the two of them. "Go for it. I'm starting to see how it helps."

Lucky smiled. "Oh, thank you. Thank you for understanding and bringing some lightness to this. As you can see, I'm struggling somewhat." Lucky held the bottle with both hands but didn't take a sip. "I used to go back in time, but now I get sent back."

Cilla blinked. Not even a swig of gin had prepared her for that. "Sorry?"

"Some people refer to it as time travel. It was something I'd always been able to do when I was small, but I didn't realize that it was abnormal. My mother didn't understand, and she became angry when I told her about it. She thought I was making excuses for running away, which I wasn't. I was just going back to other times in my life. It wasn't until my aunt explained that she could also skip back in time that I felt less guilty about it all. It's never forward, it's always back, and up until the night I lost Mira I had been able to revisit any scene of my life that I liked, but of course I could only go back for short periods or else people would know. It made me somewhat of a recluse, and then I went the other way—trying to surround myself with people so that I wouldn't be tempted to do it."

"Who's Mira?"

"Hang on." Lucky took a sip of gin and resumed her stranglehold on it. "She was my sweetheart. I was living in this little flat in London, and my housemate, Gerry, had thrown this Halloween party and there were people absolutely everywhere, and I mean everywhere: on the sofa, in the bathtub, on the kitchen bench. Death was making margaritas in the kitchen, a fairy was throwing up in the toilet, a firefighter was smoking a joint on the balcony, but I was looking for my angel Mira."

"Was she dressed as an angel?"

Lucky looked up and smiled. "An angel with a dirty halo."

"Did you find her?"

Lucky took a deep breath. "This conversation is going to send me back for sure."

Cilla decided to go along with it for now. It seemed as plausible as anything else she could think of. "But there has to be a reason you keep getting sent back. If you used to do it at will but now you can't control it, there has to have been a trigger?"

"I have to fix things?"

Cilla thought for a moment. "What type of things?"

"Change that night, but that's the thing. It can't be fixed." Lucky looked like she might cry, which made Cilla's eyes sting with the anticipation of tears.

"What happened?"

"I searched the apartment and she was nowhere to be seen, so I went downstairs and out of the front door to see if she was out in the street. Of course my little shadow, Peanut, followed me out."

"Peanut The First?" Cilla interjected.

"No, The Second."

"Wait, Peanut is a time traveler too?"

"He goes where I go."

Cilla grinned in spite of herself. "That's so sweet. Was there a Peanut The First?" She noticed the grave expression on Lucky's face. "Sorry, go on. Was Mira outside?"

"It was late but there were still people out on the street. I stood on tiptoe on the steps, trying to get a good view, and looked toward the drugstore but I couldn't see her. The problem was that she'd done that before—disappeared without a word. Once I found her standing on the edge of the bypass, looking down onto the traffic below, and she said she wouldn't have jumped, just wanted to feel something close to freedom, but I always worried when I didn't hear from her. Gerry didn't like her at all. He was always telling me she was hard work, but he didn't know her like I did." Lucky cleared her throat. "I looked back up the other way and I saw her across the street, the feathered wings ruffling in the wind, and she was walking along the pavement, one foot directly in front of the other, head and halo tipped back, nose toward the sky, arms outstretched as though she was balancing on a tightrope, heading away toward the bridge across the river. It was a strange feeling, like she was in her own world, a place where no one could reach her, and it scared me because we'd had this fight earlier because she was upset that I was away all the time, and I'd told her I felt stifled even though really she never stifled anyone. She climbed onto the parapet, which was wide enough to sit on and dangle your legs—we used to do that sometimes late at night when the house was too noisy or the moon was full—and I saw her there and it felt like she was gone, or this feeling like I'd never see her again, and I panicked. I called her name, and I have watched this scene play out so many times and I still don't have an answer as to whether she heard me or not but because a car flew past and where she had been was empty space." Lucky shrugged and looked at Cilla.

"Gone how?"

"I don't know if she jumped or fell, but she was gone."

"Dead?"

"I don't know."

"You don't know?" Cilla asked in disbelief.

"I called Aunt Nora, packed my things, and came straight home, and here I am."

Cilla wanted to ask if Lucky cared what happened to Mira, but it was clear that she did so she tried to think of a more sensitive way to word it. "Do you wonder what happened to Mira? I mean, was she your girlfriend?"

"Of course I wonder. Every day. And if I didn't, the universe or forces of nature or whatever it is that causes me to go back in time to that day remind me."

"I hope you don't blame yourself, though."

Lucky sighed. "Cilla, this is hard for me to talk about because I know it was my fault and the universe keeps hauling me back to that day to make sure I don't forget it."

Cilla thought of the article about Eleanora but decided it was better left for another time. Then she thought about what "another time" actually meant and was confused.

Lucky chewed the side of her lip, her eyes on the photo on the wall of herself outside a club. "It was my fault because Nora had warned me not to get involved."

"With Mira?"

"With anyone." Lucky's eyes were heavy on Cilla, and Cilla understood that she was trying to infer that the statement included involvement with Cilla too. "But I did. We tried to stay friends. We were friends, best of friends, but there was a tension between us that built, a compelling force, and yes, we slept together. She was the last woman I kissed, until now."

Cilla felt a pleasantness permeate her chest at that last part. "That sounds difficult." She was fighting the urge to say anything that would be interpreted as arguing, but she couldn't understand how Lucky could think that meant Mira fell, or jumped, from a bridge.

"We would fight about it, but I couldn't tell her why. In fact, I've never told anyone apart from my mother and Nora until now. The energies in my body are different to other people. I can't go around mixing them with anyone I choose. These types of things happen, just as Nora warned me they would. The only option would be to relinquish the time travel. I was too selfish, I didn't do that. I adored Mira and didn't want to be without her, so instead we fought because I would disappear and break her heart and then she would go off and we would end up back together, fighting because she didn't understand why I wouldn't yield to her as a partner and stay. Perhaps I should have told her the truth, but the times I'd tried to tell anyone as a child, I'd gotten in trouble and later my oddness had disastrous consequences for me."

"What made you tell Nora?"

"It runs in the female line of my family, but it obviously skipped my mother."

"But how long ago did that all happen with Mira? What year?"

Lucky looked over at Peanut, who was blinking at her adoringly. "1972."

Cilla worked the numbers in her mind. "But…How old are you?"

"Older than I look. See, when I go back, I'm the age I was in that period of time. Time passes here, but I come back and I've missed that time here, so I'm still the age when I left, or at least it seems that way. My hair hasn't grown, my nails haven't grown, but it's quite an adjustment landing back in this body after the effortlessness of being young again. It's probably different from what you're imagining. From what I've read it's maybe astral travel. I'm experiencing something on another plane or dimension? I don't understand the physics of it, I can only know my own experiences."

Cilla's head was swimming. "This is all so odd. I feel like any minute, my alarm will go off and I'll wake up for work and this whole thing will have been a dream. You, this time travel stuff." She rubbed the back of her thighs where they felt tight from running. "How does it feel when it happens?"

Lucky's nose twitched on one side. "Good question. Sorry, I know this is all so bonkers and you probably think I'm as mad as anything. You wouldn't be the first."

"I don't know what to think."

"Obviously I can't tell a soul. Never. I'm only telling you because…well, why am I telling you?" She let out a huff of air. "I guess because you know something's going on and"—she looked at Cilla anxiously—"if I'm honest, I'm scared you'll leave because you think I'm ignoring you on purpose. It's not that I don't like you, it's more that I do like you."

"You're scared of what would happen if we became close?"

Lucky looked down at her own hands, clutched and white-knuckled on the table. "There's that, definitely. I hope the selfishness of youth has left me, and frankly, the idea of repeating the same cycle of anguish again horrifies me. I can see how I already hurt you by disappearing recently and I never want to hurt you. You're one of the kindest people I've ever met, and you make me feel safe and seen, which has never been a combination I've experienced. Hurting people I love has been a constant theme in my life. Better to steer clear of people altogether. And also, you probably think I'm stark raving mad. You wouldn't be the first person. So, now you know my dark secret. If you leave and don't come back I won't blame you, just please keep it to yourself."

Cilla shrugged. "Not so dark, really, and of course I would never repeat anything you've told me. I've never met anyone with a superpower before. It's very exciting, to me at least. How does it feel when it happens? Physically, I mean."

Lucky unhunched slightly. "I'd hardly call being involuntarily being sent hurtling back in time to the worst moment of my life a superpower, but to answer your question, it feels like a building of anticipation, like a whole-body sneeze or a sort of tingling. I know it's about to happen when I get that sensation. I can describe it as the particles of my body are transferring from matter to another type of energy, the way water might vaporize or wood can burst into flames. It's not akin to anything else so it's hard to explain."

Cilla was still trying to process it. "So, if I was watching you do it, you'd just vanish before my eyes?"

"It's a creepy thought. I've never seen myself do it, but I assume so. Now you know why I don't get out much or drive a car. Can you imagine?"

Things were starting to fall into place. "But you went to the market with me."

"I was so nervous. I've learnt that for some reasons certain properties create a denseness that make it harder to time travel. Gin, for one, I think it skews my energies. They say it's a depressant so maybe that is something to do with it. Something in citrus fruit, primarily lemon, grounds me. When I return from the other timeline I'm always so exhausted. I have learnt through trial and error. As far as I know there's no manual on time travel."

Cilla's mouth was dry, and she could still feel alcohol in her throat. "I don't know what to think. You've blown my mind wide open, or split it into two halves. One is absorbing what you're saying like nothing has ever made more sense, and the other half feels like it's out on an island somewhere trying to paddle to the mainland. How couldn't I have noticed anything?"

A hint of a smile crept over Lucky's lips. "No, how could you have had any idea? It's outside the realms of perceived possibility."

"Can you do it at will?"

"If the conditions are right. I was a solitary child, absorbed in practicing this thing that felt more real than reality, and I got quite good at it, but I couldn't be gone for long or my mother would notice. Sometimes she did. I wasn't very well-behaved."

"How do you get back?" Cilla knew she was bombarding Lucky with questions, but they were running through her mind like a drain had been unclogged. She looked at the black-and-white photo stuck to the fridge of a young Lucky standing outside a nightclub in platform boots, wearing sateen shorts and a lacy bodice.

"By mentally tethering myself to something or someone here. Getting back is easy—Earth is dense and gravitational. It's like waking from a dream."

"What do you mean by that?"

Lucky sighed. "How's the library?"

Cilla laughed, unsure whether she was joking. The library now seemed like something from another dimension. When it appeared that Lucky was waiting for her response, she said, "Good. Nothing much changes." It seemed static after hearing

Lucky's adventures, and Cilla wondered if every experience was somehow dictated by time. Time running away, time dragging, time slowing, standing still in time. They were all expressions, but what was time? Just a concept created to quantify and order life.

"That actually sounds very pleasant to me." Lucky laughed, then reached a hand and placed it on Cilla's wrist. "You look very serious. Are you all right?"

Cilla's wrist tingled where Lucky's skin touched hers. She nodded although she wasn't sure if she was all right. The thought of Georgina had bobbed up into her head to swim around with all the other strange images that were surfacing and sinking. All the time and energy she had invested into the relationship. It was hard to let go of that, but what was it all for? If she could go back in time, would she? She felt there was some connection between that question and what was happening with Lucky, but the connecting thread was floating just out of reach.

CHAPTER TWENTY

Lucky's kitchen seemed changed somehow, like the world had rearranged itself and the objects Cilla knew as familiar were now oddities that she had to make sense of. The lemons in their bowl random shapes devoid of meaning and open to interpretation.

"Do you have proof?" Cilla asked.

Lucky's face dropped in disappointment but also like she'd been caught off guard. She removed her hand from Cilla's wrist. "You don't believe me?"

Cilla felt herself scramble back to neutral. "I do believe you, but we are butting up against decades of plain old muggle life. I can assure you I have never witnessed magic outside of performances on TV or at the library, and I've seen Marco the Marvelous rehearsing behind the shelves and it didn't seem that magical."

Lucky shrugged. "I'm not going to try to convince you. Like I said, you're the first person I have told since I was a child, and you can believe me or not. Telling you seemed the right thing to do because I can see how confused you've been. It's my fault. I shouldn't have dragged you into any of it. You turned up out of the blue—well, Benson did first—and I felt a spark of something I thought I buried a long time ago."

Cilla took Lucky's hand. "It's not your fault. I should have been more sensitive to what was going on, and you tried to warn me. I was already in too deep. I've never met anyone like you. Even time travel aside."

They both laughed, breaking the tension that had been holding the room. "Can I give you a hug?" Lucky asked.

"Of course you can. You don't need to ask."

It was an awkward hug with Lucky bending forward to hug Cilla in the chair, but it was relief and happiness and a closeness that Cilla had missed. Georgina bobbed back up to the surface again and Cilla pushed her back down. There would be a time for that conversation, but it wasn't now while they were trying to put this world to rights.

"So you're not an alcoholic?"

Lucky sat down. "No. I don't even like gin. If there was something more effective than biting a lemon or sipping alcoholic swill, I'll take it. If only I could gain control over myself again that would solve everything, but I despair of that ever happening."

"Is the key to the present in the past?"

Lucky looked down into the mint brew and swirled the liquid around. "It has to be, or why else would I be stuck in this cycle? Unless life is a pointless mess of randomness, but I don't believe that. There is order and intention in this universe. It is structured too perfectly for anything else."

It was cool in the kitchen and Cilla took another sip of tea to warm her insides. "What happens when you go back to that moment?"

"Are you cold?" Lucky asked, springing up. "I'll light the oven."

Cilla watched Lucky open the oven and light the gas for warmth, wondering if Lucky had read her mind or if the temperature had suddenly dropped or if she was just avoiding the question, but Lucky picked up the conversation again.

"It's on replay. I am back in that moment, there, standing in the street, watching Mira climb onto the parapet like she hadn't heard me call her name—or because she had, I still don't know. Then the car driving by, obstructing my vision, and then I was looking into the black sky. The thing that gets me is there was no noise."

"What do you mean?" Cilla instantly regretted asking the question, putting the pieces together in her mind as soon as the words had left her lips. There had been no surprised scream.

"Nothing, not even a splash."

"Did you look over the edge?"

Lucky shut her eyes. "I did. I did. I did. I ran around and climbed to the bottom of that bridge and waded into that cold shock of water." Her eyes opened again and she looked tired. "I called, I yelled. Nothing. Just the dirty foam and waterlogged refuse of urban living."

"Was there a search?"

"Of course, but I left. I didn't want to see it, if it was the worst. All I wanted to do was go back in time and change things, but I knew that's not how it works. I was too sad to even go back to a time before this happened. I went home to Aunt Nora and stayed in this house. I left everyone behind, even those I was responsible for."

The disappearance of Eleanora popped back into Cilla's mind. If Lucky was talking about something that happened in 1972 and Eleanora disappeared in 1943, then the two events were unrelated. Aunt Nora was not Eleanora. Cilla felt no relief. She was too heavy with sadness over everything she had just heard. How could she not believe Lucky, who was sitting there with the gray of a cemetery in her silver eyes, looking like of all the moments she could choose, this wasn't it?

"Thank you," Cilla said eventually. "I'm sorry you've had to go through all that and I'm especially sorry about Mira. What can I do to help?"

Lucky smiled. "You have been helping. You and Benson both." Benson looked over his shoulder but didn't move from where he was lying stretched out next to Peanut. "I have gone about things all wrong and I'm sorry."

Cilla's fingers tingled with longing to touch Lucky's slender forearms and scoop her up where she would be safe. "After everything you have told me, I'm not sure there is a right way, but I am glad I know the truth now."

"I guess you have some thinking to do."

Cilla surprised herself by saying, "I do." She wanted to feel Lucky close with a fierceness that sent a feverish ache through her body, but there was a calmness within her that allowed her to lean into its stillness. She had been strung out, not knowing how to feel. Now that she had more information, she needed time to process and decide what was right for her. She stood up and took her cup to the sink. She heard Benson scramble to his feet behind her.

At the front door, Lucky hugged her without asking this time, and they made no promises. Benson walked beside Cilla, only pausing a couple of times to look back at the compass point where Peanut was last standing. If they had already disappeared to London, 1972, Cilla wasn't sure. A breeze stirred discarded candy wrappers and crunchy fallen leaves. Cilla held Benson's leash in one hand and her owl feather in the other.

CHAPTER TWENTY-ONE

Lucky was not far from Cilla's thoughts as she jogged through the park the next morning. There was a mist hanging over the path ahead that felt like a destination she could never reach. The evergreens were a change from the malting golden elms and oaks. Cilla crossed the bridge over the river and broke through the foliage out into the street. She ran along the pavement, Benson bounding beside her. She noticed the real estate sign still up in front of the brick house by the church. Georgina's face grinned from a circle on the SOLD sticker, but someone had drawn a mustache and monobrow on her face. Cilla felt a little more pleased than she should. It was short-lived as she thought of Lucky baring her soul and she hadn't done the same. The least she could do was tell Lucky that she had been in a relationship with Georgina. If Lucky reacted badly then Cilla would have to deal with it. But what did Cilla want? That was the million-dollar question. Cilla had no answer, but while her burning lungs were demanding her attention, she didn't need one. Just to the end of the street, then you can stop, she promised herself. Then the end of the street came and she could keep pushing. When she arrived home, the mist had dissipated, leaving a sharp blue morning, and Cilla was running late to work.

Cilla opened the library and there was no one waiting at the door and no one to witness her lateness. She still felt hot with guilt as she hurried around preparing for the day before anyone came in. After she'd finished setting up, she saw there was a text message from Lucky saying, *Right now, at this exact moment, someone is mending a door handle*, and it was so absurd that it lifted her spirits momentarily. Cilla typed back, *That person is not me, but right now, in this exact moment, someone is putting batteries in a television remote control.* She smiled down at her phone. Whatever Lucky was, she approached life like a game without rules.

Cilla had always been open to ideas beyond her comprehension because she felt the marbles in her jar of knowledge were limited, but when presented with an idea, she did want to understand something about it. She opened up the library database on the computer and stared at the screen trying to think where she could start her research. She thought of "paranormal" but she wanted facts or scientific basis. She typed in "physics" and started trawling through all the books that bore relationship to physics. She didn't want anything dry and technical that would require prior knowledge or intense concentration. There was a book called *An Overview of Quantum Physics For Beginners* that was available on the shelf. That seemed a good starting point for Cilla. She retrieved it and began to read at the circulation desk with one eye on the door. Cilla read quickly, trying to absorb as much as she could. Her mind snagged on quantum entanglement, which to her new understanding was when two entangled particles were separated by distance, even a vast distance, they remained connected, and when one spun, the other spun too. She wasn't sure why this seemed significant, but it did demonstrate that there was more going on than what her limited senses could recognize. As she read on, she could see the link between psychic phenomena and consciousness and science. It was like someone had opened a door to a room in her mind that she didn't know existed. Even Einstein had a lot to say on the matter of spirituality in relation to physics and science. She didn't know why they hadn't taught that part in school; she might have paid more attention. Eventually patrons arrived, and Cilla tucked the book under the counter to take home, feeling only slightly guilty about reading on the job. At least if anyone asked her, she could recommend a book on physics for the unenlightened.

Emma arrived ten minutes before her shift time, went to put her belongings in the staff kitchen, and came bouncing back out, straight to where Cilla was now assisting a high school student who wanted to order a book. Emma stood impatiently, pulling orange streamers from the counter.

"So?" Emma asked as soon as Cilla had finished what she was doing.

Cilla rolled her eyes but she smiled. "Yes?"

"Don't leave me hanging. I am coming down from a sugar high and I don't have patience for games."

"Do you think we should move that plant out of the direct sunlight?" Cilla asked.

"Cilla! The fury of a whole packet of Warheads candy will rain down upon you if you don't tell me immediately what happened with Lucky. Was she home?"

"Okay, okay. If they were the hot Warheads, then I don't want any surprise attacks."

"They were."

"Ouch. Well, she was there."

"Yes?" Emma's eyes were fixed on Cilla like she had reached the cliffhanger of a movie and she had lost all concept of time and place.

Cilla came around to the side of the counter where Emma was standing and continued pulling off the rest of the streamers. "We need to get all the decorations down." She wasn't sure what she could say to Emma that would satisfy her without giving away Lucky's secrets. She moved to the bulletin board where jack-o'-lanterns grinned down like a spooky group class photo, Emma hot on her heels.

"Emma," Cilla said, turning and almost colliding with her. "Let me think about it. I'm still processing it, then I will tell you what I can."

Emma squinted at Cilla like she was tiny handwriting that needed to be deciphered. "You look happy."

"I'm not unhappy."

"Hmm…"

Cilla turned back and began to remove the staples, then lost patience and ripped the pumpkins from the board.

"I'll do the windows, then," Emma said.

"Good." Cilla was pleased the matter was settled for now. She had never been comfortable lying; even in grade school she had been the one to cave when pressed at home over little schemes she and Deb had put together. Who forgot to feed the cat? Who broke the glass and didn't clean it up properly? Deb never knew, but Cilla always gave it up within seconds. Deb was still angry at Cilla for ratting her out for stealing her parents' vodka and filling it up with water. This was different, though. This was Lucky's lifelong secret. Cilla had no intention of betraying her trust.

Emma found Cilla's candy stash from yesterday and remedied her sugar hangover with hair of the dog.

Cilla stared at the computer screen. "November first. Can you believe it?"

"We'll be putting up Christmas decorations in no time."

"Have you seen all that stuff we have to catalogue?"

Emma popped her sticky lips. "Yep."

"Do you want to do it now?"

"Nope."

Cilla opened a Milky Way. "Me neither. Let's have a coffee."

Cilla was at the point where she needed a rest from the thoughts that had been stomping back and forth like a marching band inside her head. Bugle, trumpet, drums, and all. She was more than happy to sip coffee and listen to Emma's sexcapades with Pedro the Energetic Rower while keeping an eye on the door for anyone coming in.

By the afternoon, things had picked up in the library and Cilla reflected that was another strange thing about time: the more that got thrown into a minute, the faster it went. Usually when things were fuller, they seemed bigger. She tried saying something to that effect to Emma, but Emma said all her minutes were dragging today and she needed a nap. Cilla really didn't know much about time at all, but she could tell Emma had hit another sugar slump and she threw the remaining candy in the bin. They'd eaten all the good ones anyway.

"Taco Tuesday?" Emma asked as they got ready to close up. "My treat for margaritas?"

"Thanks, but I think I'll go home and read a book. I feel wiped."

"Here." Emma handed her one of Helen Bowers's romance novels that was still in a box shoved under the counter.

Cilla looked at the cover. The heroine looked a little too Georgina-ish for comfort, with fair hair and dark arched brows. "Maybe next time." Cilla put the book back in the box. "The stack beside my bed grows faster than I can read it. I'm still hanging for the new Highgate Village book."

"You're obsessed. I don't think they're that amazing. The characters are all my parents' age."

"That's why I like them. Well, not just that. But not everyone is twenty-two and stunningly attractive. Present company excluded," Cilla said.

Emma shrugged one shoulder. "Twenty-three, actually, but yes to the other part."

Cilla gave Emma a lift home because Emma usually walked to work. Cilla had taken the car because she had been running late that morning, but she wanted to get herself organized so she could start walking to work again. As she waved goodbye to Emma, she was grateful that Emma hadn't mentioned Lucky again.

When Cilla arrived home, she noticed there was a grocery bag on the doorstep containing a pair of sunglasses, a toothbrush, and some silver earrings rolling around in the bottom. Cilla let herself inside, Benson dancing around her, and stood looking down into the bag. She felt a sad emptiness. Those three items, such paltry symbols of years of shared experiences. It felt more impersonal to have them returned than if Georgina had thrown them out. It really was final then.

She kicked her shoes off and sat down on her bed, seeing her reflection in the wardrobe mirror, slumped and creased. She had been so caught up with everyone else's drama, she didn't know who she was anymore. She picked up the sunglasses and turned them over in her hands, noticing faint scratches on the lenses. It seemed like another person who had worn them. She remembered buying them with Georgina when they'd visited the beach. Cilla had been squinting so much that Georgina had herded her into a dollar store to make her buy sunglasses. She had chosen these, cheap Ray-Ban knockoffs, but they had outlasted her other, more expensive sunglasses. It had been a fun day, walking along the beach, buying anklets made of tiny shells, and eating oysters and drinking white wine as the sun went down. Georgina, harmless and sweet in those early days, drawing a love heart in the sand with their initials inside. Cilla dropped the sunglasses back into the bag and shoved it inside her closet beside Georgina's scarf so she wouldn't have to find a place for them until tomorrow. She had been clinging to those early days for so long, expecting that if she did more or was more that they would get back there. She could see now that Georgina had no intention of getting back there. Her phone beeped a message, but it wasn't Lucky. It was Georgina saying, *I found your bottle opener and spare phone charger.* Cilla turned her phone off and tossed it back into the drawer. There was something liberating about disconnecting from phone communication, as though she was separating herself from having to make decisions or take action, even though the problems weren't going away. Benson was looking at her with the eyes of someone who would like to get their day started. She considered throwing a ball for him in the backyard but felt mean. "All right, you. Let's go for a walk."

"Groundhog day, groundhog day," Cilla sang as they walked the same streets as yesterday—same as every day, in fact—to the park. They did a lap, and by then the air was full of everyone's evening meals and Cilla was so hungry she decided to get takeout. As they got closer to Main Street she could hear voices chanting, and when she turned the corner, there was a crowd with protest signs gathered outside the real estate office. There were banners with slogans like "Green Promises = Concrete Lies" and "Trees Not Tarmac." She was surprised to see the community so vocal about the developments. She knew some small business owners were worried about the supermarkets and chains that were part of the plans, but she hadn't paid much attention. She saw a few faces that were familiar from the library and around town. Feeling cowardly, she ducked down a side street and made her way back home to a microwave meal. She didn't like the prospect of development, but she had no intention of going to head-to-head with anything remotely Georgina-related. Benson flopped on the kitchen floor at home, legs outstretched like he had run a marathon, and Cilla was glad she had let him have a run. She could feel good about getting into bed early with her physics book, which had spawned a whole lot of other books on her to-read list. The "observer effect," where particles changed their behavior when observed, was fascinating and made her rethink the idea of faith and the power of thought. It was exciting knowing that there was a whole other side to life that she had never explored, and she didn't have to go anywhere but her mind to do it.

CHAPTER TWENTY-TWO

Emma was right. Although they were yet to put Christmas decorations up at the library, decorations were out in the stores long before Thanksgiving. The crisp mornings had given way to torrents of rain, flooding the streets and swelling the river so it was gushing along just below the bridge in the park. Another day of rain and the bridge would be underwater. Cilla had tried to keep up her morning jogs, but her sneakers were sodden and even Benson was refusing to go outside. She switched to thirty minutes of yoga online just to move her body before work. There was no way she was going to the gym where she might bump into Georgina. As exciting as the transformed landscape was with its whitewater pavements and glowering skies, all the darting in and out of buildings and drying of wet clothes was exhausting. Her bathroom had sprung a leak in the ceiling over the basin, which was both convenient and annoying because she could hear it dripping at night. She shoved a hand towel in there to dull the pinging but she could hear it, accentuated by the stillness of darkness, and knew it was one more thing that needed attention.

Cilla had sloshed past Hollyoaks in the days after her discussion with Lucky and it had felt quiet and subdued, fallen leaves flattened to the damp grass and the hydrangeas left brown and drooping. Cilla didn't want to knock and find the house unoccupied, but at least now she didn't have to worry about ladders or cellars. The mailbox was empty so Lucky must have collected the mail at some point. It gave Cilla an idea. She went home and found an envelope and a legal pad and wrote Lucky a note.

Dear Lucky,

I hope you and Peanut are well and haven't been washed away. I haven't forgotten you but I need some time to think. I do want to see you again, if you still want to see me.

Love, Cilla x

P.S. At the exact moment that I am writing this, someone is on a roller coaster.

P.P.S. I think the feather works!

She had been going to write, "There's something I need to tell you," meaning the Georgina thing, but she didn't want to leave Lucky wondering. She drove past Lucky's on her way home from the library—her plans to walk to work had been a washout—and put the envelope into the mailbox, trying to avoid the wet edges of the slot. It was indeterminate whether Lucky would even check the mail in this weather. In some ways the weather felt appropriate, a forced pause to gather her thoughts and figure out her next move. The problem was that although there were vast differences between her relationship with Georgina and that with Lucky, she could see the same patterns gearing up to spin through another cycle within herself: the coming and going, the unfulfilled expectations, the not knowing who she would find from day to day. She knew she had a part to play in the dynamics, but she needed to figure out the mechanisms to see how she was enabling the patterns. Did she want to willingly put herself into a situation where someone would be emotionally unavailable to her again, or at best just plain unavailable? It was taking all her willpower to stay away as the thought of Lucky still sent waves of longing through her—as did the thought of Georgina, in a different habitual way. That's how she knew she still had some personal work to do. On the plus side, as the days ticked by and the rain finally let up, meaning she could ignore the hole in the roof again, she felt proud of herself, like she had grown in some way. That's why she was unprepared for the knock at her door on a Thursday evening.

Cilla froze like the microwave meals she was looking at and listened. The knock came again and she let the freezer door close. Benson had already raced down the hall to snuffle under the door, a sign that he knew whoever it was. Irrationally, Cilla remembered hearing that a large percentage of murders were committed by perpetrators who were familiar to their victims. The exact percentage she couldn't recall, but she knew it was high. Benson would be no help. He would be so happy to have company that he would joyfully let someone stab away while Cilla turned into a chopped turkey on the ground. "You're not a turkey," she told herself as she unlocked the door.

"Oh," she said before she could help it, because there in a cloud of Dior was Georgina, sporting red lipstick and a navy-blue pantsuit.

"Hi, Cilla. I have your things and I thought I would drop them by."

Cilla opened the door wider, wondering why she cared that her left sock had a Benson hole in the toe. "You didn't have to." Benson wagged his tail, excited to see someone he knew.

Georgina smiled softly, no teeth. "How have you been?"

Cilla was totally unprepared. "Trying to stay dry like everyone else but otherwise good, thanks. You?"

"The rain has been spectacular even though it's been slowing things down with work. Here." She passed Cilla the phone charger and bottle opener.

Cilla thought of the protest outside the office but didn't want to bring it up. "Thanks for dropping them by. I'll grab your stuff." She was still holding the door and it seemed rude to leave Georgina standing outside. "Did you want to come in?"

She couldn't have been more shocked when Georgina responded, "That would be nice, thank you."

Cilla stepped back and Georgina seemed to glide inside in the leggy way she had in her long pants and heels. It made Cilla feel short in her holey socks. Benson pranced alongside Georgina with his tail wagging, making sneezy-snuffle noises. Cilla glared at his back.

"I'll get your things."

Cilla put the phone charger away in her bedside drawer and retrieved Georgina's belongings from purgatory in the bottom of her closet. Georgina was no longer in the hall. Cilla, still holding the bottle opener, found her on the sofa in the living room. Cilla was not expecting guests. There was a rack of clothes still hanging by the heater, long dried but not put away, and a mug and plate with toast crumbs on the coffee table. The dog onesie was spread over the armchair like an animal pelt, waiting to be put back in storage. It looked like Benson had possibly slept on it. Georgina lounged at one end of the sofa, a leg crossed, looking like an art deco painting. It was such a Georgina thing to do, to arrive looking her best while Cilla, who wasn't sure if she had a hormonal hair on her chin, was feeling unfit for the public eye. She touched a finger to her chin, thinking she should find her tweezers.

"Have you still got any of my red?" Georgina asked.

"Oh, I'm not sure. I can check." Cilla picked up the plate and mug and, feeling like a criminal who was intent on hoarding other people's wine even though she didn't drink much herself, Cilla went to the kitchen and found two bottles of merlot at the back of the pantry. When she returned to the living room, Georgina was standing, admiring her own artwork which still hung over the mantel.

"Sorry, I didn't realize they were there." Cilla placed the bottles on the coffee table near where Georgina had been sitting and hastily folded up the dog onesie and placed it on the arm of the chair where it looked tidier.

"God, Cilla, where's that bottle opener? Open one up."

"I put it away. I'm not drinking much at the moment."

Georgina turned back to her painting. "I wasn't sure if you would want to return it, now that you're mad at me."

"I'm not mad at you. You can have it back if you want."

Georgina swung to face Cilla. "It was a gift, I wouldn't dream of it. And you were mad the other day."

Benson sat pressed against the armchair, grinning at Georgina like he'd found a friend.

Cilla knew she had been a little mad the other day, but she didn't know how to put it into words. "I think we were both upset."

Outside, a ripple of thunder ran across the sound of evening birdsong, heralding a return of the rainy weather.

Georgina came to sit on the sofa again and picked up a wine bottle. "Do you want me to get some glasses?"

Cilla, who still hadn't sat down yet, said, "I'll get them."

In the kitchen, Cilla thought, *Have a glass of wine, let her say whatever she wants to say, and send her on her way.*

In the living room, she thought, *Why do I always let her have her way? And why am I so attracted to her?* She knew this was not what she needed in her recovery stage. She was like an addict, and she couldn't have her drug of choice in front of her, sitting on her sofa in her damned power suit. She had been pleased that she had made Georgina so angry that she wouldn't be back, but now here she was, smiling and being nice.

Georgina opened the wine and poured two glasses, slow to stop after Cilla's reminder that she only wanted a tiny glass. The feeling that this was not a good idea was crawling all over Cilla like ants, even as Georgina clinked her glass against Cilla's and said, "To new beginnings."

"How have you been?" Cilla asked, sitting well back at the other end of the sofa.

"Things are so busy at the moment, between work, gym, having Helen stay, and everything else that's going on."

Cilla swallowed a sip of wine prematurely and it caught in her throat like desert air. "Is Helen still with you?"

Georgina's lips had left a red lipstick imprint on the glass. Cilla knew that shade; it was called "Forever." Cilla wondered if Helen's lips were stained the same color. She dismissed the thought. It was none of her business anymore.

"She's gone back home to organize the move. She's looking forward to making friends. I've told her all about you."

Cilla wasn't sure how to take that, but the speed at which Helen had entered the picture and the conversation gave Cilla the impression that there was something going on. "How did you meet Helen?"

"She's a friend of Vince's friend Jack, the one who works for Black Kettle Publishing. I think you've met him. He only has half a left leg? Anyway, they know one another through writing connections. She's published a lot."

Cilla raised her eyebrows and wondered if Georgina had come to gloat.

Georgina took another sip of wine and flicked her attention back to Cilla. "What about you? What's been happening?" A white sheet of lightning streaked across the window before the evening returned to black.

Cilla had nothing she wanted to share with Georgina. Getting vulnerable about anything that had been at her center would be a mistake. "Nothing exciting, mainly work and hanging out. I've been getting back into running but the rain has knocked me out of my routine a bit."

Right on cue, thunder cleared its throat and then spat rain against the window.

Georgina looked from Cilla to the clothes hanging by the heater. "It's a busy time of year. I can't remember having this much rain since I moved here. Why don't you give the gym a go? Plenty of treadmills and lots classes if the weather is bad."

"I prefer to exercise in private or at least by myself. Jogging through the park is horror enough." She didn't add that she didn't want people witnessing her red face and jiggling body.

"You're looking good anyway." Georgina reached for the bottle and topped both their glasses up then passed Cilla the glass, their fingers touching. Georgina's eyes flicked to Cilla's and Cilla felt a rush of something that felt like dread and familiar comfort at the same time. "Cill, we both spoke in haste that day and said things we didn't mean. Like you said, you hadn't planned it, it was a spur-of-the-moment thing. I, for one, am sorry that I left on that note because I don't think it gave our relationship the respect it deserves."

The heat in Cilla's cheeks roared to her ears, making it hard to hear. Georgina had all but scrubbed the word "sorry" from her vocabulary, so to hear it now was a shock. "George, I'm sorry too, but I think we want different things. We can respectfully be friends." She didn't believe they could at all. That was the problem. They hadn't been friends for a while.

Georgina dropped her eyes. "I have been really caught up with work and networking and my career, but you're really an important person in my life, Cill." Her eyes rose to meet Cilla's and she reached for her hand. "I miss you."

A softly burning fire was running over the skin of Cilla's hand where Georgina was touching her. "George, I miss you too, but I need to figure out who I am and what's right for me."

Georgina put her glass down, moved forward on the sofa, and slung a long thigh over Cilla's like she always used to do. She swept a finger along Cilla's jaw, drawing her close, and kissed her gently on the lips, only pulling back slightly to look at Cilla then kiss her again more slowly. She pulled back and tucked a strand of hair behind Cilla's ear. "I know who you are, and you're beautiful inside and out."

Cilla almost spilled her wine. She put the glass down and took Georgina's hand. It had been so long since Georgina had said anything remotely complimentary that wasn't backhanded. Cilla didn't know what to do. Every interaction she had seemed unexpected and confusing, like she had jumped into a book at random intervals. She felt like she was back to square one. All the work she had been doing to get past Georgina and give consideration to Lucky's situation, the objective distance that she had placed between herself and her relationship patterns— she could feel it all crumbling with one kiss. Georgina seemed so different. Maybe breaking up had made her realize what she'd had with Cilla. She gazed into Georgina's eyes, trying to divine the truth. "I'm going home to see my parents for Thanksgiving."

She took a deep breath, feeling giddy from the kiss. "Let's use that time to do some thinking."

Georgina smiled in an unguarded way that always got Cilla because she knew Georgina rarely showed her true emotions to anyone, and usually only to Cilla. "I thought you were going to ask me to come."

Cilla thought back to previous years when she had invited Georgina back home to see her family, and nine times out of ten Georgina had an excuse as to why she couldn't go. "You are welcome to join me as my friend."

CHAPTER TWENTY-THREE

In the morning, there was a note in Cilla's mailbox, written on pale-pink writing paper with embossed roses around the edges. It was dry and smooth so perhaps it was left that earlier morning, not yesterday or the day before when Cilla had forgotten to check the mail, which was now translucent with dampness. Cilla took it inside to read at the kitchen table where her cup of tea sat cooling.

Dearest Cilla,

Your note made me feel at ease. I have it beside my bed. Please take all the time you need. I would love to speak to you when (or if!) you are ready.

Warmest,

Lucky xo

P.S. Right at the moment that I am writing this, someone is cleaning a window…poor them!

P.P.S. The feather is as magical as you are.

Cilla lifted the paper to her nose and smelled traces of honeysuckle and incense. Outside, birds chirped and the sound of children playing in the neighbors' yard came traveling through the open window over the sink. The storms had worn themselves out in the night, leaving a blue sky full of thin, restless clouds. Cilla blew on the tea and watched a drop of water course its way down the bulb of a red wineglass drying by the sink. She should get up on a ladder and look at the roof. Her tossing and turning last night had been accompanied by the drip-drip of water into the bathroom basin. When she was younger, she had been handy with tools and loved making improvements around the house. Now, all she associated with ladders were falls, and her tool kit was buried under something in the garden shed. As Georgina was always pointing out, newer homes with garages were geared toward modern living. Cilla was glad she didn't have one so she would have one less obstacle to get up on the roof. Instead, she texted Georgina to ask if she knew anyone who could repair it. Georgina texted back with the names of several women who loved slinging a tool belt on. Cilla knew most of them through various connections.

Try Max. She'll give you a discount just for being cute.

Cilla wasn't sure about being cute, but she did like discounts. For once, Georgina's job was coming in handy, literally. Cilla wrote back thanking her, and Georgina said, *Are you free for dinner?*

Cilla stared at her phone screen, feeling torn. Lucky's note lay folded on the table beside her teacup. She touched the paper lightly, feeling the grain and the embossed edges. It was beautiful and old-fashioned and unique. Cilla pictured Lucky wading into cold night waters, looking for her lost lover. She had been through a lot and was still going through a lot, but she was so gracious.

Cilla picked her phone up again and typed back, *Sorry, I can't tonight.* It felt good to say no to Georgina for once. How many times had Georgina said no to Cilla? Too many to count. It did make her feel a little nervous, though, wondering what Georgina's reaction would be. She fought off the urge to overexplain. Georgina didn't need to know what she was doing.

Cilla read Lucky's note again and it lent her strength knowing that there were people like Lucky in the world. She called Benson over from where he was lying like a furry pancake by the fridge. and he happily obliged.

"Benson," she said, running both hands over his face and pushing back his ears. "Do you want to see Peanut?"

Benson's dopey expression sharpened, making Cilla laugh, and Benson began walking toward the door, looking back over his shoulder to check that she was coming. She had to follow through now. She tried calling Lucky's phone, but it went to voice mail, which wasn't uncommon. Lucky wasn't tuned in to her phone.

Cilla went to check her reflection and remembered the chin hair. Benson yapped from the door to make sure she was hurrying up as she pulled out the hair and spritzed herself with perfume, then wondered if she'd overdone it and swapped her striped sweater for a denim jacket that was less fragrance-heavy. To break the Georgina curse, she retrieved her silver earrings from where she had left them in their grocery bag in the back of the wardrobe. Now she could wear them and be reminded of Lucky instead. She checked her reflection again and vowed not to color her hair any shade of caramel ever again. Still, she had to admit her complexion was glowing and she looked better for improving her diet and starting to exercise. Maybe Georgina was right all along. Cilla brushed her teeth and rinsed her mouth with water, feeling the excitement of a first date even though all she wanted was to see Lucky and give her a hug.

* * *

There were puddles across the road and debris clogged the gutters, but the pavement was dry and already filling with leaves from the trees on either side. Benson had no time to waste sniffing light poles or cocking his leg. A withered gray balloon bounced flatly across the road, a survivor of a nearby house party.

Hollyoaks rose like a princess castle against the blue sky. The lawns were cut down to a green velvet that made the house look even grander. There was a silver SUV parked on the street in front of the house but Cilla gave it no thought. She unlatched the gate and Benson headbutted it open, trotting up the path as though he owned it. Sure enough, at the door was the sound of Peanut barking hello and Cilla didn't bother to ring the bell or knock, knowing Lucky would come to investigate. After a minute, the door opened and Lucky welcomed Benson, who only paused briefly before giving all his energy to Peanut.

"Oh, wow, Cilla. Please come in. I have company but you are welcome to stay."

Cilla's mouth dropped open and it took her a second to get any words out. "I'm sorry, I should have realized you were busy when you didn't answer the phone. We will come back another day. Benson! Benson!"

"Don't rush off, it's absolutely fine. You can meet Daisy. Come in. We were sitting out the back."

"Oh, I'll leave you to it. Call me tomorrow."

"Hush. Come in."

Cilla followed Lucky through the house out to the back porch. It took her eyes a moment to adjust to the sunlight again. Sitting at the outdoor table was a blond woman of around fifty with short golden hair with bangs, and a pretty girlish face. She smiled when she saw Cilla and stood up to shake her hand.

"This is Daisy, a daughter of an old friend of mine. Daisy, this is Cilla. Cilla lives a few streets away and her dog, Benson, and Peanut are madly in love. We have to get them together for conjugal visits, well, almost."

Daisy smiled even harder. She had a kind face with an open expression that let you know everything was okay in her world. Cilla didn't know what to make of it.

"Yes, they seem to have made Lucky's place their love nest, unfortunately for Lucky."

"I love it. Sit, Cilla. What can I get you to drink?"

"Whatever you're having would be great. I won't stay long, I just wanted to say hello."

Lucky gave a little smile and her eyes conveyed more than words could. There was an unspoken current between them that was a direct line of feeling. Lucky was letting her know that she was longing to be near her too, that she had been waiting for "hello" as well.

"I made a batch of lemonade. I'm not sold on it, it's a bit sweet, but Daisy said it's all right."

"That sounds perfect, thank you."

Lucky disappeared into the kitchen and Daisy said, "It's delicious, actually."

Cilla realized she had a British accent and took in her face again, trying to see if she should have guessed, but Daisy looked like she could have been from anywhere that people with fair hair and fair skin lived.

"This is a beautiful town," Daisy continued. "Reminds me a bit of some of the towns back home—the green hills and the woods over there."

Cilla turned to where Daisy was indicating toward the forest at the edge of Lucky's yard. Everything was verdant and glistening after the rain, the evergreens reaching up into the sky. It gave the house an even more dramatic aspect.

"It's so beautiful sitting out here among the greenery." Cilla was aware of the magic tree, changed again by the deepening of fall but still looking otherworldly with its massive trunk and widespread arms. "Where is home?"

"I live in a suburb on the outskirts of London. It's not pretty like this, but there are some lovely places a few miles on."

Lucky returned with a clinking glass of lemonade. "It's very lemony," she said as she put it on the wooden table in front of Cilla.

Cilla got the hint. Lucky had incorporated lemons into the drink so she wouldn't disappear. As soon as the thought entered Cilla's head, she marveled that she was entertaining Lucky's time travel as fact, but she was. There was nothing about Lucky that wasn't genuine. She watched her sit back down, rearranging the bangles on her wrist. Lucky made the most mundane objects look interesting. The way the bangles jangled in silvery collections on Lucky's delicate wrist would increase the sales of bangles across the country. Lucky always looked like a walking piece of art. Somehow the bold patterns and varying textures all formed a piece that was natural to Lucky and strikingly attractive. Cilla wanted to hold Lucky in her arms and touch her beneath her layers of clothes, starting with the pale skin on her wrist under the bangles. But Daisy was confusingly present, and Lucky would only disappear on her. Would it feel different knowing that Lucky didn't want to leave her? Cilla felt that it might, but she would still be entering a relationship knowing that the other person wasn't fully present, and is that what Lucky even wanted? How well did Cilla know Lucky? And now, who in the world was Daisy? She seemed lovely and down-to-earth, a good match for Lucky. And what of Georgina coming over and kissing her? Cilla took a sip of lemonade to clear her head. Only weeks ago she had been deeply invested in the relationship with Georgina while Georgina was barely present.

Cilla realized Lucky was asking her something. "Sorry, what was that?"

"I was saying that there's plenty to do around town. For Daisy, I mean."

"You're staying for a while?"

Daisy glanced at Lucky then back at Cilla. "For a few days. I hear that there's a cute market."

Cilla thought back to the bucket list that she and Lucky had been putting together and wondered if the list was still on Lucky's fridge. The last item had read, "library." Was that meant to be to visit her?

"There is, but it's not every week, maybe the third Sunday of every month or something. Lucky, is the portrait competition still showing at the gallery?"

Lucky looked at her and laughed, and Cilla realized that Lucky would be the last person to know what was going on in town.

"That sounds interesting." Daisy said.

"Do you like hiking? There are some beautiful trails through the hills and a lookout point where you can see most of the county." As Cilla spoke, she was starting to see how boring and routine-based she was. There was a lot to offer and she and Lucky hadn't even touched on the list of sights they wanted to see. She would have to relinquish her claim on that and let Lucky go with Daisy. The thought made her sad and, yes, a little jealous.

Daisy nodded. "I do like hiking but I'm not sure I brought appropriate footwear. The art gallery sounds up my alley though."

"We can do whatever you like," Lucky said.

Cilla cast her gaze back over the yard, appreciating the way the lawn rolled right out to the forest at the back, a place for wrens to tussle and preen. "The lawns look like velvet."

"It gives the whole place a lift. Daisy mowed them for me yesterday. You know how I am, I get so used to things that I stop seeing them."

Cilla felt the same way. She took several large sips of her drink, dribbling down her chin. She dabbed her chin with the back of her hand and put her glass down. "It is just gorgeous out here. Well, thank you for the drink. I had better head off. Good to meet you, Daisy." She stood up, accidentally banging the table.

"Likewise, Cilla." Daisy half rose from her seat and Cilla shooed her back down.

Lucky stood too and Cilla said, "Stay, Lucky. I can see myself out. Benson!"

Lucky followed her into the house, trailed by a reluctant Benson and Peanut. Cilla put her glass in the sink, feeling like lemonade was still glistening on her chin. She surreptitiously wiped it with her sleeve when she thought Lucky wasn't looking.

Lucky stopped Cilla in the hall. "You don't have to rush off."

"I have someone coming to repair the roof."

"Was there something in particular you wanted to chat about?" Lucky twisted a bangle around and around. Cilla wondered if she ever took them off. There were so many things about Lucky she wanted to know. She wanted to be that person who knew intimate details. Did Lucky wear slippers around the house? Did she wear her hair up at night, or loose all over the pillow? Did she like toast in the morning, or cereal? Those things seemed so out of reach. They were intimacies that were earned and discovered over time, with trust and shared experiences. What brand of detergent did Lucky use, and what did she look like when she was vacuuming a floor or reading the paper?

Cilla shook her head. "I just wanted to see how you were doing. We can catch up another time. Sorry for barging in when you had a guest." She continued walking toward the door.

"You weren't barging in, I asked you in. Daisy is…an old friend."

Cilla turned back to Lucky in the doorway. "It's no problem. Enjoy your time with Daisy. We can speak another day."

Lucky unlocked the door for her. "Thank you. We will, I'm certain." She was looking at Cilla with concern—or was it pity? She squeezed Cilla's arm.

Cilla smiled but it was only to reassure Lucky, or maybe to reassure herself. It wasn't the reunion she had imagined. The joy seemed to have gone out of the weekend.

CHAPTER TWENTY-FOUR

Max fixed the roof and put new hinges on the pantry door. To Cilla's knowledge, she didn't give her a discount, which was probably evidence that she didn't find Cilla cute, however she did ask how she and Georgina were doing, which gave Cilla the impression that she knew full well they had broken up. Roger was back from a librarians' conference in Tulsa, full of unsolicited wisdom and ideas that they didn't have the budget for, largely because he'd blown half of it going to Tulsa. Emma had taken leave to go camping with Pedro the Sex Rower, leaving Cilla to navigate Helen Bowers's reading alone. Lucky had been ominously quiet, and Cilla kept reviewing Saturday morning, wondering if she had been standoffish or petty and cursing herself for not asking for more information about Daisy, then feeling thankful that she hadn't. It was an awful place to be in limbo. She was Lucky's friend but clearly there was something there. They had slept together, but she had no claim on Lucky. Then there was Georgina, who had been keeping in touch with random witty texts. Cilla was slightly dreading Helen's reading but also curious to see what the energy was between her and Georgina. She wished Emma would be there for support, but she was no doubt scaring the nocturnal animals somewhere with Pedro, probably all night long. Cilla couldn't think of anything worse than a damp tent, bathing in a creek, and being hammered away at by someone who could use a rowing machine for an hour without breaking sweat, probably while sticks and rocks dug into her back. She must be getting old. Camping had seemed a lot more appealing when she was in college.

Roger was excited about Helen's reading. He kept uttering phrases like "we need to enhance future-focused services" and "create a diverse and inclusive space," which Cilla agreed with but was suspicious that Roger was serious about working on.

"It's fabulous we are having a lesbian author," Roger said, placing a copy of *The Well of Loneliness* on the display board beside *Fingersmith*. "I want Helen to feel right at home. It's about creating an inclusive place for all genders, races, and orientations. Cilla, why don't you swap those cowboy romances out for books with women on the covers? We want the crowd to feel welcome here. I think we could put the beanbags away. We don't want anyone thinking this is a hook-up event, though. I have a friend whose sister is that way and apparently a lot of that goes on."

Roger seemed to have forgotten that Cilla was a lesbian and he could consult her, but she couldn't be bothered to engage in any type of dialogue with him as he now knew everything about libraries and, apparently, the gay community. Cilla put the beanbags away, not because she thought Helen's writing might incite an orgy but because they were dirty from sticky fingers at storytime.

Helen arrived early with Georgina and a rolling silver carry-on, presumably loaded with books. It was the kind of luxury suitcase that someone who traveled a lot would invest in. Cilla's own carry-on was at least twenty years old and hadn't seen the inside of a plane in a good two years. Georgina had changed out of her work clothes into beige slacks, a cream shirt with a plaid silk cravat, and a trench coat. She looked elegant and sophisticated, a mirror image of Helen with her gleaming brown hair, long blue woolen coat, pale-blue shirt, and dark-blue jeans. Helen, Georgina, and the suitcase made a beeline for the circulation desk where Cilla stood like a sitting duck.

"Hello, Pricilla!" Helen beamed, showing off a lifetime of attended dental check-ups. "I'm so excited to be here."

Cilla wondered if the Miss America speech was coming next. Maybe she wanted to end world hunger. "It's great to have you. I have had some wonderful feedback already from people excited to hear about your new book." She could feel Georgina's eyes on her. "Hi, Georgina."

"Hi, Cilla. Where can we set Helen up?" said Georgina, for all the world like a devoted publicist.

"Helen!" Roger bustled over with a copy of her latest novel in hand. "Welcome! I have my copy here if you would be so gracious as to sign it. I am a huge fan."

It was the first that Cilla had heard that, but it didn't surprise her. Roger usually turned into a huge fan of whoever was visiting.

Roger produced a ballpoint pen and Helen *was* so gracious. Georgina's eyes flicked around the library, landing on the colorful displays Cilla and Emma had put up to educate children on various things such as healthy eating and good hygiene.

"Roger, I'll go organize the snacks," Cilla said, desperate to get away from the strange ensemble.

She had expected Roger to readily agree because he hated doing anything that resembled work, other than chatting, but he hissed at her. "Pricilla, these are your people. Please stay present and give Helen the author experience that writers should expect when they enter our doors."

Cilla should have known. Georgina made Roger nervous because he was never sure how to interpret her: a beautiful woman who was apparently out of bounds or at least disinterested in him sexually. That the majority of women were disinterested in him sexually anyway never entered his mind. Now he also had Helen to contend with. He had questioned Cilla earlier about whether Helen might be included under the bisexual banner, to which Cilla had responded that she had no idea and he should ask Helen, which she hoped he did. She wished Emma could be present if that interaction occurred.

Cilla wasn't sure what the "author experience" entailed but she showed Helen over to where a table had been set up with the books she had already given them arranged on display, and two chairs where she would presumably sit to sign books while someone else took the money. Cilla had Georgina penciled in for that job but she would leave it to Helen to call the shots. Beside the table, set up in front of four rows of chairs, was a lectern that Helen could use for her reading.

"What can I get you? Water, tea, coffee, wine?"

Helen opened her suitcase and began arranging more books on the table. "Water would be great, thanks."

Georgina went to investigate the lectern. "What wine is it?"

Cilla couldn't remember the name of it. "Whatever could be bought in bulk that was within the budget. Usually authors supply their own, but Roger insisted."

"With that pitch, you should work in sales. I'll have a glass of the red. Why isn't there a microphone?" Georgina stood at the lectern as though she was about to give a sermon. She picked up the sheet of paper that had Helen's bio on it and began to silently read.

"There are only about twenty chairs. I'm sure everyone will be able to hear."

Roger was hovering, looking like he was unsure whether to roll out a red carpet or go hide under the desk. "We can find a microphone if you like?"

Cilla didn't wait for Georgina to respond before going to get the drinks. Georgina sure was acting like she was running the show. Cilla supposed she was used to organizing open houses and negotiating deals but she didn't work for Helen. Cilla poured Georgina a glass and grabbed a bottle of water for Helen, deposited them on the table, and rushed back to the staff kitchen to unwrap the cheese platter and set out the wine. Roger was otherwise occupied with visitors who had begun to get settled for the reading. Helen had disappeared somewhere, and Georgina was fussing over the books on the table.

"Cilla, there could be a crowd, so please have chairs on standby. Also, here on Helen's bio you should include something about her next novel."

Cilla pretended not to hear and went to the counter to assist someone with ordering a book. She saw Helen emerge from the bathroom with fresh lipstick. She hoped by hanging back Roger would kick off the festivities, but Roger was calling her as though there was a gas leak somewhere and the place was about to blow. Cilla waited for the stragglers to come in and take a seat, and for other people who happened to be in the library anyway and wanted to know what was going on to get settled, then she introduced Helen and read from the bio, which Helen had provided herself and Cilla was not about to change. Just as she was wrapping up the last sentences on Helen's literary awards, she vaguely noticed a few more people come into the space and stand at the back. Georgina had been correct about the amount of seating. When Cilla looked up she almost keeled over, because Lucky and Daisy were standing almost shoulder to shoulder with Georgina and Vince, who had also made a late entry. Cilla's cheeks lit up like a traffic light. Guilt washed over her. She wasn't sure what exactly she felt worse about, probably that she had compromised herself by not being truthful. She was a grown woman who was single and she could be with who she wanted, but she should have been up-front and given Lucky all the information, if not Georgina. She had been meaning to, she wanted to, it just never felt like the right time. Now the universe had assembled them, she should feel pleased that Lucky was out doing things and had chosen to visit her at work and that Georgina was treating her respectfully, but all she felt was mortification and a dread that she would be exposed. Her mother's disappointed face popped into her head like it used to as a child. It was enough to make her spill any beans she had canned up.

Helen was thanking Cilla for the introduction and saying how excited she was to make the move to Twine River and meet so many wonderful people. Cilla could barely take in what she was saying. Such was her desperation that she went to stand next to Roger off to the side so she wouldn't have to contend with anyone else she knew. Roger was staring at Helen with reverence, his mouth like a cabinet someone had forgotten to close. Cilla wondered if Penny had finally been usurped. Helen drew some reading glasses from her pocket and introduced her latest novel, *Changing Tides.* The title reminded Cilla of incontinence pads, but as Helen started reading an excerpt, Cilla had to admit the writing was good. She stole a glance at the crowd, which was a mix of those who always came to their author's corner readings and some new faces, and everyone was paying attention. There was one woman coughing, which was a bit distracting, but there always seemed to be one. Cilla cast her eye to the side to see that Georgina had moved slightly away from Lucky and closer to the wine table, which wasn't surprising. Lucky had her hair twisted into a knot at the back of her neck, and gold hoop earrings with coins dangling from them. She had on pale jeans, long brown boots, a charcoal-colored T-shirt, and a bronze velvet blazer with gold buttons. There was an energetic forcefield around her that set her apart. She looked different and radiated a quiet power. Cilla wanted more than anything to be alone with her somewhere, spilling their souls into a stardust concoction and drinking it back up. Her heart beat proudly for Lucky, who was ostracized for being different but still stood in her genuine unique self.

Roger made a gagging sound like his tongue had become dry. "Do you think Helen would agree to be our diversity ambassador?"

"We can talk about it," Cilla responded, thinking for several reasons it wasn't a good idea or an effective one. She supposed Roger wanted more of Helen in his life. Cilla didn't blame him. It was easy to form crushes on beautiful women, and Cilla only had to look around the room to affirm that.

Cilla volunteered to help Helen with the cash while Helen signed books. Georgina was only too happy to eat cheese and gossip with Vince. Cilla smiled at Lucky and Daisy and gave them a wave. She wanted to speak to Lucky but didn't want the conversation colliding with one with Georgina. Daisy seemed so lovely, but Cilla felt that her self-imposed break from

Lucky could come to an end and now Lucky had inadvertently imposed one on her. It was only fair, but it didn't make it any more pleasant. Cilla was aware of Lucky waiting at the back of the room for Daisy to buy a book. Cilla took Daisy's money and, once Helen had signed Daisy's book, excused herself to go speak to Lucky. She could feel Georgina's eyes on her as she went to say hello to Lucky, and it shouldn't have modified her behavior but it did. What she really wanted to do was hug Lucky and absorb her warmth like a plant in the sun. Instead, she said a formal hello and asked what brought them to the library.

"Daisy loves to read, and when I told her that you work at the library and know all about the latest books, she searched the Internet and saw this event. I would never have thought to do that. I was hoping you would be here."

Sometimes Cilla forgot that Lucky came from a pre-Internet era, which Cilla had too, but Cilla had been surrounded by information technology and had to keep up with it for work, day-to-day life, and socialization. Cilla was part of a generation who grew up completely free of it: calling friends on a landline, getting up from a sofa to change a television channel, using a phone book to search for a number, looking facts up in an encyclopedia. Lucky had mastered sending messages on a cell phone and making calls, but searching things online was a foreign concept. She had skipped years of her life by spending them in bygone eras. That made Cilla pause, but what made her heart sing was that Lucky had hoped she would be there. It was the smallest gestures of simplest phrases that got caught in Cilla's heart, playing in her thoughts like a sweet song stuck in hear head.

"I was surprised to see you here but I'm glad you came." She smiled. "It's so nice to see you out enjoying yourself."

Lucky opened her black leather purse so Cilla could see inside. "Emergency stash."

Cilla looked inside and saw a lemon. She had to laugh. "What would you do, take a bite?"

"If I have to. Cilla, you see, it's not just my condition that makes me nervous in crowds, it's that I don't really understand this world. It seems to move so fast I can't get my balance. Books I can understand, though. Not those electronic ones, but the rest haven't changed all that much."

Cilla was about to respond but Daisy came back, clutching her book. "I'm going to read this on the plane. Lucky, you can read it before I leave if you like."

"I might get a copy too," Cilla said. "You'll have to excuse me."

She could see Roger speaking to Helen, who looked like a horse who had seen a snake on the ground and was about to rear.

"Helen, thank you so much for attending," Cilla said. "Before we pack up, I would love to get a copy of the book if I may." She inserted herself in between Roger and Helen to create some distance between whatever Roger had just said and Helen's reaction to it.

Helen gladly turned back to the table and signed a copy of the book, insisting that this copy was on her for hosting the event. Roger spied someone spilling wine on the floor and went to officiate the food and beverage table.

"I hope Roger wasn't inappropriate," Cilla said, fishing for more information.

"A little, but I can handle myself. He wanted to know if I write all my scenes from personal experience and when I said a bit of both, he, uh…offered to help should I need experience with any male characters. There was definitely a subtext." She started to giggle and that gave Cilla permission to join in.

"I am so sorry he said that to you, he is a strange man. He has a funny way of showing appreciation, but please just take it as that." She had never defended Roger so strongly before, but she wanted to set Helen at ease that he wasn't a sexual deviant or stalker.

"Cilla, don't worry about it. You have to have thick skin to be a writer, someone will always have an opinion. I will do as you suggested and take it as a compliment, of sorts." She laughed again.

She really was much more easygoing than Georgina, who was sharp but could rarely laugh at herself. Georgina had moved away from the people at the drinks table and was watching them while Vince talked to her.

"Are you all settled into your new place?" Cilla asked.

"Almost. Still some unpacking to do but the bulk of it is done. I can't believe the amount of space out here. Back in Chicago I used to write at my kitchen table because my apartment was so small—the price of inner-city living—but out here I have a guest bedroom and a home office. I love it already."

"Georgina has sold a few houses to friends, so soon she'll know the whole town."

Helen looked over at Georgina and smiled, showing off a dimple like a quotation mark. "Georgina knows a lot of people. It was a win-win for me to come here and be able to stay while I was looking for a house and then when I was moving."

"You must have found something right away," Cilla said.

Helen's brow furrowed. "No, it took a few months of searching before the right house became available. Luckily, Georgina gave me the jump on everything that was coming up for sale."

Cilla tried not to show her shock. So Helen had been staying with Georgina months ago and Georgina had never mentioned it. No wonder they seemed so close so quickly. Part of Cilla wanted to have it out with Georgina and ask her if something had been going on, and part of her just wanted to let it all fade away. In that moment she wondered if she needed a fresh start herself, away from everyone in the hopes of getting rid of any feelings she had.

"That does sound convenient. Helen, I'll speak to you before you go. Thanks again. I just have to sort a few things out."

Cilla made a beeline for the staff kitchen and shut the door behind her. She needed to give herself the pep talk that Emma would give her. "It's all in your head," she told herself. "There is no problem. If you want to know something, stop being pathetic and ask it. You're just jumping to conclusions and making yourself sick." She splashed cold water on her face then dried herself off with hand towel. She thought of Lucky bravely coming out into the new world, and here she was, acting like she was coming undone because she had a crush and her ex-girlfriend was in the building. She took a couple of deep breaths and told herself, "I am calm, I am in control, and everything is great."

Georgina must have seen Cilla go into the kitchen because she was waiting for her outside the door. "Cill, I've been giving your offer some thought, and I think we should do it."

Cilla stared at her, rapidly scanning every recent conversation she'd had with Georgina but coming up short. Her face must have given it away because Georgina said, "Going to your folks' for Thanksgiving. I'd actually like to get out of town and away from work for a couple of days. It's hard being a realtor in your hometown. I never switch off, even when I'm walking to the store."

"You want to come to my family Thanksgiving? It's the suburbs, it's not exciting."

"God, that is exactly what I need, boring streets where I don't know anyone and nothing interesting is keeping me out past nine p.m."

Cilla grinned and thought, *No offense intended*. Instead, she said, "I'm staying in the house with my family, probably in my childhood bedroom."

"I love that. I can picture it. I've been there once, remember? That *Charlie's Angels* poster is forever seared into my brain. We won't have to sleep in bunk beds, will we?"

Cilla felt the energy seeping from her body. "There's a double bed in there now. You'd be more comfortable in the motel. Are you sure you want to come? Mom and Dad are getting older, it will be very quiet, and you know, we did break up, so…"

Georgina adjusted the scarf at her neck, sending a wave of perfume Cilla's way. "We know why we broke up but, honestly, we didn't give the relationship what it deserves. I'm not saying we get back together, but we could press refresh and get to know each other again."

Cilla blinked, holding in the question about Helen staying with Georgina, then thought, *Fuck it*. "Has Helen been staying with you on and off for months?"

Georgina suddenly found her short red nails interesting. "Not on and off, but I did let her stay when she was house hunting. It's stressful enough without having to travel long distances for showings. It would have been impossible."

"Why didn't you tell me at the time?"

Georgina sighed. "I knew you'd make a big deal out of it. I can't even be nice to a friend now? Do you tell me every little thing?"

Cilla was about to say that she did, but then she thought of her friendship with Lucky and realized she had nothing to offer in defense. "Okay, I was just asking. I'm going down the day before and staying the two nights. I'm going to help Mom cook and Deb will be there for the day with the kids."

Georgina grimaced. "How many does she have?"

"Still two."

"Last time it sounded like twenty-two."

Cilla had to smile. When she took a step back from Georgina and didn't take her comments personally, she was actually quite funny. She glanced over to where Lucky was talking to Daisy, who had a glass of wine in hand. They had been joined by Helen. "Are you absolutely sure you want to come? You'll be coming as a friend, not my partner."

Georgina frowned, then shrugged. "My therapist told me to try new things."

"You have a therapist?"

"Cill, if I want to be a high-performing individual, I need to take care of myself mind, body, and soul. Anyway, I think we are all going to The Nobody if you want to join for a vino."

"Thank you, but I don't clock out for at least another hour."

As Cilla closed up the library that evening, she reflected on what Georgina had said about being a high-performance individual. It was hilarious because it came from Georgina, but there was something to it. Cilla did have to admire her total self-absorption in that she was living the life she wanted to; she was independent, successful, had solid friendships, and was in great shape. Cilla liked post-breakup Georgina better than the woman she'd been in the last half of their romantic relationship. Now that she had no expectations of Georgina, she could sit back and enjoy the pure comedy that came out of her mouth. Maybe Thanksgiving wouldn't be so bad. Although she did have to break it to her parents and, worst of all, Deb, who had never liked Georgina.

Cilla had said goodbye to Lucky and Daisy and thanked them for coming, and Lucky had invited Cilla for dinner on Daisy's last night on Thursday. Cilla was looking forward to it, but she also couldn't wait to have some alone time with Lucky. Not only was she jumping out of her skin with desire every time Lucky made eye contact, but she had so many unanswered questions.

The next evening after work, Cilla called her mother to ask if it was all right if Georgina came home for Thanksgiving.

"Georgina is just as welcome as Bryce," Cilla's mom, Patty, said.

Even though Cilla's parents had been overwhelmed when she had come out at age twenty, they had tried to keep everything fair between her and Deb, which included treating her previous girlfriends and Georgina as they would Deb's husband, Bryce, even though they never really knew how to take Georgina. It hadn't been an ongoing concern because Georgina usually avoided family gatherings. Georgina had a younger half-sister who was married to a farmer in Illinois. Georgina's parents were divorced. Her mother lived in Monaco and wasn't particularly close to either daughter, and her father had died before Cilla met her. There was no going home for holidays for Georgina, and she seemed to prefer it that way.

Cilla could tell that Patty and her father, Don, struggled to connect with Georgina, but they tried. Patty usually by involving her in the cooking and Don by talking to her about property. No one was overly happy about the arrangement.

CHAPTER TWENTY-FIVE

Benson wore his bow tie to dinner at Hollyoaks and Lucky served the dogs marrow bones outside on the back porch on porcelain plates. For the humans, she had laid out a beautiful spread on the kitchen table, which was decorated with candles in repurposed jars and old bottles crammed with marigolds and dahlias. The polished silver gleamed on her aunt's linen napkins, and she had filled crystal glasses with water and lemon slices.

"Something smells delicious," Cilla said, looking around the kitchen. "Here." She presented Lucky with the key lime pie she had made.

"I hope it is." Lucky accepted the pie and admired it before placing it on the counter. "This looks incredible. I didn't know you baked."

"Rarely, these days. I used to love to cook and garden and fix things. Now I just eat and call someone to repair things for me."

"I can't wait to try it."

Lucky was wearing a black chef's apron over a fifties-style evening gown in a deep burgundy color. She had sparkling teardrop earrings and her hair pulled back at the temples with pearl barrettes. Cilla had worn her best jeans and black turtleneck sweater that she had dressed up with a belt and gold earrings. She was saved from feeling underdressed by Daisy, who was wearing a yellow and white floral shirt with a long denim skirt.

"Are these from the garden?" Cilla asked, leaning over the table to smell the flowers.

"Yes, Daisy picked them. She's been out there doing yard work for me."

Daisy smiled. "I'm a horticulturalist, so I enjoy having my hands in the dirt."

Lucky opened the oven to check something, then stood up and undid the apron and hung it in the pantry. She had taken her bangles off this evening and wore a gold bracelet instead. She looked like an old Hollywood starlet, and Cilla was struggling to think of anything other than drawing her close and kissing her until she couldn't breathe. She wondered if she was turning into some type of pervert.

The evening was mild and the kitchen was warm from the stove. Lucky had left the kitchen windows ajar so the scents of the garden crept in on a slight breeze that ruffled the curtains and drew the candle flames up in a dance.

"Did you meet in London?" Cilla asked, her tongue loosened after a glass of pinot noir.

Daisy glanced at Lucky as though looking for confirmation. Lucky had a mouthful of chicken so Daisy answered, her voice slow as though she wasn't sure. "Sort of. Lucky knew my father and his previous girlfriend before he met my mother. She passed away, my father's previous girlfriend, I mean."

"I'm sorry to hear that." Cilla looked harder at Daisy, but she appeared to be the same age as Lucky. Cilla forgot that Lucky was older than she looked, or at least than what the calendar said.

Lucky swallowed and said, "Daisy wasn't even born when I left London." She smiled at Daisy and then turned to Cilla. "Daisy's father was a friend of mine and my then-girlfriend,

Mira. Daisy's mother, Edith, would have been newly pregnant with Daisy. When Mira passed away, everything became a blur for me."

Cilla tried to disguise her surprise. "You did mention Mira. She sounds like a wonderful person." It seemed the right thing to say even though she didn't know much about what Mira was like.

"Lucky has been like an aunt to me since we reconnected. We rarely see each other but we are loyal pen pals. It's been so nice to spend time with Lucky and hear things about my parents that I never knew. They were much more wild than they let on. They are certainly tame now."

"Cilla," Lucky said. "Perhaps you could help us. I have some photos that I would like to give to Daisy, but she suggested getting copies done. Is there anywhere in town that does such a thing?"

"Sure. The drugstore can make copies for you. I can make copies at work, but they won't be as professional. But, they won't cost you anything."

"I'm happy to pay for them. If you could help me with that process, I would appreciate it."

"It would be my pleasure."

Cilla felt relief to know what Lucky and Daisy's relationship was, but she was also curious as to how they had reconnected and what had happened in the intervening years. Did Daisy have anything to do with Lucky getting stuck in a time warp? Lucky had said that she hadn't told anyone about her "condition," as she called it, so she didn't want to say the wrong thing in front of Daisy.

Their chat turned to Helen's reading. Lucky said she had started the book and it was nice to read something more modern than the classics she had on the shelf. Daisy tried to explain about e-readers, but Lucky couldn't grasp the concept of a virtual library. As they were laughing at Lucky's interpretation of what Daisy had just said, the doorbell chimed. The dogs started to bark and everyone froze, looking at one another. It was so comical that they all started to laugh again.

"Would you like me to get it?" Daisy asked.

"No, no. Stay and keep Cilla company. Maybe it's a lost soul looking for another house. The street numbers here make no sense."

Cilla listened to the creaking of the floorboards under Lucky's footsteps and the sound of the door being unlatched. "Hello?"

"Hello, Luciana. Apologies for the late knock at the door. I work long hours."

Luciana? Cilla's stomach clenched. She knew that voice. Daisy had paused to listen too.

"I'm not selling," Lucky said. "And I have company. Goodbye."

"I'm aware that has been your stance, however I'm giving you the opportunity to reconsider as we have some developers interested in the piece directly behind you."

"It's not for sale. I own it and I would die rather than sell to developers."

Georgina scoffed. "Not the back, you don't. Check the measurements of the block on the deed. Your land ends a yard or so before that old tree. Just think of how nice it will be to have a strip of condos that look out onto that forested area."

Cilla quietly stood up and moved closer to the doorway.

"You're mistaken. I'll find the deed. This has always been my aunt's land, acres of it."

Georgina laughed. "Did she tell you that?"

"I'll find the title, I know I have it someplace."

There was a pause, then Georgina said, "Whose dog is that?"

Cilla's heart dropped. This wasn't the way she wanted things to go. She should have cleared things up weeks ago.

"Never you mind," Lucky said. "Now if you'll excuse me."

"Benson?" Georgina said.

Cilla groaned inside.

Daisy whispered, "Who's that?"

"This isn't your dog," Georgina said. "Give him to me or I'll call the police."

There was the sound of paws scrabbling and a dog yelping. Cilla couldn't hide any longer. She straightened her spine and walked out into the hall.

"Georgina," she called. "Benson is here with me."

Georgina looked up from where she had been trying to pull Benson up by the bow tie. Benson had laid down on the floor as though heaven's light was shining directly on him. "Cilla?" Georgina let go and stood up tall. She brushed her hands together, then wiped them on her trousers.

Lucky moved aside to allow Cilla room to come through to the entrance. She looked flustered and like she might cry. It was the second time she had been accused of stealing Benson. Daisy appeared in the hall to see what the commotion was about.

Cilla tried to keep her voice even. "George, it's late. Let's talk tomorrow, yeah?"

Georgina looked from Cilla to Lucky to Daisy. "Are you going to introduce me to your friends?"

Cilla felt sick. "Georgina, this is Lucky and this is Daisy. Lucky, Daisy, this is Georgina." She knew Georgina wanted the full introduction that included relationships, but she felt like a sinking ship rapidly making its descent toward the ocean floor.

"Lucky?" Georgina asked.

"Sorry." Cilla clarified, "Luciana."

They stood awkwardly: Lucky wide-eyed, Daisy looking at the floor, probably wishing she had stayed in the kitchen, Cilla with folded arms, Benson playing dead, Peanut standing over Benson, looking from face to face, and Georgina like a pin-striped warrior about to run into battle.

"Georgina," Lucky said after a moment. "This is an inconvenient time and I don't wish to discuss anything right now. The house and adjoining land belongs to me. If you have anything to say, you can take it up with my solicitor. Otherwise, if you would be so kind, our dinner is getting cold."

Georgina looked at Cilla and then said, "A representative from Finegrove Property will be in contact. Thank you for your time." She stepped out through the door and Cilla followed her out, grabbing her sleeve to stop her from walking down the steps.

"George, wait."

Georgina shook her off but stopped. "You should be careful who you associate with. Some people are not normal."

"I'll call you tomorrow."

Georgina looked at her with an icy rage in her blue eyes. "This isn't going to go well for your friend, you know. Finegrove is a huge corporation with a whole legal team."

The Cilla boat had hit the ocean floor. "Lucky is a good person. This house has been in her family a long time. Just leave her be, please."

Georgina sucked air in through her nose and looked Cilla up and down. Cilla knew that face, when Georgina was crunching something in her mind. Eventually Georgina said, "It's interesting whose side you're on here."

"I'm not on any side." Benson came to stand beside her as though Cilla did have a side and he was on it. "Let's talk tomorrow, okay?"

Georgina shrugged. "Whatever, Cilla."

Cilla watched her make her way down the steps, then turned and went inside. Lucky and Daisy were seated at the table, slowly eating their food like children who'd just been chastised by a parent.

"Sorry about that." Cilla sat down and looked at the delicious food that she now had no appetite for.

"Why are you apologizing?" Lucky said. "Let's just forget it and enjoy ourselves."

"She was at the reading, wasn't she?" Daisy asked.

Lucky looked at Cilla and Cilla nodded. She felt like she couldn't put anything in her mouth to eat until she'd burped up the truth, but she couldn't put Daisy through that. She would have to do it tomorrow after Daisy had departed.

Conversation flowed, but to Cilla, Lucky seemed to be lacking some of her sparkle. They ate the pie and Daisy told Cilla about her job working for the local council, and Cilla regaled her with Roger stories until she was howling with laughter. When it was time to go, Cilla gave Daisy a hug, and whether Lucky had said anything to Daisy about her feelings for Cilla or not, Daisy made herself scarce so Cilla and Lucky could say goodbye.

Cilla took Lucky's hand by the front door—where only an hour ago Georgina had stood—and said, "I've missed you."

"We should talk. I think there's a lot that has been left unsaid."

Cilla wasn't sure what that meant. "Are you free tomorrow evening? I could come after work, or you could come to my place."

Lucky squeezed Cilla's hand and let it go. "Daisy has a late flight. We could get together the following day?"

"Pencil me in. Would you like to come to my place for dinner? I can pick you up around six."

Lucky smiled. "I'm sure I can walk, just give me the address."

"I will message you. Lucky?"

"Yes?"

"Have you been here the whole time, or...traveling?"

Lucky's gray eyes were like planets, worlds of their own to be traveled. Cilla wanted to imbibe Lucky and draw her in like fluid. Her body throbbed with the wanting to be even nearer to Lucky, but she was aware of Daisy making herself scarce and the chasm of unspoken truths between them.

Lucky's lips parted as though to speak, then she closed them again and leaned forward and took Cilla in her arms. She took a deep breath and Cilla wrapped her arms around her. They stayed like that for half a minute, then Lucky pulled back. "I've been here with Daisy for now, but it's there like an itch, the pull to go. I wish it wasn't. I'm tired, Cilla, and now this business with the land…"

Cilla heard Daisy making what seemed like deliberately loud noises coming back into the kitchen. Cilla and Lucky stepped farther apart, and Cilla said, "Will you still come to my place?"

Lucky smiled. "There are many things pulling at me at once. Some stronger than others. Yes, I will be there."

Cilla felt light as she walked home, buoyed by the wanting she saw in Lucky and the knowledge that it wasn't just her battling desires. Cilla knew she also had Georgina to contend with, and for some reason the image of Eleanora Bromwell, with her dark hair and languid eyes, was intruding on her thoughts. Jumbled pieces of a puzzle on a table. She needed to find the corner piece to start to join them together in a way that made sense.

CHAPTER TWENTY-SIX

Emma stood behind Cilla with a hair color brush poised over her head and looked at Cilla in the bathroom mirror. "You have become very secretive, and I know there's something juicy inside of that caramel-colored melon of yours."

It was dawning on Cilla that Emma had insisted she color Cilla's hair so she would have her captive to squeeze out information about Lucky. She knew she would have to give her something or risk having hair chemicals burning into her scalp forever. "Georgina is being all weird."

Emma squinted at her in the mirror. "How so?"

Cilla tried not to flinch as the cool concoction was buttered over her hairline. "She wants to come to my family Thanksgiving and would not take no for an answer."

"You said yes?"

"I was caught off guard."

Emma's eyes bugged and she raised her brows. "That is not Georgina-ish. Wild horses couldn't drag her to anything that mattered to you, and now she's wanting to hang out with Ma and Pa? Maybe she's getting a glimpse of life without you and it's not so great after all."

Cilla used the corner of the old towel that was draped around her shoulders to wipe some color from her ear. Emma had not tidied her bathroom for Cilla's benefit and Cilla didn't mind one bit. There was a damp pink bath mat scrunched up in front of the shower and a used razor on the bathtub. The basin had a blob of blue toothpaste on the rim, and a pair of nude-colored tights hung over the cold tap in the shower. Cilla used the corner of the towel to smooth off the toothpaste blob. "She's been hounding Lucky to sell her land for development."

"No way. Does she know that you know Lucky?"

Cilla sighed. "She does now. When I had dinner there, Georgina randomly showed up to essentially bully Lucky into selling the land to whatever their company is called, and Georgina saw Benson and it all went down."

"Wait, what? Why didn't you tell me at work? Don't move. I'm going to get the plastic wrap."

Cilla moved her face side to side, trying to see if Emma had gotten the color on all parts of her hair. Cilla no longer wanted to be a caramel latte; her natural pale brown hair would be fine. She would have been happy to go to the hairdresser this time, especially after Georgina's comments about cutting corners, but Emma was so excited by their salon evening that Cilla gave in. Her father used to tell her she had a rubber arm, and Cilla knew he wasn't wrong. She helped herself to a pretzel from the cup that Emma had balanced on the basin beside the soap.

Emma returned with the plastic wrap and began to encase Cilla's head until Cilla had a view of what she would look like with a facelift. She eased some skin back out so she didn't look so startled, but it just made her forehead scrunch into a frown. Emma sat down on the bath and took the cup of pretzels, and Cilla explained what had happened when Georgina showed up. "And there's something else." Cilla opened up her phone and typed "Eleanora Bromwell" into the search bar. "Do you think this is peculiar?"

Emma slid her glasses back up her nose and took the phone and read the article, her lips softly moving. At the end, she looked up and passed the phone back. "It vaguely rings a bell. Maybe we did something about it in school or one of my friends talked about it years ago. What's it got to do with Georgina, though?"

Cilla looked at the photo of Eleanora. "Lucky disappears and she has an aunt named Nora, and this woman is Eleanora and she disappeared from around here."

To her credit, Emma seemed to be considering it. "That is weird, and I see a link, and you know I love a good true crime show, or book for that matter, or podcast…" Emma looked thoughtful. "There's something there, but it could easily end up being nothing if you ask the right questions. Why does Lucky disappear, and what happened to Nora?"

Cilla glanced at her watch. "How long does the color stay in?"

Emma stood up and smoothed the plastic wrap. "I set a timer for forty minutes. Let's go sit in the living room."

As they walked downstairs to Emma's living room, which was not far in the tiny townhouse, Cilla said, "I can't tell you where Lucky goes because I was sworn to secrecy, and I'm not sure about the aunt. Do you think it could be the same person?"

"Could she be a great-aunt? That was like, a hundred or eighty or whatever years ago. Do you want a drink?"

"Water, please."

Emma returned with a glass of water with a straw in it and a bottle of nail polish. "I'm going to paint your nails. This is a salon, remember. Do you need to pee first?"

Cilla assured Emma that she was fine and allowed Emma to take her hand.

"How old is Lucky anyway?"

Cilla watched Emma paint a pearly white onto her thumbnail. She wondered if this was what it would be like to have a daughter. Then she remembered fighting with her own mother about clothes and hairstyles and let go of the idea. She didn't actually know the answer, so she said, "Around my age."

"So, unless she's from a long line of vampires, Eleanora is not her aunt."

"Yeah, you're right," Cilla said, but she knew that Lucky hadn't aged like normal people and perhaps her aunt hadn't either. "It's an intriguing story, though."

"I am going to look it up. I wonder what other grizzly secrets this town keeps. Someone must have known who murdered her."

Cilla's finger twitched, and Emma held it still. "Murdered, you think so?" Cilla asked.

Emma looked up from under her blond bangs. "It's always a young, attractive woman in a small town snuffed out by some misfit who works as a handyman or runs a gas station seven miles away. Trust me, I've seen the shows."

"Maybe that's just the ones they show because the pretty murders get the ratings?"

"Either way, there's a lot of them. I had to search Pedro's room while he was in the shower to make sure he wasn't hiding cable ties or photos of his mom with the eyes scratched out."

Cilla made a face. "That seems extreme."

"Well. I wasn't too worried because he is an accountant, but they are fastidious people and he does have good upper body strength. He could be the type to dissect me and add a lock of my hair to his catalogue of fallen nymphs."

"If you feel unsafe—"

"I've been camping with him. If he wanted to murder me, he missed his opportunity. Other hand."

Cilla obediently swapped the hand resting in her lap for the now pearly nailed one. "Life is strange, isn't it? Imagine doing some mundane task at home like unpacking the dishwasher and not realizing that's the last thing you'll ever do because you've got a matter of minutes left."

Emma nodded grimly. "I think about that a lot, like, what if we all had a timer above our heads counting down the minutes left on this earth and I spent mine vacuuming the floor or chopping carrots? I picture myself like the reenactments on crime shows. There I am, sliding the diced carrots along a chopping board into a pot and then there's a bang at the window. Anyway," she said, switching cheerfully, "there has to be more info on our strangled aunt. There's always a rabbit hole to go down, and as for you, you might be begging for that bang at the window if you take Georgina home with you to see your folks."

Cilla had been beginning to feel alarmed with all the murder talk, but the thought of Georgina at her parents' was a sobering one. She smiled anyway, remembering Georgina at the library. "She actually makes me laugh. You can only take her with a grain of salt."

"Maybe you could tell her about all the murders in your hometown and it'll put her off."

Cilla's smile turned grim. "I'm hoping to get her to release her grip on Lucky's land. I know she has some type of KPIs she has to meet, and when it comes to sales she's like a dog with a bone, but there's no way that Lucky would ever sell her land."

"Surely there's some type of heritage listing on that house. If there's not, there should be. Do you want to watch *Evening Shadows over Beach Lane* while your nails dry? I'm on episode four but I'm happy to start again."

"Maybe just while the color sets, but watching those shows makes me jumpy."

Emma flapped her fingers over Cilla's nails. "It's about some nut called Dermott Dewayne who thought he had magic powers that would take him into different dimensions. He thought certain girls were evil spirits, so he killed them and then thought he was getting away with it because he was skipping into other dimensions or times or something."

Cilla's chest constricted so her breath came out in a double sigh. She had come so close to confiding in Emma, and it was only that she had sworn to Lucky that she wouldn't that she hadn't. Her voice sounded far away when she spoke and she forgot her nails for a moment, smudging her pinky against her ring finger. "Actually, I had better go home and feed Benson. He's been alone all day."

"What about your hair?"

"It's easier if I jump in the shower. Thanks for a fun evening. I…" She looked around for where she had left her purse. "I will see you at work."

Emma handed Cilla her phone, which was on the arm of the sofa. "You've scraped your nail, hang on. Won't you at least wait until your nails dry?"

Cilla stood and let Emma repair the paintwork.

"Is everything okay?" Emma asked at the front door.

"Yes. I feel bad about Benson and I want to get up for a run in the morning. I'm sorry."

At the car, she got a glimpse of her gleaming wrapped head in the reflection of the driver's side window, looming ridiculous and distorted. She drove home, leaning forward so as not to stain the car seat with the color, which she could feel oozing down her neck.

Benson was excited to see her when she arrived home, but he stayed by the threshold, looking over his shoulder at her and swiping a paw at the front door in request to visit Peanut.

"Not tonight, Ben. Come on, dinner."

Benson gave a mournful look toward the front then followed Cilla as slowly and dejectedly as he could toward the kitchen. Cilla sat at the table with the noises of Benson crunching kibble and the microwave whirring as it heated a frozen shepherd's pie. The sound of the neighbor calling their cat in drifted through the open back door with the scents of garlic from someone's home-cooked meal. Cilla thought about what Lucky had told her. Lucky seemed so sane, but what if she was delusional? Was Cilla enabling it? The microwave beeped but Cilla didn't move. Despite her resistance to the idea, she knew she was falling for Lucky—or had fallen—rather quickly. She thought about her all the time, imagined spending time with her, touching her, kissing her, making love to her here, there, and everywhere. She knew Lucky wasn't quite of this world, but Cilla knew herself to be a humble creature, and she couldn't help but place Lucky into the sweet domestic life she had always wanted with Georgina and never achieved: grocery shopping, doing chores together, going to the movies or out for dinner or to a ball game. She wanted to be the person who had the privilege of being driven mad by Lucky coughing in bed at night or by Lucky leaving a wet towel on the ground. She was self-aware enough to realize that she was putting herself into another situation where it was still unattainable, and that was the rub. She wanted what she probably couldn't have, but where there was a glimmer of hope, she couldn't help but strive for it. If Lucky was crazy, then Cilla wanted a life with a crazy person.

As far as Georgina was concerned, Cilla felt confusion. Part of her still desired Georgina and thought she always would. There was a chemistry between them that had always been a push and pull, but Cilla would no more trust her heart to Georgina than she would put Dermott Dewayne in charge of a Girl Scouts' hiking trip.

Benson had finished his food and was now standing by Cilla's chair to see if she had any scraps for him. Cilla stood and removed the pie from the microwave and placed it on the table. Outside, a car alarm began to yell and Cilla stood again to shut the door. She would have to cook something better than a frozen meal for Lucky tomorrow night. The thought of Lucky sitting at the table in her home felt strange and remote but also exotic and exciting. Cilla looked around the kitchen with its potted plants and knickknacks that Georgina despised, and its odd glasses that had formed a team over the years as Cilla had broken glasses from sets. Now there were two orange palm-leaf-engraved tallboys, a crystal stemless wineglass, a fine blue thin glass, and two plain tumblers that she had got on clearance at Target that were remaining from the original six. She wasn't elegant and stylish like Lucky. She didn't have an instinct for harmony of the senses. She knew how to identify it when she saw it all right, but she was at a loss how to create it. She took a bite of the pie, but the meaty smells were mingling with the chemical waves coming from her head. She ate mechanically just to eat something, then scrapped the rest into Benson's bowl and went to wash her hair.

CHAPTER TWENTY-SEVEN

Cilla cleaned like she had never cleaned before. As soon as she started cleaning, she realized how much there was to do. There were cobwebs on the crown molding and dust on the wainscoting. The windows were streaky and the walls marked. Cilla had a pot roast in the oven and a cheese platter waiting in the fridge with white wine for Lucky's arrival. She also had a jug full of water and lime. It felt a bit strange and she hoped Lucky wouldn't be offended, like she was trying to drug her into staying. Cilla had been saving the candle that Lucky had bought her at the market, but now it glowed in its pearly glass on the coffee table in the living room, permeating the house with a summery sweetness. Cilla felt jittery with excitement at seeing Lucky again and also nervous about what Lucky might say. She would surely have questions about Georgina, and Cilla knew she owed her an explanation. There was also the Thanksgiving trip in a few days. Cilla wished she was taking Lucky instead, although she wasn't sure what Lucky would make of the pedestrian suburb that Cilla had grown up in with her white-bread family, including now her sister's rambunctious children. They were Cilla, though, a part of Cilla's life, and Cilla couldn't hide from who she was. She was the person with the mismatched cups and the splotches of hair color on her ears and sideburns, the person who loved easily and long and still got out of breath when she ran.

The doorbell chimed and Cilla smoothed her hair, which now shone pale brown, and tried to walk normally to the door even though she seemed to have lost all sense of how her body usually contracted her muscles and moved her joints to walk. She opened the door and Lucky was standing under the porch light with a posy of flowers in her hands and crimson in her cheeks from walking in the cold. Her skin was cool as she leaned forward to press her cheek against Cilla's but her breath was warm on Cilla's ear. Cilla took the flowers and showed Lucky inside. Benson and Peanut bounced around on stiff legs, kissing each other until they began their zoomies.

"Oh, sorry!" Lucky yelped as she saw through the living room doorway, Peanut careening off the sofa and rumpling the floor rug. It was followed a second later by Benson crashing into the coffee table, making the candle flame grow and stutter, then shrink again.

"They don't have the space here that they do at your place. Maybe I'll open the back door for them. Come on in."

Lucky looked around her as they walked along the hall to the kitchen, glancing into the open doorways of the living room and at the partially shut door of Cilla's bedroom.

"Hopefully they will settle," Cilla said, letting the dogs into the backyard.

"Your house is divine," Lucky said. "Oh, you still have the feather."

Cilla followed her gaze to the owl's feather that was poking from the top of a jar filled with tiny seashells she had collected at Marco Island one year. She wasn't sure if an owl's feather belonged with seashells as much as a gull's feather would, but she just didn't have a knack for these kinds of things. Lucky seemed delighted anyway. "Of course," Cilla said, trying not to smile too openly at Lucky's delight. She found a vase under the sink and set the flowers on the table.

"And look at your potted plants, they're so happy here by the window. I can never get my indoor plants to flourish like that, the house is too dark."

Cilla brought the wine from the fridge and held it for Lucky to see. "Would you like a glass?"

"Why not?"

Lucky continued to cast her eyes about as Cilla poured. "I didn't realize how close our houses were."

"Let's go into the other room where it's warmer," Cilla said, handing Lucky a glass. "Yes, we are only a couple of streets over."

"I love the stained glass," Lucky commented as they walked back through to the living room.

Cilla contemplated the blue and yellow art deco style fans patterning the windows by the front door. She remembered how she had fallen in love with them when she bought the house. "Thank you. When the afternoon light is right it makes lovely colors on the floor."

There was a moment of awkwardness as they sat on the sofa, Cilla unsure how close to get to Lucky. She wanted to sit close enough to touch knees, but she found Lucky hard to read. She hadn't seen Lucky interact with enough people to measure how she behaved with anyone else. Did she smile so easily and look about her so warmly? Cilla guessed that she might, but she hoped some of those smiles were just for her. She watched Lucky's elegant fingers with their clusters of rings lightly grasping the stem of her wineglass. Her bangles played out their tune as Lucky lifted the glass to take a sip. Cilla watched the ripple of her throat then hastily looked at a photo of Benson as a puppy on the mantel so she wouldn't be caught staring.

"This house has so much charm. The fireplace is beautiful," Lucky said, craning around to take it all in.

"It is pretty, but I haven't used it in years."

Lucky's gaze traveled to Georgina's painting. "That's an impressive work of art. Did you paint it?" Cilla must have looked startled because Lucky quickly said, "Not that it doesn't look professional, I just thought perhaps you were into painting. I have always had a fondness for it myself."

"I didn't paint it but I know the artist. It was a gift…" The words slowed to a halt as though Cilla had run out of the power to project them, but she knew she shouldn't let this opportunity to come clean glide by. "My ex-partner painted it. See, the thing is…well, you know Georgina?" She could hear desperation creep into her own voice. "From the other night?"

"Yes," Lucky said. She had grown still, even her restless fingers holding her glass unmoving on her thigh.

Just then the dogs came trotting in. Benson had leaves and twigs stuck in his coat. "She, she was my…we were together. I should have told you."

Lucky looked down into the green gold of her wine. "You don't owe me a view into every nook and cranny of your life." She looked up to meet Cilla's eye. "Your life is yours to live as you want."

"I know, but I've been meaning to say something and the timing never felt right and then when she showed up, I was full of remorse. You had mentioned her in relation to real estate, and I should have let you know back then."

"No need, Cilla. We all have pasts, and we haven't made any commitments to each other."

"No, we haven't," Cilla said miserably. She wished they could, but she didn't see how. "I do want to get to know you, though, and I love hearing everything about you so I want to share…" She paused to wonder what exactly she wanted to share. "I want to share who I am with you so that you might do the same because you seem such a mystery to me."

At those words, Lucky seemed to draw back into the couch cushions. "There's not much to know. I've been terribly boring, just keeping to myself. Printing photos is probably the biggest outing I've had of late."

A beat passed. Cilla didn't want to switch away from the deeper subjects to talk about trips to the drugstore, but she sensed a reluctance in Lucky and was afraid that if she pushed too hard she might push Lucky beyond the couch cushions and into another dimension. "How did it go?"

"Daisy seemed to know what to do. Did you know that you can just plug phones in and put photographs onto a computer?"

Cilla laughed but wasn't sure if Lucky was joking. Lucky shrugged and Cilla decided she wasn't. "Cars that drive themselves, vacuum robots…What will they think of next?"

It was Lucky's turn to laugh. "That's what I need, a car that drives itself. Then maybe I would leave the house."

"If you ever need a ride, I'd be happy to take you anywhere."

Lucky leaned forward to touch Cilla's knee. "Thank you. I know."

The little gesture soothed the tension, and before Lucky could lean back, Cilla took her fingers and gently held them. Lucky clasped Cilla's hand back, and Cilla felt a warm melting in her chest. In Cilla, a window was flung open and she could see Lucky again clearly as the person she had witnessed who felt lost to her. The words *oh my darling* sighed across Cilla's mind like a soft breeze, ruffling the curtains of the open window, and she watched Lucky's lips softly part like a flower opening. They shuffled closer together, and Cilla had a feeling that auras were real because she seemed to be enveloped in a sensation that was emitting from Lucky.

"I'm sorry that you keep getting caught in the quickly changing weather. I know how it is to be with me—one minute the sun is shining and the next you're in a bleak wind."

"I'll bring an umbrella," Cilla said, her eyes full of Lucky.

"It's no life standing alone in a storm."

Cilla's concerns seemed distant with Lucky's hand warm upon her knee and the swell of her being filling Cilla's senses. "I think I'm already too deep into the garden to mind the weather."

"Winter is no concern during spring."

Cilla's hand moved to Lucky's thigh. "I know, I know. What about you? Is there nothing we can do?"

"I've been trying. Spring is so beautiful."

Cilla could feel Lucky's breath on her, and she leaned forward, their lips finding each other's. Cilla's critical mind sat back and let spring sweep through: violets, roses, gardenias, jasmine, freesias. Oh, my darling. That's why it was called spring. From nowhere, she was in bloom. Lucky's soft lips, her tongue, the feel of her skin brushing Cilla's. Not a speck of snow in sight.

When they pulled apart, Cilla was still giddy and Lucky's skin seemed to glow with the smile on her lips. Lucky's eyes were tender as she reached to run the pad of her index finger lightly along Cilla's brow and down the side of her face. "It is very hard to stop, but I do feel conflicted."

"I'm a big girl."

Lucky sat back a little and looked down at Cilla's hand still in hers. "You are, but your world is so rich and I wouldn't want to bleach it out with my strange one. I wouldn't feel right knowing I would let you down."

Cilla's mouth still tingled. "I understand. There must be a way. What about FIFOs and businesspeople who constantly travel? No one stops them from relationships."

"FIFOs?"

"Fly-in, fly-out."

Lucky still looked confused, but she squeezed Cilla's knuckles. "I certainly hope so but…Oh, I don't know, I don't know."

Seeing Lucky's consternation, Cilla uncurled her legs, which had crept up onto the couch in an effort to get closer. "All I know is kissing you is a feeling that will stay with me for a long time. Perhaps after dinner we can solve the world's problems. I actually cooked, which is something of a miracle in itself."

Lucky brightened immediately. "I feel honored to be a guest at the miracle dinner."

"You haven't tasted it yet," Cilla said, standing and drawing Lucky to her feet.

"It has been decades since someone cooked for me. I shall love every mouthful."

Cilla laughed, and as they walked through to the kitchen she marveled that Lucky was here in her house and only moments before they had kissed on her couch. Yes, winter couldn't have been more distant right then than if they were strolling a Bahamian beach in July. She thought to herself, *Right now, in this very moment, someone's heart is bursting with happiness.*

* * *

There was too much food. Cilla wasn't accustomed to cooking for two anymore, and the dogs ate better than both Lucky and Cilla, who chatted between loosely paced mouthfuls until their plates were almost empty but not quite. The apple pie Cilla had made sat cooling in the oven, and they returned to the sofa where it was comfortable and warm. Cilla wanted to kiss Lucky again. Even Georgina's painting hanging reproachfully overhead could not deter the feeling, but the room seemed to bring out a reticence in Lucky as if the meal had given her time to gather her resolve. Cilla wanted a sense of security that Lucky was on board for seeking a resolution that would provide consistency. She didn't want to ruin the evening, but the wine had added a boldness that may have not come to the fore sober. She should have felt relief that she had told Lucky about Georgina, but Lucky had swept it aside in a way that was confusing, and Cilla feared there would be another week, or more, of unanswered questions. "Lucky…" Cilla paused to frame the question, but Lucky was looking at her expectantly, and she couldn't think of a better way to say it now that she had Lucky's attention. "Your aunt…Was Nora short for Eleanora?"

The color seemed to drain from Lucky's face except for two sharp spots of crimson on her cheekbones. When she spoke, her voice had thinned and her eyes were unblinking. "I wouldn't know. Well, I suppose Nora could be short for…Yes, perhaps. Why do you ask?"

"I saw an article and, of course, it's not your aunt, but it was about a woman who went missing in Twine River and her name was Eleanora."

"How peculiar." Lucky put her wineglass down and looked around the room.

Cilla wished she hadn't said anything. "Would you like dessert?"

"You know what? I am feeling slightly feverish. I am sorry, as I know you have gone to so much trouble and something smells divine, however, I think I should get home."

"Of course. Are you okay?"

Lucky stood, banging her knee of the table. "Peanut!"

"Wait, I'll take you in the car."

Lucky was already surging forward with a wild blindness about her. "A walk in the cool air will do me good. Peanut, come!"

Peanut came uncertainly, ready to walk but unsure about leaving his playmate.

Cilla grabbed her car keys from her purse. "I'll drive you. You will be home before you know it."

Lucky seemed to sag against the doorframe in a half faint and Cilla grabbed her waist, but Lucky's weak hand pushed her off, leaving a clammy spot on Cilla's wrist. "No," Lucky whispered. She wrenched open the front door.

"Let me know you're home safe," Cilla called after Lucky's disappearing form, catching Benson by the scruff of his neck as he dove after Peanut.

She watched Lucky vanish from sight and then turned around and want back into the living room. The cushion was on the floor and the wine in Lucky's glass still seemed to be vibrating with movement. Cilla felt sick to her stomach herself. Her first impulse was to text Lucky, but instead she called Emma.

"She ran off!" Cilla said by way of greeting. "I asked her if her aunt's name was Eleanora and she ran off."

There was the sound of people talking in the background. Emma said, "She's a weird one. Let her go. You've had enough drama with your other weird one. We'll go to the movies tomorrow and watch the new Disney, then we'll get fucked up on cheap wine at The Nobody. I'll get us tickets to an early showing."

"Okay," Cilla agreed but her heart wasn't in it.

"And I'm going full stalker on this Nora business. There's something weird there. Did Lucky do her disappearing trick?"

"We were having a nice time, or so I thought, then I mentioned her aunt and she said she felt unwell and stood up. To be fair, she didn't look great. She was all shaky and she wouldn't let me give her a ride back to her place." Cilla heard voices in the background again. "Sorry, do you have people over?"

"I'm watching *Shrek 2*. You're my annoying talking animal."

"Right, thanks, I think. I'll let you get back to it."

Emma burped. "Sorry, gummy bears. Cill, forget her. You can come annoy me tomorrow."

"Thanks. Night."

Emma burped again. "Does Donkey remind you of Roger but cuter?"

"I've never seen *Shrek*."

"Cilla! I'll tell you about it tomorrow. How's your hair?"

Cilla picked up the shiny ends of her hair. Lucky hadn't even mentioned it. "It looks great, thanks for taking the time."

"All good." Emma laughed at what was on the television. "Oh, Roger."

"Talk tomorrow."

After Cilla had hung up, she took the still full glasses to the kitchen and tipped the wine down the sink. Benson lay by the front door with his head on his paws. She felt like a divorced parent who was making her child choose. She sat down beside him and patted his soft head. She knew how he felt.

CHAPTER TWENTY-EIGHT

"You know what?" Emma said as they left the mall the next night, a plastic spoon full of ice cream in her mouth. "Eleanora was crazy."

"How do you know?"

"Ghhhurgle."

Cilla looked at her. "Google?"

"Yeah," Emma said, pulling her spoon from her mouth, a tightrope of saliva joining her lip to the red plastic. "Most of the articles online were almost identical, but there was one that mentioned something about her being a lunatic."

"That's harsh." Cilla licked her own chocolate-mint cone. It wasn't the weather for ice cream, but she'd managed to convince Emma that it was a more suitable accompaniment to a Disney movie than dry wine. She kept having flashes of her kiss with Lucky, and it was like a sharp blade of pleasure being pushed into her middle.

"But it makes sense, right? If she was mentally unstable, she may have jumped off a bridge or drowned herself or something."

"That's morbid." Cilla chewed a chocolate piece, distant alarm bells sounding the correlation between Mira jumping off a bridge and Eleanora jumping off one.

Emma pointed her spoon at nothing in particular. "The whole story is morbid. I should have searched her husband. You know it's usually the husband. Maybe he offed her because she was a nutjob."

"The way Lucky spoke about her aunt, she seemed like a ballsy old spinster, not a young married person who disappeared. It probably doesn't matter now anyway. Are you sure we parked over here? Didn't we pass the bowling alley?" Cilla stopped walking to look toward the mall parking structure.

"My bad. We were down where the arcade is. Timeline doesn't fit for aunt, so maybe grand-aunt or something?"

They changed course toward the elevators. They always made Cilla nervous at night.

The elevator doors opened and Emma pressed the button to go down a level. There was no one to scare Cilla. "Maybe craziness runs in the family," Emma said.

"She's not crazy," Cilla responded, happy to leave the remark behind as they exited into the basement. She had called Lucky to ask if she was feeling better, and Lucky had assured her that she was fine. They had spoken for a few minutes, but Cilla still had the feeling she had hit a nerve.

Cilla dropped Emma home and couldn't resist driving past Lucky's house. It was past eleven p.m. and the steeples of the house rose clear and sharp against the darkened sky, the forest rippling under the gentle torments of the wind. High up in the turret, the window glowed with light through the fabric of a curtain. It made Cilla feel both calmer and anxious to see it—calmer because she knew Lucky was there and anxious because she felt a need to check. She wanted so badly to be close to anything associated with Lucky, and it scared her. She remembered how, as a child, she was always bringing home birds with broken wings and stray cats and abandoned dogs, and after the cat had attacked Rusty the one-legged robin, Cilla's father had yelled that it had to stop. The memory was unsettling, and

Cilla didn't want to think too hard about why it had popped up now. Everyone was shaped by their experiences. Maybe they all had a bit of crazy in them and maybe the urge in her to heal a wounded robin was still there. Cilla took one last look at the turret window, waiting to see if any shadows were shifting behind its coverings. She thought of Eleanora disappearing in mysterious circumstances and of Mira disappearing in mysterious circumstances and then of the cat who had slinked off with a tattered ear and never messed with a one-legged robin again. She turned her attention from Lucky's space back to her own to put the car in drive. There was a gray fluffy feather with a red tip fluttering against her windscreen. She leaned forward to peer at it, but a gust of wind swept it back up, and it disappeared into the night.

* * *

Thanksgiving weekend seemed a long way off and then it was suddenly upon them. The library was staying open on the Friday, but Emma was working due to her recent camping adventures taking up her vacation days. Both Cilla and Roger were taking off the Friday as well as the Thursday to see family. Cilla wondered if Roger was the strange uncle who brought unwanted books to birthday parties and then remembered she was always giving Deb's kids unwanted books at birthdays and realized she might be the strange auntie. Thinking anything was preferable to the mental imagery of Georgina sitting in her parents' dining room. Why did she get herself into these uncomfortable situations because she didn't want to disappoint people? Her own people-pleasing had made her grumpy and she told herself she didn't care if she was short and direct with Georgina, but as soon as Georgina pulled up in her dark-blue Mercedes SUV, Cilla's people-pleasing took over and she greeted her with a big smile. After all, Georgina was her guest and Cilla had a responsibility. Breaking it to Deb had been another thing, Cilla's desire to please and have peace sent her into a turmoil of competing priorities. Georgina had insisted on driving, which would have been more pleasant if Cilla wasn't stressed about Benson in Georgina's car. She knew he would behave but also that Georgina wouldn't enjoy having him there.

After all her agonizing, seeing Georgina actually made her relax. Her anxiety had built Georgina up into a monster, but Georgina greeted her warmly and got out to help load her things into the back seat so Benson could go on a blanket in the cargo area. He hesitated with one paw up and looked at Cilla.

"Up, Benson," Georgina commanded just like she used to when they would go out together, and Benson leapt into the SUV and sat, trying to catch Cilla's eyes with his sad ones. Georgina shut the liftgate before he could.

"I bought you a cappuccino. It should still be hot," Georgina said as they hopped into the vehicle, which smelled like new car and warm coffee.

"Thank you, that's so thoughtful," Cilla said, lifting the warm cup and holding it between her cold hands as Georgina drove away from the curb. She hoped Benson wouldn't change the chemistry of aromas mingling inside, now with the addition of Georgina's perfume.

"No problem. I saw Roger at the café, He is an odd little man, isn't he?"

Cilla was still recovering from the surprise that Georgina had gone out of her way to do something kind for her. "He is very Roger-ish. He's a bit scared of you."

Georgina gave a dramatic shudder and reached into the cup holder for her coffee as they cruised to the end of Cilla's street. "I'm glad he's scared. He has no sense of personal space. He was eating a gingerbread man—which is odd enough for a grown man—and sprayed crumbs on my jacket when he said hello, then he got awkward and stood there staring at my breast where the soggy mess had landed and said nothing else. It's a Valentino jacket!"

"He spat on Valentino?" Cilla asked.

"He did," Georgina confirmed. Then as an afterthought, "And my breast."

Cilla gulped her coffee. She didn't want to think of Georgina's breast. But, as always, Georgina was dressed for the runway. While her Valentino overcoat was spread neatly over their luggage in the back, she sported a navy blue sweater with the sharp mustard shirt collar poking over the top, very fresh dark-wash jeans, and navy-and-white sneakers. Creamy pearls sat primly at her earlobes. That knack for fashion that Cilla didn't possess, Georgina oozed. When they first met, Georgina had loved to dress Cilla up like a Barbie doll, but Cilla had never felt comfortable in Georgina's attire and was always wiping off dog hair, and by now she was surely too fat. Cilla couldn't be bothered anymore. As long as she was clean and comfortable and presentable, she was happy to admire the color that the Georginas of the world brought to the neighborhood. Cilla realized she had been carrying a lot of mental pressure to keep up with Georgina. There was still a hint of it, but she looked down at her own white-ish sneakers with her near-enough-matched socks and wiggled her feet. If Georgina was a luxury vehicle, she was a beat-up SUV that had been on more than a few camping trips. Both were appreciated in life. It was a novel experience being driven; she felt a bit out of control that she wouldn't have her car for the weekend, but she knew her hometown like the back of her hand. It did give her a chance to admire the scenery from a different perspective as they motored out of town. The red station wagon in front of them had a bumper sticker that read "Trees Not Tarmac." It bumped stubbornly along ahead of them, refusing to turn onto any side streets, but if Georgina noticed she didn't comment. Eventually, it indicated to turn into the driveway of a house on the main road where a man was mowing the lawn around a swing tied to a tree branch and a small girl wearing a yellow parka was drawing with chalk on a lamppost in front of the house.

Cilla's head followed the scene as Georgina maneuvered around the turning car. "Isn't it exciting when you see a car turn into a driveway?"

There was silence so she turned back to Georgina, who had both hands on the wheel and was looking at the road as though Cilla hadn't spoken.

Cilla continued in case Georgina hadn't heard. "It's a snapshot of someone's life. Especially when I see certain cars in town or at the library all the time, and then you think, *Oh, that's where you live. You have a wind chime hanging from the porch or you love to garden.* You know what I mean?"

Georgina's arched brows attempted to draw together. "I see people in their houses all the time. I don't think about it. We all live somewhere."

Cilla didn't bother trying to explain further, but that was exactly it—they all lived somewhere, and she had just seen a vignette of someone's life. She imagined telling Lucky the same thing, and she knew Lucky would get it. It wasn't Georgina's fault, though, they were just different. Cilla took another sip of coffee and turned to check on Benson, who was watching the scenery go by much as she had been. Sensing her gaze, he turned to grin at her with the beginning of a pant. Georgina's window was already lowered an inch, and Cilla did the same to hers in case the car should begin to smell like dog.

"How's work?" Cilla asked, attempting to make conversation. It had been weighing on her mind to say to Georgina that they couldn't kiss again, but sitting there in the car with Georgina cool as a cucumber in her designer outfit with her beautiful profile crisp against the window glass, Cilla felt foolish even mentioning it. Georgina should save her kisses for Helen or any of the other women who were Georgina's match.

"It's all going really well. The development has been a blessing. The lots are almost selling themselves, and sometimes I like selling houses in town just for the thrill of the chase. It's a great feeling when you land a buyer at a premium price or when you finally close on a stubborn listing that's been sitting for months."

The large freeway signs appeared, and Cilla felt a surge of excitement at seeing her family. It had been so long, and she had barely felt any anticipation in her anxiety about recent events and bringing Georgina home.

"Do you think it'll change the town?"

"Hopefully for the better. The aim is to keep the quaint charm—there'd be no point losing that or else who would want to move here? But eventually there'll be an aquatic center and supermarket and increased public transportation. We could finally get Uber Eats and more than one cab out here. Imagine a really nice open-air shopping center with some boutiques, better restaurants. There'd be options."

"You don't think it would drive the local businesses out? How could they compete with the chains?"

Georgina turned onto the freeway and accelerated to beat a cattle truck. Cilla kept her eyes averted so she wouldn't have to see the piteous cows behind the manure-stained bars.

"Cilla, that butcher could use some competition. I tried to buy a couple of chops the other day and he wanted to charge me twenty-two dollars. There'll even be a new sports complex with a football field. You can go for runs along the project's vast new green spaces. They're putting in a lake, even. Benson can chase the ducks."

"I hope it all works out, but it does make me nervous as I love the area so much. I'm happy to pay Frank twenty dollars for chops, he has a great variety and everything is so fresh. He always gives Benson a free bone when we go."

Georgina picked up her coffee cup and took a sip, leaving a lipstick kiss on the lid. She held her cup in one hand, the other on the wheel. "It was twenty-*two* dollars, and I think having some competition won't kill him. That's just standard business. You can't monopolize sales completely."

Cilla thought that's exactly what Georgina and Finegrove were doing but she didn't want to pick a fight. "There's still the option to drive out to Winnerly to go to the supermarket. I'm not against increasing facilities or letting others come and enjoy what we are lucky to have, I guess I'm just cautious."

"I think you're stuck in some gloom-and-doom rhetoric from hearing all the hippies and the oldies in town complain. It's exactly what the town needs. Your place will shoot up in value, just watch."

Cilla knew Georgina was watching her own property shoot up in value, which was fair enough, but Cilla didn't feel as motivated. She had moved to the town for its natural beauty and small-town atmosphere.

The freeway whirred by grayly outside the window. A message tone sounded on a phone, and Georgina twitched but didn't move. Cilla realized it must be her own phone and took it out of her bag. She could almost feel Georgina's curiosity leaping off her body. Cilla looked at the screen and her heart swelled gladly. It was Lucky wishing her a fun and safe trip. Cilla quickly typed out a thanks and wished her an enjoyable day and put her phone back in her bag. Her phone dinged again, and there was a stifling ten seconds while Cilla ignored it and Georgina didn't say anything. Cilla felt awkward reaching for her phone but just as strange ignoring it.

"Everything okay?" Georgina asked.

"Yes. Everything okay with you?" Cilla responded because she didn't know what else to say. Maybe bringing Georgina home for the weekend was the worst idea ever.

Georgina laughed. "*I'm* fine." The scenery raced by as Georgina pushed the gas pedal to the floor. Then, "How's your *friend*?"

Cilla knew exactly who she meant by the inflection at the end of the question. "Which friend?"

"Your dinner pal from Christopher Street."

"I'm sure she's well."

Georgina didn't take her eyes from the road, but her brows reached for her hairline. "You know, there's no point holding on to all that land. It's just sitting there growing wild."

"Isn't that how forested areas should be?" Cilla knew she shouldn't take the bait, but she couldn't help herself.

"If it's a forest, maybe. Anyway, she'll come around when she sees what they will offer her. How do you know her?"

Cilla pressed her finger into the sipping hole in her coffee cup, feeling the outline sharp against her finger. She didn't want to discuss Lucky with rational Georgina. Georgina was waiting for a response, so Cilla just said, "Through the dogs. They like to play together."

"That's cute," Georgina said. "Plenty of room in that yard." She checked her side mirror. "Why people want to get on a freeway and drive like they're on their way to their own funeral,

I don't know." She accelerated and overtook the car in front, sending Benson clattering to the side in the back. "Maybe we could all take the dogs out for a walk soon."

Cilla studied the oval imprint on her fingertip. When she looked up, she caught sight of herself in the mirror. She looked grim, her mouth a thin line. She took a breath. "We could go for a walk tonight. Every time I go home, it feels like the neighborhood has changed again."

"It's funny that you still call it 'home.' Why don't we go for a run? I'll go mad if I don't exercise."

"That's where I grew up and that's where my family is. It feels like an anchor point in my life. You know that feeling when you walk in the door and you feel relaxed and comfortable?"

Georgina laughed. "Yeah, I do. At my own home. I don't want to be tied down to one thing, just go where opportunity is. I don't have that sense of home like you do. My mother wasn't much of a homemaker, bless her. She'd prefer to be waited on at the Ritz than make toast or do laundry."

"The Ritz does have its appeal, especially in this weather when nothing dries outside."

"Absolutely. Give me a spa treatment, room service, a nice bar, and a fully equipped gym. Let the concierge carry my bags. Remember when we stayed at the Waldorf in Vegas? I'd go back there in a heartbeat. That was a great trip."

Cilla could remember it. It had been a great trip, Georgina like a pampered racehorse at its peak. They'd had so much fun, gorging themselves on fine dining and good wine, swimming in the pool, shopping, touring the Grand Canyon...having mind-blowing sex. Cilla hadn't thought about that trip in a long time. It had been an absolute indulgence, but it had been early on when she was high on love and deep in the Georgina experience. "It was a lot of fun," she said. "Feels like a lifetime ago, now."

Georgina's lips were flattened by a small smile at some memory that Cilla didn't want to explore. "Life is for living, right, Cill?" Georgina glanced over at her.

"It is," Cilla agreed even though she didn't know anymore what that meant.

CHAPTER TWENTY-NINE

The house Cilla grew up in was just like every other house in the street: unassuming, neatly tended, older cars parked in the driveway, the odd windchime on the porch or flag by the front steps. The lawns were wide and shorn to a green carpet, the trees established and shady over the slightly cracked pavement. It reminded Cilla of riding her bike as a child or playing in the street with her friends, many of whom had settled in the area. There was a time when she had longed to show Georgina off to them, but she had let that go. It was ironic that she was returning with Georgina as her friend—if that's what she was.

"I'm looking forward to seeing your family, it's been ages," Georgina said as though it was something she had been meaning to do recently. She parked the car out front of Cilla's parents' place and turned to squeeze Cilla's knee, smiling like she was showing off a recent filling, then she turned and flipped the visor down and checked her face, smoothing the skin under her eyes.

Cilla could see Deb's car parked behind her parents' old station wagon in the driveway. She felt a responsibility for whatever situation she was about to unleash, but to her surprise, they were greeted warmly at the door by her mother and Deb. Georgina kissed them on both cheeks and seemed genuinely happy to see them. Deb's children came bounding out to briefly acknowledge them before lunging at Benson, who stood tolerantly, his tail waving as he was hugged and rubbed. Deb looked similar to Cilla, except Deb was shorter and fairer with paler eyes and ashy blond hair like their father had had before he lost most of it. Her children had ended up skinny and freckly with bright blond hair like their father, but their little faces looked like Deb's at that age.

"Come in," Patty said. "Don's in the den. I don't think he heard the doorbell."

No sooner had Patty spoken than Cilla's father appeared in the corridor. "I heard it, Patty." He walked more slowly and hunched than Cilla remembered, making her heart lurch. "She thinks I'm deaf," he said as he came to clutch Cilla's arms and slowly kiss her cheek. "Hello, Georgina," he said, leaning in to give her the same treatment.

"Hello, Don. Happy Thanksgiving." Georgina thrust a bottle of red wine at him.

"Thank you, very thoughtful." Don held the wine at arm's distance, trying to read the label. After a moment he handed it to Patty, who read aloud, "Chat-ewe Rauzan Segla. Oh, I can't read French. I'm sure it's a lovely wine, thank you, Georgina."

Deb started to laugh. "Whatever that was, it wasn't French, Mom."

Patty swiped her away. "I said I don't know how to say it."

"No one does except for the French," Georgina said.

Deb looked at her sideways as though she had ruined the joke.

"Come in, we don't have to stand here like we are reenacting the Nativity," Don said.

Deb's youngest, Jacob, who was four, popped up beside Don and looked at Cilla. "If we're acting the Nativity, can Benson be Baby Jesus?"

They all laughed, and Cilla said, "Sure, if you can get him to sit in a crib long enough. He might be better off as a camel."

Jacob looked up at Georgina. "You can be Mary because you're pretty and you have a cool belt."

Georgina tried not to look too smug and Deb tried not to roll her eyes. Cilla could almost see her thinking, *But you're no virgin.*

"Patty's made up your room," Don said to Cilla.

"There are fresh towels in the bathroom, and I cleared some space in the closet for you," Patty said to Georgina.

Cilla blushed, thinking of her childhood clothes being pressed up against Georgina's attire. "Mom, we're only here for two nights. I'm happy to take the sofa so Georgina can have more room."

"The kids are on the foldout. There's a double in your room now, it's the guest room."

Patty looked concerned, so Cilla thanked her, then she and Georgina made their way to her old bedroom. It felt smaller with the large bed in there. Patty had removed the posters of Cilla's youth from the walls and put her trophies and certificates and toys into storage, but the window she used to look out from onto the backyard still had almost the same view, and the carpet and wallpaper brought back memories.

"What, no Farrah Fawcett?" Georgina asked, a crooked smile lifting one side of her mouth.

"Shut up," Cilla said. "This is painful enough." She surveyed the bed with its pink floral bedspread. "There's probably still an air mattress in the crawl space."

Georgina placed her suitcase on a chair by the window and unzipped it, shaking out a shirt. "It'll be fine. You take one side and I take the other. It'll be good for us to just hang out. I've been caught up in work, and it's been years since we took a vacation."

Cilla eased open the closet and peered inside to see if there was anything embarrassing in there. It had been cleared out apart from some winter coats and matching dresses that her mother had made her and Deb for church when they were little. She opened the closet wider and handed Georgina a hanger. "Things can just be natural between us. Don't force them one way or the other. I don't need you to start spending time with me, and I don't think sharing a bed is what we need." She wanted to say that they shouldn't kiss but Georgina was looking at her with a hardness in her eyes. "Sorry, I just want us both to be who we are, and if those two people want to hang out, then great. But if you're drawn to other things and I am too, then that's the natural course of things."

"I came because I want to be here with you, but trust me, I'm not going to lose control in the night. I'm not an animal. But if you don't want me here, I can leave." Georgina had placed the shirt over the hanger but now she held it to her chest as though reconsidering whether to hang it in the closet. Her face looked stricken, and Cilla felt a little stab in the heart. There were moments when the abandoned child in Georgina would flick to the surface or Cilla felt the closeness of accumulated years of shared experiences, and she wanted to hug Georgina to her.

"Don't be silly, I do want you here. All I'm saying is, let's just relax and take the experience as it comes."

Georgina continued to clutch the hanger and stare at Cilla, then after a moment she softened and said, "I did hope the experience would involve Charlie's Angels."

There was a knock at the door, and Deb's voice said, "Lunch is ready. Mom wants to know if you want coffee or lemonade."

Cilla jumped as though they were doing something private, and Georgina looked at Cilla and mouthed, "Lemonade?" and raised her brows. Cilla bit back a smile and shook her head at Georgina and went to open the door. "Sure, we're coming out now."

Deb glanced past Cilla to where Georgina was still holding the shirt. "Sure."

Deb left them and Cilla felt like a teenager who brought a date home. It wasn't such a bad feeling, really. As a teenager she would have drooled at the thought of having Georgina in her room. "Do you want something to drink?"

Georgina finally released the shirt from its duty as armor and hung it in the closet. "No, thank you. I have my alkaline water. I brought extra if you want one, because last time the tap water was sketchy."

Cilla's mouth opened to defend the tap water, but she thought better of it. "Let's go out anyway and be social. You know how Mom is with the constant food."

"I will, as soon as I've finished hanging my clothes up. It's you they want to see anyway."

As Cilla walked along the passageway to the kitchen, she thought of a few nicer ways to phrase that such as, "Why don't you spend a few minutes catching up and I'll be out shortly?" but Georgina was Georgina. Smooth as the custom paint on her Mercedes if there was a deal involved. She could hear her mother and Deb talking in hushed tones, probably about her and Georgina. Cilla paused to finally check the message on her phone that she had received in the car. It was from Lucky, saying, *At this exact moment, someone is trimming a hedge into a swan*, which made Cilla smile and take a moment to ponder if that could be true. Were there really that many swan-shaped bushes on the planet that someone would be shaping one at the exact moment Lucky had sent the text? Cilla quickly typed back, *At this exact moment, someone is wearing a sweater their grandmother knitted with a kitten on it.* She couldn't wait to ask Lucky about the driveway thing. It seemed like something she would have thought about too. Cilla put her phone into the back pocket of her jeans and purposely made some noise entering the kitchen so whatever secret conversation was going on could be halted. The table was laid with homemade bread, various condiments, cold meats, cheeses, and salad ingredients.

"This looks incredible, Mom. What can I do to help?"

"Nothing, it's all done. Is Georgina joining us?" Patty asked, taking a seat at the same round table that Cilla had grown up eating at every day of her young life. Only the cushions on the wooden chairs had been upgraded, and over time new appliances and new cupboard doors had been added to the kitchen, but everything was more or less the same. Now Jacob and Winnie's drawings and school photos were pinned to the fridge where hers and Deb's had been.

"She's just putting her clothes away. Where's Benson at?" Cilla felt herself immediately falling into a lazier way of speech with her family.

"In the den with the kids watching cartoons."

Cilla laughed. "Benson heaven."

"Lemonade?" Patty asked, reaching across the faded polkadot tablecloth for the perspiring jug of lemonade.

"Sit, Mom," Deb and Cilla commanded in unison, and Patty sat back and flung her hands up, then placed them in her lap.

Georgina appeared and exclaimed over the food and was told to sit beside Cilla.

"I'll get Dad," Cilla said, casting a look at Georgina to make sure she would be okay without her, but Georgina was looking around the room as though appraising it for sale. She could almost hear Georgina thinking, *Established neighborhood, proximity to schools and public transportation…renovators' delight!* Georgina caught her looking at her and smiled. There was a moment of connection that felt like old times, and Cilla stood up and placed a hand on Georgina's shoulder as she squeezed by her.

Don was in the den with the kids, idly stroking Benson's head as he stared at the colorful images on the television screen. Benson looked up at her, grinning, and Don noticed her enter. He'd always protested that dogs should be kept outside only, but he had been a fool for puppy-Benson right from the start.

Winnie scrunched herself into a ball and rocked onto her back and rolled around for a second, then said, "Auntie Cilla, I do gymnastics now."

"And I do too," Jacob said.

"Do not," Winnie said, sitting up indignantly. "He doesn't," she assured Cilla.

"Well, I go there," Jacob said.

Winnie gave Cilla a look of forbearance that said she put up with that kind of nonsense every day. Benson left his massage station to hover over Winnie and make sure she wasn't having some type of fit, and Winnie pushed him aside so she had Cilla in her line of vision again. Benson happily tolerated it as another form of massage.

"It's lunchtime. Dad, come have something to eat."

"Oh, right." Don placed his hands on the couch beside him and tried to leverage himself up. Cilla sprang to assist him. "I can do it," Don said in a tone that reminded her of Jacob.

"I want to watch the end of this," Jacob said.

"How long has it got?" Cilla asked. "I think your mom wants you to come out."

Winnie stood up. "Mom said we can eat in the den because there's not enough room at the table because of you and Georgina staying."

"Winnie, we have the big table in the dining room," Don said.

"Let's just go ask Mom, okay?" Cilla said, pulling Benson out of the way so he wouldn't get under Don's feet and trip him.

Winnie took Cilla's hand. "Do you believe in witches?"

Cilla blinked. "Why did you ask that?"

"Because the witch on the show we're watching lost her powers because she was sad because the kids at school bullied her. Hey, look." Winnie stopped and turned to Cilla and stuck her tongue through a gap where her front tooth had been. "I got two dollars from the tooth fairy."

Don was walking slowly ahead of them, and he chuckled.

* * *

There was so much food and the conversation was flowing as people reached again and again for the homemade bread. As usual, Don peppered Georgina with questions about the property market and was tickled pink when Georgina said their house would be worth a lot of money now. Then he engaged Georgina in his political rants, and Deb's husband, Bryce, turned up from repairing the garage door for the elderly couple across the road, and they all scooted aside and squeezed him in at the table. Cilla felt a sweet sadness because this was the life she had wanted, one big happy family. Looking at her father, who was chuckling with apple cheeks at Georgina's political assassinations, she wondered how it had passed her by when it was right there in front of her.

After lunch, Bryce announced that he needed to go to Home Depot and get some trellis for Mr. and Mrs. Kransz because he noticed theirs had rotted by the front door and the roses were coming loose over the path.

"Take the kids," Deb said.

"I love home improvement stores," Georgina said.

"You're welcome to come along," Bryce said good-naturedly. Cilla had been wondering how to entertain Georgina after lunch, so she was relieved when Georgina said she'd love to. Cilla stood and began to clear the table, which prompted Georgina to begin taking plates to the sink.

"I'll go round up the kids," Bryce said.

"Let's go in my car," Georgina whispered to Cilla as they put condiments back in the fridge where the turkey for tomorrow sat like a giant among Lilliputians.

Cilla knocked over a bottle of ketchup and righted it. "Oh…I thought I might hang back."

"Come with me, Cill. It'll be fun. You love Home Depot."

"I do," Cilla admitted. She felt torn. She wanted to spend time with her parents and Deb, but she did like the idea of driving through her hometown and browsing the homewares with Georgina.

"Yay." Georgina turned to survey the kitchen. "We'll be back. Does anyone need anything while we're out?"

* * *

Cilla had almost forgotten what shopping with Georgina was like. Unconscious of the stares she drew from men and woman alike, Georgina became totally absorbed in the detail of each product she viewed, visualizing it in her home, searching a price and quality comparison then discarding it as she had extracted the enjoyment she wanted merely by considering it. "Cill, look at this brass door knocker. This would look great on your front door."

"It's cute," Cilla said without enthusiasm. She didn't want to make any purchases. The roof repair had cost enough—especially without the "cute" discount—and Christmas was looming, which meant buying presents for the family. She had also been giving a vacation serious thought. She needed to change something in her life, and temporarily relocating to see new sights and think new thoughts, far from everything she knew, seemed somewhat appealing.

Georgina marched them to another aisle to look at planters for indoor plants. Cilla caught sight of Bryce looking at trellis while Jacob, who had a plastic bucket on his head, was purposely crashing into Winnie, who was kicking at him.

"I love this." Georgina lifted up a white planter with a scalloped pattern for Cilla to see.

"I can picture that at your place."

Georgina turned it over to look at the price underneath. "Bargain. Vince and I are starting up an interior design business. We're going to stage houses for sale. I'm going to get this pot. We can use it in the business but I can keep it at home."

Cilla was slightly taken aback that Georgina had made a significant life decision without telling her what she was planning, but she fought to recover before Georgina could notice. After all, they weren't together and Georgina didn't owe her anything. Plus, she should be used to it; Georgina had always used knowledge sharing as a power play. Cilla's voice came out a little too cheery and she was annoyed at herself. "That's a wonderful idea. You already have the knowledge and connections."

"Exactly. I don't know why we didn't do it earlier." Georgina dusted off the base of the pot then hugged it to her and turned to look at hanging baskets. "I'm buying a block of land and building. It's a great time to get into the area because it's going to boom. If you're interested in doing something similar, I can show you where the best parcels are." She tapped a display basket so it swung back and forth. "I'm on a powerful upsurge at the moment. You should jump on my coattails."

Cilla didn't need to be told about Georgina's momentum, she could see it. A man had stopped midsentence to gaze at her. Georgina strode on, oblivious of the effect she was having. Georgina paused to watch Jacob headbutting a sack of potting mix with his bucket. "Is that child all right?"

"You go ahead to the register. I'll see if Bryce needs a hand."

"I'm not done yet."

Cilla walked off, happy to deal with a small bucket head rather than witness any more of Georgina's power surges.

Bryce was grateful for some assistance as he carried trellis to the counter while placating a crying Winnie, who had gotten in trouble for kicking Jacob. Cilla loved her niece and nephew, but it was times like these that she was content to be a single person. She snapped a photo of Jacob as a bucket head before removing the bucket and placing it on a tall shelf. She found a piece of gum in her bag to distract him and sent the picture through to Lucky saying, *Right this moment someone has been freed from a life inside a bucket.*

Sometimes truth was stranger than fiction.

On the way home, Cilla nursed Georgina's planter on her lap so it wouldn't roll around in the trunk. Between her feet was a peace lily in a pink planter that Georgina had bought for Patty. Cilla had peeled the orange discount sticker from the bottom of the planter and was now rolling the sticky label around her thumb, up into the skin under her nail. She had put her phone on silent but she had checked it several times, and Lucky hadn't responded to her bucket-head photo.

As they drove through the familiar streets of Cilla's childhood, Georgina commented on various houses and returned to the subject of the value of Cilla's parents' house. "I could do a search of comps in the area and give them an idea."

"If you want to, but they don't plan to sell," Cilla said.

Georgina checked her reflection in the rearview mirror at a red light. "It's funny how many people's plans change when they see a large number with a dollar sign in front. They're getting old, Cill, it'll happen eventually. I'm just trying to support where I can."

Cilla puzzled over that as they turned onto her parents' street and pulled up to the house in question, which looked an unlikely prospect for any windfalls with its seventies frontage and cracking driveway. It still gave Cilla a warm feeling of happy memories.

Patty was pleased with the plant, her face turning a similar shade of pink to the planter in the same way Cilla's did when she was embarrassed. She placed it reverently on the counter by the fruit bowl while Cilla flicked the label she'd rolled into a ball into the trash. Patty went all pleased and quiet, which showed Cilla how much they still took her mom for granted. She hadn't expected Georgina to show her that. Benson swam around them, happy to be reunited.

"Mom, why don't you find something to do, and Deb and I will cook dinner tonight?"

Patty was already putting the kettle on and fussing around. "Your father and I thought we could just have something light because we need to finish preparing for tomorrow. I thought I might make a chicken salad, and there's some garlic bread in the freezer that the kids like."

Georgina went to the fridge, opened it up, and peered inside. "Let us do that, Patty." She opened the vegetable crisper on the bottom and looked at the salad ingredients. "We can go to the store and get some extra things."

Patty's blush bloomed again. "Oh, you don't have to do that, you're our guest."

Georgina closed the fridge door. "It's our pleasure. You've been so kind to have me come and stay. Cill, should we go get some stuff to make a Caesar? I have a super healthy version that I can whip up."

Cilla gave Benson's head a rub. She supposed she would get a chance to hang out with the family soon. "Let's go."

"Wait, let me give you some money and I'm sure I have a coupon." Patty said. "Don! Don!"

"Mom," Cilla said, trying to quiet her.

"Don't be silly, Patty, it's my treat. We'll be back."

* * *

"Isn't this the best?" Georgina asked as they drove to Walmart. "This trip is a great reminder of what it's like to slow down and enjoy the simple things in life. I love being here with you." She smiled at Cilla. "We've had a lot of adventures over the years, but sometimes it's the simple moments, not doing much at all, that seem the most significant."

Cilla felt that way and had thought Georgina was all about the extravagant times, but she had always held dearest those intimate moments of not doing much, just the two of them together. She had kept it to herself because it seemed silly to covet those tiny glimpses of a mundane life together, but it felt like Georgina's heart had jumped an octave to connect with hers again. She didn't want that painful sweetness, so she said, "Even a trip to the supermarket is an adventure. Let's see if Mom can stay out of the kitchen long enough for us to get a meal on the table."

In her hand, her phone lit up with a message. *He's wonderful. Those stores make me want to put a bucket over my head too! Looking forward to hearing some stories when you're back.*

CHAPTER THIRTY

Dinner was a success, even the children ate most of Georgina's salad, and Deb appeared to have warmed to Georgina. After dinner, Cilla and Georgina took the kids for a walk with Benson while Deb and Bryce cleaned up under Patty's supervision. When they returned, Deb herded the children off for bath time, Don brought out the wine that Georgina had given them, they set up the poker table and played a few rounds while they waited for Deb to report that the kids were in bed. Unsurprisingly, Georgina's poker face and love of winning made her a card shark, which delighted Don no end. Despite Lucky's recent tutelage, Cilla wasn't great at cards. Her facial expressions were too open and she felt bad when she took everyone's chips. She was having a great time, though. Even her mother was laughing and silly with wine. Georgina was on form, telling horrendous stories about homes she'd seen and the people she'd dealt with, making Deb cry with laughter the way she used to with Cilla as a teenager. Bryce was amused by the situation, and Cilla sat basking in it all, feeling love for everyone at the table: her aging parents; her only sister and her kind husband; and Georgina, her energy and warmth lighting up the table. At one point, Georgina's hand reached for Cilla's under the table and Cilla clutched it on her knee, feeling Georgina close, back on her team.

After they called it quits for the night and crept past the living room where the kids were sleeping on the foldout, the prospect of sharing a bed with Georgina seemed both comfortable and daunting. While Georgina was in the shower, Cilla gave herself a pep talk, Emma-style. The wine had softened the edges of her thoughts, and she was finding it increasingly hard to remember what was so bad about Georgina. When Georgina emerged from the bathroom in nothing but a towel tucked around her breasts, her face as naked as her legs, Cilla covered her eyes and said, "George! Put some clothes on."

"I'm not ashamed of my body. It's nothing you haven't seen before."

Cilla grabbed her toiletries and pajamas and fled to the bathroom, thinking that it was something she didn't need to see again. In fact, she was trying not to even remember it.

Cilla was much more reserved and arrived back in the bedroom fully clothed. Georgina was already in bed, lying on her back, which was how she slept so she wouldn't get wrinkles. Cilla was relieved to see the blue collar of her T-shirt peeking over the top of the bedspread, indicating that she was at least half-clothed. Georgina snapped the lamp on and Cilla turned the overhead light off. She felt very strange and took her time putting her things away in her bag, hoping Georgina would fall instantly asleep. Of course Georgina, who was fully wired all day every day, power surge or not, was not asleep.

"I'll just stay on this side," Cilla said unnecessarily as she climbed into bed. Georgina turned to her, impossibly pretty and mellow in the lamplight. Cilla felt like fifteen-year-old her was having some type of surreal dream with her eyes open and the alarm clock was going to ring and wake her for school. Cilla had always melted when faced with bare-faced, gentle Georgina, quieted by the silence of impending slumber. Georgina smiled at her, and Cilla felt her own face, like a Kewpie doll with large swiveling eyes, not knowing where to look. Not at Georgina's pale lips or shining eyes. She cleared her throat and pushed the covers down between them like spongey divider.

Georgina's smile gathered amusement. "What are you doing?"

"Keeping out the cold air." Cilla's voice came out all gruff.

"Right, right." Georgina drew her features down and nodded sarcastically, then reached a cold toe to land on Cilla's shin.

Cilla yelped. "George, don't. We should get some sleep. I want to get up early and help out with some things."

"Sure, I'll get up with you. I might go for a run."

Georgina's cool fingers found Cilla's waist under the covers and she wriggled closer. Cilla could smell Georgina's minty breath and see the lamp lighting up her flaxen hair in a halo. Beyond that was her own childhood walls and the window frame still painted green, where she used to sit her figurines and collectibles from cereal boxes.

"Cilla," Georgina breathed, one leg pushing between Cilla's.

Cilla's heart was thumping, and she started to ache and tingle. Georgina's hand traveled up Cilla's rib cage and her mouth found Cilla's lips. For a delicious second Cilla let herself be kissed in a way that was familiar and sent her body into well-worn responses, but she didn't feel right. She gently took Georgina's hand from her waist and pulled back.

"George, I can't."

A cool burst of air hit Cilla's chest as Georgina raised her hand to touch Cilla's bottom lip. "You want to."

Cilla took Georgina's wrist, kissed the pad of her thumb, and held her hand. "I do want to, but I also don't want to." Georgina's eyes were like a vacant blue sky. There was sadness there, but Cilla couldn't let Georgina's drop of sadness be the reason she would swim in her own ocean of sadness. She kissed her hand once more, then drew it back beneath the covers and placed it against Georgina's chest. "Good night."

Georgina was very still, then she said, "Good night," rolled over, and turned the light off.

Cilla blinked into the darkness until she could make out the curve of Georgina's shoulder and the wisps of her hair against the faint glow from the street. Then she rolled over too, feeling a warmth in her chest, knowing that she had done the right thing even though part of her still wanted to do the wrong thing. She thought, *Right now, at this very moment, I am saving my kisses for the person who deserves them.* Then she remembered that Georgina was now the last woman she had kissed, and she couldn't wait to see Lucky to set it all straight.

* * *

In the morning, Cilla woke disoriented from a dream where she was at work and she realized she was wearing Georgina's shirt but it had no buttons and her breasts were hanging out. She opened her eyes, not knowing where she was. Slowly, the room arranged itself from abstract forms into familiar shapes, and Cilla turned to find Georgina's pillow bare and a warm furry body curled up down near her feet. The door was partway open, and Cilla guessed that Georgina had gone out for a run and left the door unlatched. Benson's eyes rolled to meet Cilla's, and she sat up to give him a rub on the head before casting him off. Patty didn't believe in dogs on beds.

Cilla checked the time on her phone. It was just after seven, and she got up and quietly picked her way through the house to let Benson out into the backyard. She could hear voices coming from Deb's room and the vague sound of the television in the den. She changed the filter in the coffee machine and filled it before going to the back door to watch Benson sniff around the lawn, ascertaining who or what had been there overnight. Outside, the sun was finding its way through the wispy clouds, beckoning Cilla out into the day. She inwardly sighed, not wanting to follow Georgina's lead, but a short run would do her good because thoughts about Georgina last night and how she would react were cycling through her mind.

By the time Cilla returned from her run, Georgina's car was gone and there was a text saying she had gone to get a "real coffee." The run had prevented Cilla from dwelling on half-naked Georgina in bed kissing her, and released some welcome endorphins. In Georgina's absence, Cilla was happy to have some time at breakfast with the family, eating cereal out of the same comforting bowls that she had eaten from as a child at the same scarred table. When Georgina returned she was behaving normally, but when Cilla caught her eye, she returned her gaze evenly and unreadably. After breakfast, they all crowded in the kitchen to get the food prepared, the kids peeling potatoes and carrots at the kitchen table while the adults chopped and basted and arranged. The turkey barely fit in the oven, but after it was in they cleared a space for the kids to bake cookies with Patty, and Cilla got a chance to be alone with Georgina in the den as they turned on a movie. Benson lay on the floor at Cilla's feet, dozing and twitching.

Cilla wanted to get things out in the open. "Is everything okay?"

Across the other side of the sofa, Georgina kept her expression blank. "I'm okay."

"After last night," Cilla added even though she knew perfectly well that Georgina was aware what she was referring to.

"Why wouldn't it be?"

"Because…" Cilla began, then thought better of it, then decided they should air it out. "I don't think you really want to be with me, do you?"

Georgina shrugged peevishly, signaling to Cilla that she would get nothing from her. "I didn't say anything about it either way. You seem to keep changing your mind."

"I haven't changed my mind about anything, but relationships are complex and I'm trying to retain the parts we can. Sex would only confuse that."

Georgina had been staring at the television but she turned to Cilla, her diamond earring catching the light. "What's complex about it?"

Cilla tried not to show her frustration. "Trying to be friends and not hurt each other and do the right thing by each other."

"I don't find that complex."

There was the sound of footsteps, and they were saved by Bryce and Don coming to join them. Part of Cilla felt relief that Georgina and her patterns of behavior were no longer her concern, and part of her wanted to smooth things over. There was no point persisting, though. Georgina would keep twisting things around like a constrictor with an antelope, trying to invalidate Cilla's feelings in the hope of making her drop it. Deep down, Cilla had a feeling that Georgina was manipulating, probably playing hot and cold to keep Cilla invested. If Cilla gave in to the romantic notion of a fresh start, Georgina would collapse back into her old ways, leaving Cilla farther from where she was currently standing. Even though she generally had fun with Georgina, changing moods aside, she missed Lucky and thought how different the trip would be if she was there instead.

"I guess you girls want to watch one of those romances with that blond lady in them that your mother likes," Don said.

"You secretly love them, Dad," Cilla said.

"I watch them to keep the peace."

Georgina passed Don the remote. "I can't sit still for a whole movie anyway."

They settled on a nature documentary that was equally semientertaining but mostly boring to all. Don fell asleep in his chair and Georgina started scrolling on her phone. Bryce excused himself and went to check on the kids.

"I might go see if it's time to put the vegetables in," Cilla said. "Do you want to come?"

Benson led the way to the kitchen where Deb was wiping flour off the counter. Through the window, Cilla could see Bryce outside throwing a football with the kids. Cilla went to fill the sink with sudsy water to wash the mixing bowl and spoons. Georgina stood by the back door with her arms folded, watching the ball fly back and forth while the muffled shrieks of play came through the glass. Benson went to stand beside her, wet nose on the glass, his tail slowly waving.

"Why don't you take him out, George? You can show the kids your ball skills."

Georgina kept staring outside for another minute until Cilla was preoccupied with the dishes, then let herself outside. Cilla watched as Georgina joined the game, turning the scene into a happy nuclear family, with Benson casing the perimeter of the yard.

Deb picked up a tea towel and began to dry beside Cilla. "She's all right with that football."

"She's good at everything."

Deb didn't look at Cilla but seemed to be taking an extra-long time drying the wooden spoon. "Are you back together?"

"No."

They watched Georgina running backward to catch a wide shot from Winnie while Benson cavorted along beside her.

"Well," Deb said. "She seems like she's trying. Does she want to get back together?"

Cilla picked up a juice glass from the counter, dripping soapy water, and dunked it into the suds. "I don't know."

"Do you want to?"

Cilla rinsed the glass and set it on the rack for the water to run off so Deb could dry it. "I don't think it's a good idea."

Deb took the glass and started to dry it. "I used to worry about you with her."

"I know. You didn't hide it."

Deb bumped her hip against Cilla's affectionately. "Looking out for my sis. Seriously, though, I know I gave you a hard time about her but I just want you to know that we like Georgina and I'm sorry if we had any influence on your decision to break up."

Cilla pulled the plug and listened to the water gurgling down the hole in a bubbling shriek. She rinsed out the sponge and began wiping around the sink. "Georgina and I aren't good for each other. There may always be some spark between us, but I'm too deep and homey for her, and she's too surface level and works against me instead of working as a team." She squeezed the sponge out and put it on the rack.

Outside, Bryce had abandoned football in favor of showing Winnie how to rake the lawn. Jacob was running back and forth holding a leaf in the air. Georgina was standing back, looking at the house, probably assessing what work would need to be done prior to sale.

"Yes," Deb said, watching Bryce coach Winnie through her raking style. "You need someone who's on your team."

Cilla's thoughts went to Lucky. She hoped she wasn't lonely over Thanksgiving, but she had to remember that Lucky had been taking care of herself for a long time before Cilla came along.

"Yeah, I do. I forgot what that's like. Even being here with you and Mom and Dad and Bryce and the kids, that feeling of belonging, being okay with who I am."

Deb considered Georgina through the glass again. "It must be hard to keep up with that, and I'm not talking about what's on the outside, I mean the inside too. Like I said, though, if you choose Georgina then we will welcome her to our team. She has been a welcome addition this trip."

Cilla smiled and said, "Thank you. I wasn't sure how it would all come together but it's been fun so far." Outside, Georgina was peering over the side fence, probably appraising the neighbor's yard. "Deb, do you remember when we did that séance in the den and something knocked on the wall and we ran upstairs screaming?"

Deb laughed. "How could I forget? We didn't go into the den for about a year after that. The den still gives me the heebie-jeebies when I'm alone." She moved to the oven and cracked the door open to check how the turkey was doing. The small of roasting meat wafted into the room, and Deb shut the oven door again.

"Do you believe in all that stuff now?"

Deb straightened the tea towel hanging over the oven handle and said, "Yes and no. I mean, I still get freaked out going into the den alone and I do believe in intuition or a sixth sense. Why do you ask?"

Cilla shrugged and pushed away from the counter she had been leaning against. "I guess I've been thinking about it, like, things that are invisible to our senses but there still there, you know?"

"Like what?"

Cilla saw that the group outside were making their way toward the back door, led by Benson. "How you can only hear a radio station when you tune in but the music is there in the air the whole time, or like, I dunno..." She looked around the kitchen and saw the crystals hanging by the window, casting their rainbow refraction onto the counter. "A rainbow."

"All explained by science," Deb said as the back door opened to a tumble of children and dog.

"Isn't everything, eventually?"

"I guess," Deb said, but she was already making sure muddy jeans were going in the wash and hands were going to the sink.

Georgina had Benson by the collar. "He's all dirty."

Cilla sighed. She loved Benson's coat but sometimes it worked like a dirt catcher. She picked him up like a big heavy baby and carried him into the laundry to wash his paws and belly.

* * *

As always, Thanksgiving seemed to be lighter on the thanks and the giving and heavier on the eating. Everyone proclaimed themselves full, but within a matter of hours leftovers were being heated and the feast continued in the den. Belts were loosened, naps were taken, and then by the evening Georgina was getting itchy feet and suggested they take Benson for a walk. Cilla would have been happy to become one with the couch, but a digestive walk would probably do her good. Don and Patty stayed behind but the rest of them pulled on jackets and gloves and braved the crisp evening air. Georgina strode on ahead while Deb wrapped her arm through Cilla's and they walked slowly, catching up on hometown gossip. Deb always knew what was going on, largely because between the preschool set, the school set, and work at the hospital, she had most bases covered. Cilla learned who was pregnant, who was divorcing, who said what to whom. It meant little to her, but it was fun to gossip all the same. Watching the white pom-pom on Georgina's beanie bobbing under the streetlights, Cilla took the opportunity to tell Deb a little about Lucky. Not much, but just enough to let her know that she had a friend she cared about a lot, letting Deb read between the lines. The kids ran shrieking into the park, and Cilla kept an eye on Benson while she spoke to Deb and Bryce pushed the kids on the swings. Georgina, hands shoved in her pockets, came back along the path toward them, and Cilla let the conversation drop. Together, the three of them walked a lap of the park while Benson snuffled around, the calls of the kids to go higher and the creaks of the swing growing fainter and then louder again. The cold was biting, and everyone was happy to return to indulge in more dessert, watch a movie, and go to bed.

This time in bed, Georgina didn't kiss Cilla. They lay on their sides, looking at each other, and Cilla said, "What do you want out of life?"

Georgina didn't act surprised and answered as naturally as if she had been waiting for the question. "To be happy. Isn't that what everyone wants?"

Cilla's hands were pressed into prayer beneath her cheek. It felt oddly okay to be here with Georgina in an intimacy that was only warm to the touch. Cilla could let it go, the idea of Georgina being hers. "Maybe. What does happiness look like for you?" She was asking now because maybe she had never asked before. Maybe she had been too scared to ask because she wasn't sure if she would like the answer.

"I like to have a goal to work toward, money in the bank, and a beautiful woman in my bed." Georgina smiled at Cilla.

"Well, two out of three ain't bad."

"I'm doing all right tonight, aren't I, Cill?"

Cilla huffed in amusement. "We've had our moments."

Georgina studied Cilla's face. "Yes, we have."

"Will you sell your townhouse if you build?"

Georgina scrunched her nose up. "I'm right on Twine River's millionaire row—that's how I picture it in ten years, anyhow. It's right by the stores on the main strip. If anything, I'll rent it out and go traveling once Vince and I get the business established. The block of land is only an investment. I don't actually want to live in plastic-dump-truck-sand-box-suburbia."

Cilla stifled a yawn. She still felt full. "I didn't think it was your scene."

"It's all in the visualization. I can picture how I want the business to be."

Georgina's words were far away and Cilla's senses were growing dull. She murmured good night.

CHAPTER THIRTY-ONE

Cilla felt heartbroken leaving her family. It had been a case of out-of-sight, out-of-mind but after spending a few days with them, she felt the strength of the connection returning. She even felt closer to Georgina for the experience, but in a nice way that made her realize how much anxiety she had held before. They closer they got to home, the more she was thinking of Lucky. She couldn't wait to be in her presence again, see her lit-up face and be swept up in her energetic flow. Georgina dropped Cilla and Benson home, and Cilla spent a few minutes unpacking then asked Benson the question he had also been longing to hear.

As Cilla unlatched Lucky's gate, she could see that the mailbox had some envelopes poking out. She plucked them out and continued up the path to the house. The sun was out, warming her back and bringing out the smell of the winter jasmine crawling up the porch railing. Benson made a beeline straight for the door, already standing with his tail waving in anticipation by the time Cilla made her way up the stairs. As always, Peanut was better than any doorbell, and before Cilla could lift a hand, Lucky was opening the door. Seeing her face was similar to the feeling of sun on Cilla's cheek. They briefly embraced and Lucky stood aside for Cilla to come in.

"Here." Cilla passed Lucky the envelopes and Lucky put them down on the cabinet in the hall while Cilla hung her jacket on the coatrack.

"Thank you. Come through, the kitchen is lovely and warm."

They followed the scent of sugary baking to the kitchen where the light was coming in to land on the table and a cake was cooling on the counter. It was so cozy and inviting by the warmth of the oven.

"How is your family?" Lucky asked as they took a seat at the table.

"They're good. Dad has slowed down a lot and has trouble hearing, though he won't admit it, but otherwise it was so nice to spend time with them. I forgot how much I enjoy it."

Lucky's face grew pained, and Cilla wondered about the aunt who had passed away.

"It is difficult watching loved ones grow old. At least he and your mother have each other."

Cilla nodded. "They argue a lot, but they've always been like that. Deb does an amazing job, which makes me feel guilty. It's a bit of a thing between us now. I do consider moving back there sometimes. If Dad gets worse, I may have to. It's not fair to Deb, and as she's always reminding me, she does have two kids to look after as well."

"It is a concern. I'm sure they loved having you home for Thanksgiving. And, dare I ask, how was Georgina?" She grimaced.

"On her best behavior. We got along the best we have in a long time."

Lucky stood, turning her back to Cilla to put the kettle on the stove. Cilla watched her, fascinated by the thought that Lucky had been raised in a very different world where today's technology probably wasn't even someone's dream yet. Lucky turned back to Cilla and took a deep breath. "Will you get back together?"

Cilla was surprised. Her thoughts had been in a completely different place. "No, of course not. If anything, the closeness I felt to Georgina there showed me how lacking it was before."

Lucky's face relaxed and her shoulders seemed to spring up as though she was stretching invisible wings. "I did wonder, but I wouldn't want to interfere. Tea, coffee?"

"What, no gin?"

Lucky froze, then she realized Cilla was joking and she laughed. "Don't you worry, there's always some on hand."

"I would love a coffee, thank you. Would you like some help?"

"How are your cake-cutting skills?" Lucky opened a drawer and found a knife.

"I wouldn't put my knife skills on a CV, but I've managed to get this far in life."

Cilla cut two slices of cake and put them on plates while Lucky made a pot of coffee and they sat back down. Cilla still felt out in no-man's-land, wanting to sweep Lucky up and consume her like a dessert, so instead she kept her hands and mouth occupied with cake and coffee, silently vowing to go on a cleanse tomorrow. Cilla was conscious of the laundry she had to do at home and Benson's empty kibble bowl, so after they had finished, she made her excuses and stood to leave. Cilla called Benson, and as they walked to the hall, Lucky turned as though she had forgotten something. By the front door, Cilla reached to take her jacket from the coat rack and as she did so looked down at the envelopes Lucky had tossed there. One was from the bank, which didn't pique her interest, but the other was from Two Fountains Publishing. Cilla heard Lucky's footsteps and quickly shrugged into her jacket, zipping it up as Lucky appeared, holding a wedge of cake on a plate. "Please take some, I can't eat it all. I made it for you, really."

Cilla took the cake, their hands brushing. "Thank you. I will definitely eat this, probably all in one sitting, and I will bring your plate back."

Lucky smiled. "I don't have far to go to hunt it down."

Cilla smiled shyly, wanting to kiss Lucky but still not knowing if she should, then she remembered Georgina's kiss like a stamp of ownership and wondered what she was waiting for to kiss Lucky—an invitation? She gently grabbed the back of Lucky's head and planted a firm kiss on her mouth, then pulled back and said, "I have been wanting to do that since I arrived."

Lucky looked slightly stunned, and as Cilla turned to go, she smiled and said, "Wait. Is that it?"

Cilla didn't need to be told twice. She put the plate down on the side table and took Lucky in her arms and kissed her like she would never see her again. When they finally broke apart, Lucky said, "That was worth waiting for."

Cilla didn't feel like leaving at all, but as she drove home, she reasoned that the second-best thing after spending time with Lucky was speaking to Lucky, and the third-best thing after speaking to Lucky was thinking about Lucky, which she could do all day long.

* * *

After a weekend spent with Lucky playing cards, going for walks, cooking, cuddling up on the couch, and feeling absolutely blissful, neither Benson nor Cilla were feeling so cheerful about reality asserting itself on Monday morning.

The library seemed to have more people dropping in than usual, and almost all of them were asking for a Highgate Village mystery. They were Cilla's favorite books so she could understand why people wanted them, but the urgency seemed out of sync with usual borrowing habits. She went into the system to see if any other library branches had any extra copies, but they were out everywhere. Roger was preoccupied showing a plumber the broken hot water system, so she couldn't defer to his superior knowledge of all things.

She wanted to text Lucky, but her phone was in her bag locked in the kitchen. She dashed to retrieve it from the cupboard and brought it back to the counter and quickly typed, *Right now, someone is reading a Highgate Village mystery, I hope it's you.* She had told Lucky all about them and wanted her to get reading so they could discuss the new book when it came out. Thinking about Lucky always gave her the happy tingles.

Roger resurfaced with the plumber in tow, and Cilla hastily shoved her phone into the pocket of her black slacks.

"Well, there goes an unnecessary hunk of the budget," Roger announced as the plumber walked toward the exit.

"Very unnecessary hunk," Cilla said, smiling to herself as she watched the plumber's broad shoulders disappear out of the door.

"We only use the hot water for washing things that don't go in the dishwasher, but apparently for legal reasons we need hot water," Roger vented, coming to stand behind the counter with Cilla.

Cilla moved aside to regain some personal space. "We could use the large pot to boil water for dishes and add some cold."

Roger irritably clacked at the space bar of the keyboard to wake up the computer screen. "Didn't you listen to what I said? There's no choice, we *have* to have a functioning hot water system."

Cilla wondered if Roger's irritability over the expense was partly to do with the fact he had blown a large portion of the budget going to the conference in Tulsa, which she knew he would have to justify for auditing purposes. "Where is the plumber going?"

"He has to order a new system. This one is ruined."

"Ruined?" Cilla said in amusement. "As ruined as a young Victorian woman having a baby out of wedlock?"

"Yes," Roger said firmly. "*That* ruined." He looked down at the unlocked computer screen where Cilla had been looking up the Highgate Village books. "They're all out and have wait lists. We could order more, but that hot water system will blow our budget. Besides, by the time we do, the hype will be done." He scratched at a dry spot on his cheek, sending tiny skin flakes floating down toward the keyboard.

Cilla moved farther away, feeling the oatmeal turn in her stomach. She wanted to check her phone to see if Lucky had responded but it wouldn't be worth the lecture from Roger about using phones during work hours. "What hype?"

"The author of the Highgate Village Mysteries was unveiled, right in our hometown. The bookshop will be raking it in today.

Make a note, Cilla, you should call the publisher and set up an author reading. We have that science fellow coming next week but we could easily bump him. Science isn't going anywhere."

Cilla felt like her blood cells were throwing a parade in her veins. "What do you mean, 'in our hometown'?"

"The author is right here, probably lives around the corner. Where have you been all morning? The local paper ran a story and it's gaining momentum on social media."

Cilla felt like the blood cells had moved their party up into her face. She could scarcely believe that her favorite author was here. "Who is it?"

"The pigeon lady. I always said she wasn't crazy. What I keep wondering is if it was her at Helen's reading. You know that Helen broke the story? We really are ahead of our times at this library and we don't get the credit we deserve. The director should visit more often and see that for a small facility we are under-resourced and over-extended. At the conference—"

Cilla cut him off. "There's a lot to unpack in what you just said. Do you mean the woman with the long hair who lives nearby?"

"Yes, that one. As I was saying, think of what we could do if we actually had the resources…"

Cilla didn't stay to think about what they could do with extra resources. She fled to the bathroom and stood at the sink, staring at her pink-faced reflection, even more colorful against the bland white walls. She took her phone out and immediately remembered her last text to Lucky, to which there was no response, then thought back to the conversations she had had with Lucky to encourage her to read the books. She cringed at the memory. She opened her browser, and as she did the phone began to silently flash with Emma's name. Cilla rejected the call. She wasn't ready for that. Instead, she typed "Highgate Village author" into the browser and right away breaking news stories popped up. She clicked the first one: "Highgate Village Series: Author Helen Bowers Rips The Cover Off Local Author's Secret." Cilla's oatmeal continued to churn as she began to read. A text came through from Emma, but she swiped it away for later.

The article had a posed author photo of Helen looking about ten years younger with glossy hair and a calm, knowledgeable expression. Then there was a photo of Lucky walking down Main Street, with her face tipped to the ground like she was fleeing from something. The article alleged that Luciana Raphael was the author who wrote under the pen name of Marena Orellebowl and that she purposely kept her identity hidden to generate intrigue and publicity. The publisher had been contacted but had declined to comment.

The door swung open and Cilla jumped, but it was just a woman wanting to use the restroom. Cilla shoved her phone in her pocket and washed her hands, then dried them with paper towel and walked out. Roger was hovering by the bathroom door, pretending to look at a book, but she had the impression that he was been waiting for her to emerge. She took the elastic hair tie from her wrist and pulled her hair back into a knot. Every sensation seemed to be bothering her as though she had been physically and mentally overwhelmed by what she had read. She could see a young man sitting at a computer, looking around for assistance, so she walked over on autopilot to assist. He was trying to search jobs online, and she helped him navigate onto a job-seeker platform. She felt numb, like the words were coming from her mouth but she had no connection to them. Her mind was racing with thoughts of Lucky and Helen. Was it all true, and if so, why had Lucky kept it a secret from her? She bitterly wished that they were better resourced, as Roger had complained, so that there would be more staff and she could leave for the day and see Lucky. Her lunch break couldn't come quickly enough. Lucky still hadn't responded, and Cilla had a feeling sitting in her gut like a rock that Lucky would be nowhere that she would be able to find her.

As soon as Roger finished his break, Cilla grabbed her things and raced out to the car, thanking her lucky stars that once again she had been running too late to walk to work. Her poor car almost skidded on the damp pavement as she peeled out of the car lot toward Lucky's house, her windshield wipers ineffectively moving around the light drizzle. She hit the usual traffic on Main Street and ducked around through the side streets up to Christopher, wondering how clogged these roads would get once the housing developments were completed and full of new residents. There was only one main road in and out of town to the freeway.

Lucky's house appeared to rise slowly from the misty rain. Cilla could already sense a quietness over the place. The light was on in the front living room, but she felt a heavy dread, much like her childhood fear of going down into the den alone. She parked the car and got out even though it was cold and wet. She unlatched the gate and made her way up the path where weeds were starting to sprout again after Daisy's ruthless tending. There was no barking as she rapped on the door and there were no footsteps hurrying along the hall. She shivered as she stood on the porch with the rain-muffled sounds of afternoon traffic and the drip-dripping of the eaves. She tried the door and found it unlocked. It eased open with a creak, and Cilla called out for Lucky again. There was no answer, so she wiped her feet on the mat and walked into the house, shutting the door behind her. The house seemed to hold its breath along with Cilla as she stood in the entranceway. The grandfather clock in the hall ticked out the seconds for Cilla only. There was no one else in this house who would experience them. Cilla had barely noticed the creaking of the floorboards before, but now her every footfall seemed to cause them agony. She peered into the living room on the left, but of course it was as motionless as a still-life painting so she continued down the hall, peering into rooms along the way to the kitchen at the back of the house. The back door was ajar, and Cilla stopped to watch the tree with its darkened trunk and outstretched arms. She wondered if she stood all day, would she see Lucky materialize like the sun from behind a cloud or a rainbow after a storm? She concentrated as hard as she could, trying to summon Lucky back from where she was, back here to the present, if that's what it was.

Cilla closed the back door but left it unlocked and walked back down the hall. She was about to leave but instead put a hand on the carved banister and began to ascend to the next level. This time at the landing, she went straight over toward the windows where the desk was and looked down at the pile of papers sitting under a glass paperweight. She peeled back the corner of the blank sheet on top and looked at the handwritten words beneath. She read the words "Laura-May had rarely" and let the edge of the paper fall back down. She had read that name countless times before in her favorite series. Feeling like a snoop, she opened the desk drawer and found a bunch of envelopes inside. She remembered handing one just like them to Lucky the other day. The envelope and letter inside it bore the Two Fountains Publishing logo in the top right corner. She pushed the letter back into the envelope without reading it.

Beneath the envelopes were stacks of letter paper with yellow Post-it notes on them, held together with large binder clips—manuscripts sent back for final review before typesetting. Cilla's hand shook as she closed the drawer, and she felt ill as she made her way back through the house to the front door, along the path, and out the gate to her car. She sat for a moment, staring at her hands on the wheel, before she started the ignition.

* * *

It was two full days of buzz around the Highgate Village story breaking, and Cilla felt glad that Lucky wasn't around to be harassed. The press must have worked out where Lucky lived, and there was an inordinate number of cars parked on Lucky's street. Cilla drove past as frequently as she could to make sure no one entered through the unlocked door. She'd considered locking it but was too scared that someone would see her or that Lucky would reappear elsewhere and be locked out. Even the town seemed more populated by strangers than usual. Cilla had called Georgina, who claimed she knew nothing about any of it, and of course Emma was all across the coverage, giving Cilla constant updates. Apart from going to work, Cilla made herself scarce. She didn't want to be part of the gossip. All she wanted was for Lucky to come home, or to be able to peer into a secret portal and talk to her. She had been slowly digesting the fact that her favorite author and her favorite person were one and the same. Missing Lucky felt like a dull ache, and it seemed every little thing reminded her of Lucky. Her fingers itched to tap out a text to Lucky, and Benson had taken up his pound-puppy look again, moping by the door and shooting Cilla pathetic looks. Cilla didn't have a child, but she could understand how parents' hearts broke when their children's did too. Cilla had taken to having imaginary conversations with Lucky like a mad person, telling her about the perfect rose she saw or the funny old man who had spoken to her at the crosswalk. Whether Lucky could hear her, like a spirit in another realm, remained doubtful but not entirely impossible, seeing what Lucky had told her. In her room at night, Cilla had even tried willing herself into the past to see if it was possible, but the only thing that happened was a slight headache from scrunching her scalp too hard. She had finished the physics book and had started to read it again to try to piece it all together.

On the third morning, Cilla woke to a text from Lucky. *I have to tell you something.*

Cilla pushed her pillows back against the headboard and sat up. *I think I already know.*

To which Lucky responded, *Phew, I think.*

Cilla was about to reply when her phone rang in her hand. She lifted it to her ear and said, "Hello?"

It was Lucky. "Do you hate me?"

"Why would I hate you?"

There was a silence, then Lucky said, "Because I disappeared again and I was untruthful about the books. I should have told you when you were telling me about them, I just didn't know what to say. You were so sweet and enthusiastic, and I felt completely silly. I'm used to keeping my cards close to my chest."

Cilla had thought all these things through and more. "I wasn't forthcoming about Georgina initially, so maybe we're even."

"I didn't mean to disappear again. I think I became overwhelmed. This is why you and me…"

"We're not going back to that, are we?" Cilla asked. "I don't care anymore. I accept you as you are." This time the silence was so long that Cilla said, "Are you there?" Benson peered up at her, his tail thumping against the mattress.

"I'm here. Come around after work, we can talk."

"Do you need anything? I can pick you something up from the store."

"Thank you, I'll let you know."

* * *

For once, Cilla wished she didn't work in a library, she was sick of the whole Highgate Village scandal, as it was now being touted. The articles were getting bolder and more ridiculous by the hour, and even though Emma had put a lid on it at Cilla's request, Roger was utterly fascinated as it involved Helen, his latest fixation. Even Penny seemed to have lost some flavor now that he was getting celebrity castoff thrown onto his ego from his association, albeit tentative, with Helen. Closing time could not come around quickly enough, and Cilla waved across the room at Emma and left. She raced to the store and got some essential grocery items, then stopped off to pick up Benson and continued on to Lucky's street, which she found still populated with people hanging around in cars. Cilla drove by Lucky's house without stopping, wondering how she could get in without being accosted by press. She called Lucky from the car. "Is there a way to get in the back door without being seen?"

"Gosh, you normal people are hopeless," Lucky quipped. "Can't you just jump in through another dimension like the rest of us?"

"Wishful thinking. If I jumped, my butt would probably remain behind, no pun intended."

"Not intended but appreciated nonetheless. You could come up through the trees behind the house? It might be a bit of a walk. I'll wait for you by the back door."

Cilla parked the car down farther, and she and Benson walked the long way around, coming up via the walking track through the trees until they found Lucky's land. "How did life get so weird?" Cilla asked Benson, who was not remotely listening because he was getting closer and closer to Peanut. Twilight was seeping all around, the sky melting into peaches and mauves and the stars appearing sharp and bright. Cilla stopped to touch the rough bark of the magic tree on her way past, keenly aware of the skin where her hand had touched the tree as though she had dipped it in warm honey.

Lucky was waiting at the door, her generous mouth cracked into a smile. She held her arms out, and Cilla put the bag of groceries down on the porch and tumbled into them. She could smell wildflowers and woodsmoke in Lucky's hair. Lucky held her close and their bodies melted together. "I missed you," Cilla whispered.

"Thank you for coming. Don't let me leave again. I want to be here with you."

Cilla tightened her grip as though Lucky might vanish in her arms. The only thing that made her loosen her embrace was so she could kiss Lucky, completely forgetting that the whole reason she had snuck in through the backyard was so she could avoid detection. Here they were falling deeper and deeper into the moment until Lucky remembered and pulled Cilla inside. Once inside, Lucky locked the door again and they went through the darkened ground floor to peek through the front curtains at the people sitting in cars, leaning on cars, standing on the sidewalk, smoking, talking, eating. They had camped out for the night.

"All this fuss for me?" Lucky whispered even though no one could hear them.

"As I keep telling you, they are good books! Obviously I'm not the only one who reads them."

Lucky watched a pizza delivery car pull up, then a man get out of a white van and go to the car to collect his pizza. "But they're just books."

"Not to the fans they're not. Surely you know your books do well."

"Isn't that clever?" Lucky said, still watching the pizza exchange. "All I know is that they pay to keep the utilities on and the groceries delivered. That's been my goal because there's not a lot else I can do behind closed doors to earn money. By myself," she added, turning to look at Cilla.

"You'd be surprised these days." Cilla laughed. "There's plenty. In fact, it's probably half the Internet these days."

Lucky looked puzzled. "I know I don't know, but I also know that I might not want to know."

"Yes, that," Cilla said. "Oof, disgusting." A man had unzipped his jeans and was urinating into the gutter. Cilla let her side of the curtain drop. "Bad timing, but are you hungry? I didn't know what you needed so I just brought essentials. Sooner or later you will have to accept that you're famous now."

"My plan is to wait until they go away. It's a theme in my life."

"Lucky," Cilla said firmly. "We are breaking old habits and starting healthier new ones. No more dwelling in the past, and no more hiding from the present. Let's begin with eggs and toast."

"I'm starving," Lucky admitted. "I'm ready to agree with anything if you'll give me food."

Cilla cooked eggs by candlelight, as much because they enjoyed the ambiance as because they didn't want anyone knowing they were there. Cilla loved the feeling that she could say anything and Lucky didn't judge or grow moody. She loved watching Lucky light candles and eat eggs and tell a story. Everything she did seemed so special and Lucky-ish. Cilla realized with a not unpleasant jolt that she was falling in love. She couldn't picture how anyone who beheld Lucky wouldn't fall in love with her. She was a living work of art, so different from anyone Cilla had ever met. To Benson's delight, Cilla did not drag him off home but left him sleeping curled up with Peanut while she disappeared upstairs with Lucky.

* * *

If there was one thing Lucky knew how to do, it was lay low, and the press eventually went away without any fresh material or salacious photos. Cilla was relieved, as coming and going through the bushes like a spy was losing its cloak-and-dagger appeal. Being holed up with Lucky hadn't yet, though. She had known in her bones that Lucky was someone she wouldn't tire of, that she would be endlessly fascinated. She spent half the workday drifting around in a daydream of Lucky, and Benson was happy to play house with Peanut while she was gone. Lucky had time to edit her manuscript that was due to go back to the publisher soon. They had been breathing down Lucky's neck as they wanted to strike while the iron was hot and release the new book while there was a buzz. Presales were already strong. Even realizing that Lucky was a person with deadlines was a stark change of reality for Cilla.

Georgina had tried to meet Cilla for dinner a few times but Cilla had put her off, so Georgina had tried calling and texting to see if Cilla could arrange a meeting with Lucky to negotiate a sale of Lucky's land. Cilla had a feeling Georgina's recent affection toward her had actually been to worm her way closer to Lucky. Cilla thought back to Thanksgiving and felt utter relief.

Lucky finished the book and it hit the shelves with a bang, just in time to be wrapped up and put under the tree for Christmas.

CHAPTER THIRTY-TWO

Cilla leaned against the bar at The Nobody, waiting for the bartender to bring her glasses of champagne for Emma, Pedro the Sex Rower, Lucky, and herself. It was a book launch party for the latest Highgate Village mystery, and Lucky was the guest of honor. On the wall were various pictures of the old grain store that had once occupied the building. Cilla had never paid much attention before, but now she looked with renewed interest. The bartender placed four glasses on the bar and made a show of popping a fresh bottle before pouring the champagne with a confident flourish. Cilla tipped him, and when he moved off to the next customer, Cilla noticed a plaque on the back wall among the grain pictures. She leaned closer and squinted, but it was still blurry and Cilla wasn't sure if it said what she thought it said. Emma popped up beside her, ready to help carry the champagne.

"Emma, can you read that plaque on the wall there?"

Emma pushed her glasses more firmly onto her little nose. "I'm two glasses deep already, but I'll try." She waited for the bartender, who was picking up a bottle of whiskey, to move out of the way. "It says, 'The Saint Nobody, named for Nora Bromwell, who vanished in 1942 and we hope haunts this building to this day with her good deeds.'" Emma turned to look at her and whispered, "Nora."

Cilla felt a chill prickle over her skin. "The general store…it was right next door. It was owned by Aunt Nora's husband, who must be Dudley Bromwell."

The bartender sauntered over and placed his hands on the bar. "Anything else, ladies?"

"No…" Cilla was temporarily lost for words. She remembered seeing Lucky in the shadows on the night of Vince's birthday.

Emma was rarely lost for words herself. "We were reading that plaque behind the bottles. Do you know anything about Nora Bromwell?"

The bartender glanced over his shoulder. "Not really. I think she was a young woman who disappeared and they never found her, but apparently some of the town thought she was a healer who could help people and some thought she was mad as a box of frogs. I guess Theo, who owns this place, chooses to believe she was a healer. Nicer story. It'd be cool if she was a ghost, but I've never seen her."

"Thanks," Emma said. "It is a cool story."

They took the champagne glasses and moved away from the bar to allow other patrons to order drinks.

"Don't say anything to Lucky. This is her special night," Cilla said as they walked back to the table where Lucky was sitting with Pedro. Lucky was looking up into the faces of two excited fans who were talking animatedly. Cilla smiled and placed Lucky's drink on the table as unobtrusively as she could and then stood back to talk to Pedro and Emma. More groups came to talk to Lucky, bringing books for her to sign. Lucky occasionally looked at Cilla for help, but Cilla stood back and smiled, letting The Saint Nobody who had become A Big Somebody deal with the adulation. It was a full-circle moment for Lucky to be in the bar, receiving recognition for her hard work and celebrated for who she was. Cilla could see she was finding the limelight overwhelming, but it was up to Lucky to act for herself—and she did, eventually escaping and coming to stand beside Cilla, who had positioned herself near the table but at a respectable distance. "I'm not used to so many people. What time can we leave?"

"This is your party," Cilla said. "Those people over there came all the way from New Jersey for the book launch. There's a line outside to get in here."

"One woman asked me to autograph a magazine article about it."

Cilla could see the fear in Lucky's eyes and she had an inkling what was driving it. "You're Luciana Raphael, and there's interest in that at the moment. No one has any proof or means to say you're anyone else other than Marena Orellebowl, which is your pen name. It's a sensational story, the mysterious recluse who wrote everything by hand. You created intrigue."

"Inadvertently," Lucky said. "I was trying to do the opposite and remain anonymous."

"There's a buzz around the story but it will die down. You're safe."

Lucky looked at her and Cilla gazed back evenly. After a moment, Lucky smiled sadly and blinked at her in a silent thank-you, and Cilla saw that Lucky felt she understood something deeper about her identity. Cilla was aware of people hovering with books in hand. "Go hide in a bathroom stall for five minutes and take some deep breaths," Cilla said. Lucky stared at her for a second, then nodded once and fled before the next group of fans could besiege her.

* * *

That night, Cilla lay in Lucky's bed up in the turret room, feeling like she had stepped back into another era herself. Lucky lay with her head on the pillow beside her, her hair coiled at the base of her neck, the salmon-pink cusp of her ear lit up by the lamp behind her. Their legs were wrapped together and their fingers intertwined. Cilla brought their hands closer and kissed Lucky's fingertips then returned her hands.

"Look at you," Lucky said. "Did you fall out of the pages of a fairy tale?"

Cilla laughed. "The troll."

"No, no, no," Lucky said. "You're not allowed to say those things anymore. You are the most beautiful woman I've seen in my life, and I'm going to put you in a story."

Cilla blinked back tears stinging at her eyes. She didn't want Lucky to see and think she was a sap. "You are the most beautiful woman who ever existed."

On the nightstand behind Lucky was a stack of books with new covers the publisher had sent that had the author's name in larger type than the title, which Cilla knew was a big deal. She looked at *Marena Orellebowl* written along the spine in thick white letters, and something niggled at her. She read the name again in her mind, and the letters rearranged themselves. She flicked her gaze back to Lucky, who was studying her face like she really was about to describe it in print. "Marena Orellebowl," Cilla said out loud. Lucky's eyes stopped on Cilla's, and Cilla said, "Eleanora Bromwell." Lucky flinched but Cilla held her hands. "Luciana Raphael."

Lucky took a sharp breath. "When did you know?"

"I'm not sure. Tonight at The Nobody I saw the plaque on the wall, and just now I was looking at the spine of a book behind you and the letters of your pen name seemed to stand out to me. Will you tell me now?"

Lucky's eyes traveled Cilla's face, and after a moment she sighed and said, "I will." She untangled her fingers from Cilla's and began to worry the edge of her pillow instead. "Yes, my name was Eleanora—Nora—named after my aunt, who was very special to me. I was born in 1920 but I suppose I've spent only half that time here." Lucky smiled and a sparkle leapt to her eye. "So, I'm at once very old and young. I have seen more things than most people yet at the same time know less than most. I could show you how to start a car with a hand crank or how to knit lace, but I couldn't tell you how to make a purchase over the Internet. To go back to the time that set things in motion, I was a young woman when I got married, only twenty, and looked younger still. I never wanted to marry Dudley, I didn't want to marry anyone. My parents insisted, thinking it would curb my wild ways, but all it did was make me and Dudley miserable to the point that I would disappear into happier times. Dudley thought I was running away from him, and when I tried to explain what I was really doing, he claimed I was a lunatic and went about having me committed. It was an easier out for him to say his wife was mad so he could be rid of her. I wasn't an obedient wife and I had no intention of getting pregnant, so finding creative ways to dodge sex was difficult."

"But couldn't other people see that you weren't crazy?" Cilla asked.

"Oh, yes, those who knew me, but Dudley was an established and respected member of the community. Women were still second-class citizens and essentially a woman belonged to her husband. I knew that, and I never wanted one. It wasn't Dudley's fault. He wasn't a terrible person, just an unimaginative soul who was regimented and had firm beliefs about family and society in general. He wasn't alone in that way of thinking. This was an even smaller town than it is now, don't forget."

"What happened?" Cilla asked. She felt that her mind was alive with so many questions at once, jittering like loose ends waiting to be woven into a tapestry.

"Oh, golly, it's all coming out now, isn't it?" Lucky blinked against a tear and ceased worrying at the pillowcase to begin picking at a fingernail.

Cilla took Lucky's hand in hers again. "I won't tell anyone. You're safe here with me."

Lucky raised the back of her hand to wipe at her eye. "Thank you, I know. Well, I had no intention of being committed to an asylum, so I buried all the money I could find in a jar under the tree in my aunt's garden and disappeared. I stayed sheltered in another dimension of time, lived carefree years of my life over, gone from this plane, as though in a dream. When I returned, I had to be careful not to be spotted. By then Dudley had remarried. I dug up my money from under the old oak tree and caught a ship out to England. My new friends used to call me Lucky because they said I had nine lives, the way I would get out of trouble. We had a magnificent time, and it was total liberation from the way I had been raised. My aunt was the only one who understood. We used to write letters, but even in letters we never openly discussed our condition. After Mira passed away there was nothing there for me, and I returned home. Of course I returned as Lucky because I couldn't return as myself. I continued living with my aunt until she was gone, and my secrets died with her."

"What about your family?"

"That was hard. I had to remain a recluse, because if they had seen me they would have instantly recognized me, even though they had aged and I barely had at all."

Cilla breathed out slowly, trying to order things in her mind. "But what about Mira? Why do you keep going back to that moment? I mean, I get that it was traumatic, but by the sound of what you said, there were a few sudden events that were triggering."

Lucky clasped her hand tighter then let it go and rolled onto her back, staring at the ceiling. The bedside clock ticked out the seconds before Lucky spoke again. "If there was one thing I was never supposed to do, it was have a child. My aunt was firm on that. How could I raise a child? I couldn't, and I didn't. But Mira, when I met her, had a small child, a baby, really. She called her Baby, which seemed fine at the time but I'm not sure if she would have loved it all through life. You have met Daisy, and, well, this is where it gets complicated, but Daisy and Baby were half sisters. Mira was free-spirited and unique and fun to be around, but she was not a stable mother for Baby. She refused to tell Baby's father that he had a child, although it was generally suspected who he was. Instead, she had this well-to-do fellow James something thinking he was Baby's father. Anyway, this had all happened before I met Mira. I thought I could be a second mother to Baby, and I mostly was, but the lifestyle and the people around us weren't healthy for a tiny child. When

Mira vanished I should have stepped in, but I didn't know what to do so I left." Lucky chewed the corner of her lip. "I have never gotten over that. I wrote a letter with no return address to Adrian Bishop letting him know Baby was his daughter because he was a lovely man, he just wasn't flashy like James. It was a terrible, terrible, selfish thing to do. I tried to find Baby but I was never successful. The closest I could get was Daisy, who has been helping me search, but all we learned was that Baby ended up with the well-to-do fellow who was on her birth certificate. No one knows where he went, but Daisy knows she has a suspected half sister out there somewhere. I carry that guilt with me. I should have stayed to look after Baby."

"Nobody puts Baby in a corner." Cilla smiled but Lucky only looked at her blankly. "*Dirty Dancing*. Patrick Sway…never mind."

"Sorry, I think I missed that one."

"We can add it to the list. Never mind. In terms of Baby, it wasn't your situation to fix," Cilla said.

"I should have done better, and try as I might, I can't change the past. I can only learn from it."

"Is there something you can do in the present to make up for the past?"

Lucky blinked up at the ceiling then rolled back to Cilla. "I have been thinking about something. The Highgate Village books are mysteries that were inspired by my London life. I originally wrote them as an outlet, but when they got picked up by Two Fountains Publishing, I realized it was a way to support myself. Now that the royalty checks are becoming larger, I have all this money saved and I've been thinking I would like to give a portion of it over to Baby and Daisy. I know it's just money and it doesn't mend the past, but it might give them more freedom here in the present. If I never find Baby, well, Daisy can have the lot. I certainly don't need much for myself."

Cilla smiled. "I think that would be lovely. I still can't believe that my favorite author was right under my nose this whole time."

"I can't figure out if Helen did me a favor or a disservice by outing me."

Cilla thought about it. "Do you feel freer now? There's nothing to really hide now. No one can prove you're—I can't believe I am saying this—one hundred years old."

"More, actually." Lucky grinned, looking closer to nineteen than one hundred. "Am I a cradle-snatcher or what?"

"I'd find it difficult to get in and out of a cradle at this age, although soon I may have as many teeth left as an infant."

Lucky kissed her. "I'll always think you're beautiful, even when you're ancient and toothless."

Cilla's heart expanded. "Oh, I hope you stay. Don't go and be lost to me again."

"I'm trying my best to stay here with you. I don't want to go anywhere, I'm so tired from jumping in and out of life. I want to focus on this life here with you."

CHAPTER THIRTY-THREE

It was Saturday morning, and Cilla and Benson had slept at Lucky's place. Despite being up half the night, tangled with Lucky like the ivy around the lamppost out front, Cilla was determined to keep up her morning jogs. She pulled on her sweats, dragged a comb through her hair, and went downstairs to where Lucky was clanging around in the kitchen, suddenly possessed by a desire to make pancakes. Benson and Peanut were hovering by the stove like furry vacuum cleaners on standby. Seeing Cilla in her running gear, Benson looked torn; food and walks were his two favorite things.

"I'll take the dogs," Cilla said, deciding for him. As soon as the words left her mouth there was a knock at the door, creating a more insistent priority, and the dogs skedaddled across the tiles and out into the hall, barking.

Lucky looked at Cilla and Cilla frowned, remembering when Georgina had shown up unannounced. She dimly registered that Lucky had flour on her cheek, but Lucky had already started for the door and Cilla followed close behind, ready to tell Georgina to leave them alone. Instead, when Lucky opened the door, it was Helen standing on the porch, clutching a manila folder. Cilla's first thought was that Helen was now working with Georgina and had come to harass Lucky in her place, but she instantly dismissed it. She also wondered if Helen wanted to take photos of Lucky's house or write more gossip. She sternly told Benson to come back when he went to greet Helen. He didn't know that she was a traitor who had sold Lucky down the river for five minutes of self-promotion for her book.

"What is it, Helen?" Lucky said.

If Helen was surprised to see Cilla there, she didn't show it.

"I know you probably hate me right now, but I think it's time I cleared up a few things."

Cilla hadn't forgiven Helen, and she thought, *Right now, at this very moment, someone hates Helen.* Then she immediately felt mean.

"You can clear up your things out here," Lucky said, not moving from where she stood in the doorway, righteous despite the flour streaked on her face.

"R-right," Helen stuttered, and Cilla noticed how frazzled she looked despite her impeccable clothes, which once again reminded Cilla of Georgina. Helen opened up the folder, her hand shaking, and drew out a piece of paper. When she held it out to Lucky, Cilla realized it was a large photograph. "Please," Helen said when Lucky didn't move to take it.

Lucky sighed and took the photo, and Cilla moved closer to discreetly look over her shoulder. "I don't have my glasses. Is this some ghastly photo you've taken of me to sell to the press?"

"N-no."

The colors of the image were washed out, but it was a photo taken of a group of people sitting in a room that had wallpaper patterned in brown and orange flowers that looked like it would have been fashionable in the sixties or seventies. There were seven people: three women, three men, and a toddler. Cilla did a double take, because sitting cross-legged on the white-carpeted floor with a guitar on her lap was Lucky.

Lucky held the photo at arm's length, then closer, then back out again, and blinked at it. After a moment, she said, "How did you get this?"

Helen was pale and her eyes looked watery. "From my father."

"Wha…" Lucky looked back at the photo.

"James Buchanan."

Lucky looked back up at Helen then back at the photo. "That's me and that's Mira." She tapped a finger on a fair-haired woman sitting beside her, holding a tall glass. "And Baby. Oh, look at her. Yes…James, I had forgotten his last name, but Buchanan could be it. That's him."

Helen came to stand beside Lucky and pointed to the fair-haired toddler standing beside James. "And that's me."

Lucky looked at her, and said, "That's Baby. That's…" She trailed off, still looking at Helen.

Cilla looked from the grainy photo back to Helen, but she was confused. She put an arm around Lucky's waist.

"Do you need to sit down?" Helen asked Lucky, although she didn't look too stable herself.

Lucky said, "I think I might."

They walked over to the sofa on the porch, the dogs trailing along, uncertain what was going on and whether a run was still in the cards. Cilla and Helen sat down either side of Lucky, who was still clutching the photo.

"But this photo…I don't understand," Lucky said.

"Here, try mine." Helen opened her purse and pulled out a glasses case and opened it.

Lucky put the glasses on and looked again. "But I know these people."

"And that is me," Helen said again. "When I was a baby."

"That's Baby."

"Also known as Helen."

Lucky took the glasses off, placed the photo down, and looked at Helen. "Mira's daughter?"

"Apparently."

Cilla's own pulse was racing and her mouth was dry. "How did you become Helen, and how did you find Lucky?"

"I grew up knowing next to nothing about my mother, all I knew was that her name was Mira, she was British like my father, and she was dead. I grew up in Chicago with my dad, James, and my stepmother, Audrey. It wasn't until Dad had health complications that I realized he wasn't my father at all and started to wonder who I was and where I came from. I knew Dad came to the States for work when I was a baby and then he met Audrey, and that's about it." Helen glanced back at the photo. "I went rifling through everything from Dad's past, including old photos."

"I think I might know who your father is," Lucky said. "If you want to know his name I will tell you, however, please bear in mind that I'm only going by what Mira told me in confidence."

"You do know?"

Lucky nodded, her eyes heavy. "I have an idea, and I can tell you what I know."

"Can I ask you something first?" Helen looked like she might cry.

"You can ask."

"Why did you leave me? Why didn't you take me with you?" Helen blinked and a tear wobbled. Cilla didn't know what to do, but Lucky reached to squeeze Helen's hand.

"I couldn't, and I knew you would be safe with James."

"But he wasn't my father." A whine had crept into Helen's voice, and Cilla was reminded that there was a small child in Helen who had been carrying this confusion around.

"And I wasn't your mother. James had money, and he was who Mira chose as your father. It wasn't my business." A tear fell down Helen's cheek and Lucky rubbed her own eye. "I'm sorry. I've always felt bad about it. If only you knew how it has tormented me all these years. I can't change the past, but I can tell you now."

Helen sniffed and tilted her face away as though ashamed of her tears. Lucky moved her hand to rest between Helen's shoulder blades and craned forward to see her face.

Cilla stood up. "I should let you two have some privacy."
Lucky took her hand. "Stay. I don't have any secrets from
you. Is that okay, Helen?"

Helen nodded but didn't look up. Cilla sat back down
uneasily.

"Helen, the way I heard it, your father's name is Adrian
Bishop, and if that's true, you have a half-sister. Her name is
Daisy and she is remarkable woman, only a couple of years
younger than you. In fact, you've met her."

"When?" Helen asked, looking up sharply.

"At the reading you gave at the library. She bought your
book."

Helen's face had been transformed by emotion and she
barely resembled the cool, clever woman who had delivered a
talk at the library.

"She lives here too?" Helen asked, then looked at Cilla as
though it might be her.

"No, unfortunately, she lives in London, but she was visiting
me here. We reconnected through her father—well, your father,
too. She's been wondering about you."

"About me?"

Lucky nodded. "I'll speak to Daisy, but I'm sure she will
want to connect with you if you're willing."

Helen's expression took on some hope. "I would love that. I
can scarcely believe it."

Lucky clasped her hands together. "I read the article you
wrote about me, and I've been wondering why you wrote it and
how you found me."

Helen said, "I wanted to find this mysterious woman who
apparently was like a mother to me. Any connection to who I
actually am and where I come from seems like gold dust. When
I read the Highgate Village Mysteries I fell in love with the
characters and the stories, but there was something else that held
me when I read the books—there was a striking similarity to my
own life. I can't explain it, but the characters and the dynamics
were so similar to what I knew, and Morgan reminds me so
much of what I had heard about my mother that I couldn't get

it out of my mind. At the very least I wanted to know who was behind it all. I went to my publisher and asked them what they knew, which wasn't much at all, but through my connections I did some digging into Two Fountains Publishing and this mysterious author, who apparently was a recluse in Twine River. Ask anyone around here and they will tell you who the town's eccentric recluse is. As soon as I saw you, I recognized you from my father's old photos that had my mother in them. You haven't aged a bit. I came to Twine River to get a glimpse of you myself. The town is so charming, and seeing you made me feel like I was connecting with my past. Then I met Georgina when I started house hunting, and it turns out we have a friend of a friend in common. I wanted to put some distance between myself and Chicago, so I decided to make some changes." Helen took a breath, cleared her throat, and looked from Cilla to Lucky. "I'm sorry about that article, but I guess I was angry that for so long I lived under a shroud of other people's lies that I wanted to lift it off and let the truth be told, at least about this. I know it wasn't mine to tell, but that's journalism. Georgina said it would be great publicity for the both of us, and truly, she hasn't been wrong."

Cilla stood up again. She didn't want to hear any more about Georgina. She touched the crown of Lucky's head and Lucky looked up at her. "I am going to go for that run with the dogs. You two have a chat and I will be back later. Goodbye, Helen. I'll see you again soon. You have a lot to process, I'm sure."

Helen looked up at her and smiled sadly. Color had returned to her face, and she looked much more Helen-like.

* * *

Cilla's mind was reeling as she jogged off down the street, happy to leave the intense conversation behind. She wondered how long Helen had known about Lucky. Up ahead, the dogs bounced along, silly and unaware of the revelations at Christopher Street. Cilla wanted to be temporarily unaware too. She put a playlist on and tried to lose herself in keeping her breath regular and her pace consistent. Her thoughts kept intruding, however, and then when they got to the park she wasn't concentrating and Benson splashed into the river after a bird and Cilla had to call him five times before he acknowledged her. She got back to it and struggled through another lap of the park before calling it quits and jogging back home to give Benson a bath before she would let him back inside Lucky's house. By the time she finished blow-drying Benson's blond mane, it was lunchtime and Peanut had resigned himself to waiting by the front door in case anyone should try to give him a bath. Cilla walked back to Lucky's with the dogs on a leash so Benson wouldn't roll in anything disgusting and undo her hard work. By the time she got to Lucky's, Helen had left and Lucky was upstairs, writing at her desk. Cilla paused in the doorway to watch her surrounded by her antique things, like looking back into another time. Lucky must have heard her because she turned. They just looked at one another for a moment, Cilla in her gym gear and Lucky with her fountain pen, like two eras about to collide. After a long moment, Lucky stood up and Cilla went to hug her.

"Sorry, I'm all sweaty."

"I don't care. I wanted you to stay."

Cilla kissed her temple. "I wanted to stay but it was between you and Helen. How did it go?"

Lucky let go of Cilla. She pursed her lips and looked back down at the notebook she had been writing on. "I'm writing my thoughts down to straighten them out in my head." She frowned at her curling scribbles. "Although if I can decipher my own writing, it will be a miracle."

"Does it feel like Helen is the missing piece of the puzzle for you and Daisy?"

"I realize now there was something inside of me that I didn't know I was carrying. I feel lighter. Things will always be hazy because half of my present has been the past, but I hope now I can let that moment go. Daisy's gone and Baby is no longer frozen in time as a helpless child. She was loved, cared for, and grew up to be Helen. An author like me!" Lucky laughed, which quickly turned shaky, and Cilla drew her back into a fierce hug.

"Who knew Twine River was so exciting? I only moved here so there would be room for a dog and because they were looking for a librarian, but it's like *Days of Our Lives* out here."

Lucky's sobs turned back to laughter, her body bumping against Cilla's. "I don't know what that is."

"After we finish watching *Dirty Dancing*, we can watch an episode. I'll tell you what I know, which is limited. Suffice to say it's a soap opera—you do know what that is, don't you?—where not much time passes but lots of drama occurs."

"Sounds like my life," Lucky said and laughed.

Cilla laughed too and held her even tighter. "Oh, I love your life."

"I think I'm done now. Done traveling. Mira is gone and I know that Baby is okay. I want to be here with you."

CHAPTER THIRTY-FOUR

Cilla stopped her car at the traffic light and glanced down at the piece of paper with Lucky's handwriting, marveling that this same flowery lettering had written each and every word of her favorite books. Lucky had doodled two dogs trotting over a rainbow in the corner. Cilla felt her heart expand with love. The paper was held loosely in Lucky's hand on her lap in the passenger seat as they drove.

"Cilla," Lucky said calmly.

Cilla looked up and noticed the light had gone green. "Crap, thank you." She glanced in the rearview mirror as she took off into the intersection.

"Everything is so different," Lucky said, her eyes transfixed like a child on the changing scenery. "None of these houses were here, it was just fields and trees. I can't imagine the falls themselves have changed much."

Cilla tried to picture what it was like for Lucky, losing chunks of time and seeing the landscape unrecognizable. "When was the last time you were there?" Cilla noted a sign up ahead directing them to Singing Falls Park.

Lucky saw the sign too. "Well, it wasn't a park then. You had to fight your way through vegetation along an infrequently used path. When I was a girl, we had an old dog called Pepper who used to be game for any exploit I had in mind. He used to come with me and saved me more than once from stepping where I shouldn't."

"I'm no Pepper, but I hope I can keep up. Maybe with less panting. Although, who knows?"

Lucky laughed. "You'll receive no judgment from me. The only exercise I've done is pulling weeds and lugging a vacuum cleaner up and down the stairs."

"Time to break those shoes in."

Lucky looked down at her feet and tapped her new sneakers together. "I feel so bouncy."

Cilla smiled at the memory of Lucky trying on sneakers at the mall. It had been a short trip as soon as the mall opened so there were fewer customers. Lucky had walked slowly, her head swiveling, trying to catch everything. She had remarked that even accounting for all she'd seen, the fashions had changed and the lights were so bright, and why was every surface so white it hurt your eyeballs? Cilla didn't have answers for her questions, nor did she think the mall was the best place to gauge societal development, so here they were, off on another adventure. They had been to the portrait gallery, which seemed less abrasive, and now they were going to walk the Singing Falls trail because Cilla had never been and now maybe Lucky could show *her* around.

A misty drizzle had started to fall as they parked the car and stepped outside into the parking lot. Cars were parked here and there but there was no one around. Everything smelled of rain, and the damp air clung to their clothes and curled Cilla's hair. Lucky wore a dark-green baseball cap, and Cilla couldn't get enough of looking at her fine features under the curved brim. She had cut her hair short, and it curled up at the base of her neck.

Lucky caught her looking and laughed. "If you think I look silly now, you should see the pillbox hat I used to wear. Back then I thought I looked wonderful."

"I was actually thinking that you look great in anything. You look cool in the baseball cap. It suits you."

Lucky looked around to make sure they were alone, took Cilla's face by the cheeks, and kissed her sideways so they wouldn't bump hat brims. "Not as cool as you."

Cilla took Lucky's hand and they set off for the trail.

"None of these signs were here and certainly no restrooms," Lucky said.

The ground was slick and the trees were silent under the heavy sky. Birds still sung out to one another overhead, and off in the distance Cilla thought she could make out the sound of rushing water. As they walked, Lucky reached to caress the textures of varying leaves and stopped to look at insects on branches. The drizzle stopped, leaving the air close and everything shiny and damp. With Lucky at her side, everything felt magical and new.

Cilla twirled the end of a leaf in her cold red fingers as she walked. "It must have been hard finding your way through the forest. Everything looks the same."

"I knew if I got really lost I could find the river and follow it back. And there was Pepper, remember? He was a stout old thing and knew what time his dinner was. There was no way he'd be kept out too late."

"Pepper is sounding more and more like me. I think I am your new Pepper."

Lucky squeezed Cilla's elbow. "Do you like your ears being stroked too?"

Cilla scrunched her nose up. "Not particularly. You can rub my neck anytime, though."

Lucky stopped in her tracks. "Can you hear that?"

Cilla held her breath to listen. There was a distant roar of moving water. "Yes, let's go."

They picked up their pace, pushing at the young sinewy foliage that was reaching over the trail. They rounded a bend and jumped in fright as they almost collided with a man and woman coming back the other way. Both groups laughed a greeting, and Cilla and Lucky found the wooden stairs, darkened and soggy with rain, leading to the lookout high above, the view of trees giving way to a cliff face of thundering water. The roar was deafening, and Cilla and Lucky clutched hands again, picking their way up the stairs to the lookout point. Overhead, the dense foliage was replaced with a lake of gray sky, and down below was a churning black pool, frothing white where the water pummeled it. The air was thick with river water and the smell of decaying leaves and bark. Cilla could feel the exhilarating power of the water crashing. They let go of their hands to clutch the railing and let the sensations and sights envelop them. The air was cold, but Cilla was warm beneath her clothes. She was grateful that they had the spot to themselves in this sacred space. She was smiling so hard she felt her cheeks like ripe plums that would burst at any moment. She looked over at Lucky, but Lucky had a tear on her cheek.

"Lucky, what's wrong?"

Lucky wiped the tear away with her fingertips. "Nothing. It's beautiful here with you. I'm just thinking of the strange life I've had and how I've spent it avoiding the present, afraid of what it could be when all along it is unexpected and wonderful. It's an unlimited feeling standing here with the water crashing down to form the river it came from again. It's a reminder to me that energy can never die, only transform, and all the fear I was holding on to was a false sense of control."

Cilla thought over what Lucky had said before responding, watching the clouds crack apart, letting down a ray of light that hit the aura of mist around the waterfall, creating an iridescent rainbow. "You've had an incredible life which you've navigated with grace, and I think you're absolutely right, in my experience, the need for control is human nature, but the joke is that once you relinquish it, things fall perfectly into place. It's taken me a long time to see that too." She took a long breath of forest air. "Nature has a way of putting things into perspective. Nothing is that important. Come here." She drew Lucky into a hug, with Lucky's wet cheek pressed against hers.

When they pulled apart, they looked back at the light show the sun and the cascading water was putting on. "Selfie?" Lucky asked.

Cilla burst out laughing. "Don't tell me I've created a modern-day monster. Okay, let's do it."

Lucky fished her phone from her pocket. "What do I do again? Remember, I'm very old. You have to show me."

Cilla instructed her how to hold the phone and they angled it to get the rainbow over the falls into the shot. After they had taken it, they looked at the picture. Cilla was grinning like an idiot and Lucky had a damp spot under her eye from her tears, but it was a lovely photo. Their first photo, Cilla realized.

They heard voices, and the next minute a group of teenagers' heads appeared climbing the steps. Lucky and Cilla looked at one another, and without a word Lucky put her phone in her pocket and they both began the return walk to the car.

"The boys would have loved that," Lucky said, meaning Benson and Peanut.

"We can take them for a walk later."

Cilla didn't worry about Benson when he was at home with Peanut. She reflected that she and Lucky had spent almost every minute of the past two weeks together, apart from when Cilla was working, and all she felt was more and more love for Lucky. So far, Lucky had stayed put, despite kicking the gin and citrus habit. In fact, she said she couldn't look at a gin and tonic or a lemon for a long time.

As they drove, they passed houses already decked out for Christmas, reminding Cilla that she hadn't made any plans with her family. Part of her had been holding out, unsure if Lucky would be alone and would want to be with her for the holidays. She'd thought of inviting Lucky to come, but after all the years of Georgina's excuses for family gatherings, Cilla was hesitant. She let the thought go.

Back at Cilla's house, she made sure Lucky was comfortable on the sofa with a throw blanket and the heater on, then went to collect the microwave popcorn from the kitchen. Her trusty microwave hadn't had much use lately.

Back in the living room, she handed Lucky the television remote and said, "Go for it."

Lucky looked at it for a long moment and then pressed the power button. Cilla instructed her how to find *Dirty Dancing* on the streaming service.

"See?" Cilla said. "The main character is called Baby too."

Cilla had seen the movie a few times over the years. The blond dancer, Penny, had a touch of the Georgina about her but Cilla was okay with it. She was preoccupied with surreptitiously watching Lucky instead. Lucky, who had barely watched television since the 1970s, was captivated. Her mouth was silently moving and her eyes were like saucers. When the credits finally rolled, it was as though she came to life again. She turned to Cilla like an imploring child. "I used to love dancing."

Cilla laughed. "Put it on the list. There has to be somewhere to go out dancing around here."

"Yes!" Lucky squeezed her hands in and out of fists. "I think I was gripping the throw really hard."

"You're funny. What time are we meeting Georgina and Helen in the morning?"

"At ten. Georgina said she'll bring the contracts."

Lucky had decided to buy the land surrounding her property so no one would encroach on her or ask her to sell her property again, and Cilla was going to put in too. Helen had been instrumental in getting Georgina to drop the idea of acquiring Lucky's property, but through Lucky's purchase instead, she'd hit her targets anyway.

"You're going to have your own oasis among the suburban jungle."

Lucky leaned back against the couch cushions and put her hands behind her head. "I can thank Helen for all the attention my books have received. They are all back on the charts."

"You watch, Hollywood will be calling soon, wanting to make them into movies and television series. I had to order more at the library because the wait lists to borrow are so long."

"Thanks for the extra sales." Lucky laughed. "I can't believe I'm a person who thinks about sales now. I only ever wrote the books to put some order to my thoughts and keep myself in bread and milk. I did get some curious looks from the staff at the bank the other day."

Cilla nudged Lucky's knee with her own. "Next, you can conquer the world of online banking."

"Remember I did those self-serve checkout things at the big store in Winnerly the other day? But I didn't really care for it. I like to say hello to a person."

Cilla laughed at the memory of Lucky's surprise when the checkout's robotic voice spoke back to her. "How could I forget?"

Lucky sat back up and leaned closer to Cilla. "I've been thinking about something."

"Yes?" Cilla wondered what else Lucky could possibly make happen.

"I haven't met your family, unless you count Georgina."

"I don't."

Lucky smiled. "Okay. Well, I'm pretty keen on the idea of meeting your parents and Deb and the children, and, well…"

"Sure, I'd love for you to meet them. They would adore you, and Deb has read all your books. I know because I kept giving them to her on her birthdays."

Lucky looked relieved. "I was thinking maybe they could come to my place for Christmas. There's loads of room, and I have old boxes of decorations in the attic that are begging to be enjoyed. And there's the magic tree that we can decorate with lights. The kids would love it because it is especially magical and wish-granting at Christmastime."

Cilla thought she might burst with joy. "We could ask. I think Mom was going to make her usual Christmas dinner but they might be able to make the trip down with Deb and Bryce instead."

"There's a sled around somewhere too. If it snows, the kids can take it out on the hill."

"Your hill."

"*Our* hill. Or it will be after about ten o'clock tomorrow."

Cilla smiled. "I'm not sure how I ended up here. Everyone seems to be doing incredible things, particularly you, and I'm just the same person."

Lucky ran her eyes all over Cilla as though drinking her in. "You," she said, "are exactly the same person, and I am eternally grateful for it. You were, and are, the lighthouse in a storm. I have never met anyone who makes me feel as loved and seen and safe. You're my best friend, and you give others the strength to be themselves. You are amazing."

Cilla was slowly getting used to Lucky's affection but it still made her feel bashful. She changed the subject. "Dad loves to play cards. Even though my card-playing skills have brought the family into disrepute, don't go into a game of poker with Dad unawares."

Lucky smiled. "You think they might come?"

"Let's call them together."

"Do they know about me?"

"Of course they do," Cilla said truthfully. "Mom said she's never met anyone famous before." Cilla grinned, and Lucky slapped her arm playfully.

"Stop it."

"She did." Cilla nodded earnestly.

CHAPTER THIRTY-FIVE

Even though Lucky had come up with the idea, Cilla worried that she would be overwhelmed by a house full of people for several days. Cilla needn't have worried, though. Lucky was welcoming and warm and kind and made a fuss of the children, finding old curiosities from the attic for them to play with such as dolls and tin soldiers and trains. Deb marveled that the kids hadn't asked to play online games once. Cilla and Lucky had decorated the outside of the house with strands of holly and ivy, and Cilla had introduced Lucky to the wonder of solar-powered LED lighting, which they had wrapped around the oak tree. The inside of the house glowed warmly with candles in lanterns, and they had decorated the house with Lucky's aunt's beautiful old wooden and glass ornaments. Lucky had made up a downstairs bedroom for Patty and Don so they wouldn't have to go up and down the stairs. It hadn't taken Patty long to recover from meeting a famous person, and it made Cilla's head swim to think that Lucky had been born before her mother. That part was her and Lucky's secret. Patty loved looking at Lucky's paintings and photos. Don and Lucky bonded over card games and because Lucky didn't give a hoot that he smoked cigars in the living room, which Patty never let him do at home.

On Christmas Eve, Lucky generously opened her hospitality up to not only Georgina and Helen but also Emma and Pedro. Cilla had drawn the line at Roger, even though it was sweet of Lucky to suggest it. They all sat in the living room by the fire, eating snacks and drinking wine while the kids raced around excitedly, full of pre-Santa adrenaline.

"You know what we should do?" Lucky said, clapping her hands as the kids came thundering in. She paused dramatically while everyone waited for her to say more. "Go outside to the magic tree and make a wish."

"Yessshhh!" Jacob shrieked, and Winnie asked, "Will it come true?"

"It will if your wish is honorable," Lucky said. "And you know what I'm going to do to personally guarantee it?"

"What?" Winnie asked.

"I'm going to tell you all my wish, and when you hear what my wish is and that it's come true, you'll know yours will too."

"I thought wishes don't come true if you tell them?" Winne said.

"It will for me this time because I'm an expert wish-maker with my very own wishing tree. Now, what do you say?" Lucky looked at Helen.

Georgina said, "Are you going to tell us what your wish is?"

"At the tree I will."

"All right," Don said, easing himself up out of the chair. "Jackets on, kids."

There was clatter and chatter by the back door as they pulled on jackets and shoes and made their way out, the dogs bursting through first. The tree was pretty in her Christmas attire, and the lights added a warmth to the freezing garden.

"All right," Lucky announced, placing her hands on the tree trunk as everyone looked on. "Oh, Magic Tree, I am so grateful for the oxygen you give and the shade in summer and your strength and beauty. My wish tonight is for a white Christmas so we can go sledding."

"Yay!" Winnie said.

Lucky turned to them and smiled. "Who's next? You can just think your wish or say it softly to yourself."

"Me!" Jacob said, putting his hand up.

They all took turns one by one, even Georgina, who passed her wineglass to Cilla to hold, and Don, who had the pursed lips of intense concentration as he approached the tree, the words silently forming as he closed his eyes and pressed his hands to the trunk. Cilla went last. She wasn't sure what to wish for. She felt so happy, which made her think back to Georgina's criteria for happiness: a goal, money in the bank, and a woman in her bed. Cilla wasn't sure if that was her definition of happiness, but looking at the people around her she could only feel overwhelming love, so she pressed her hands against the cold bark and wished that the love she felt would touch everyone present and keep on going and going. She wasn't sure if she was getting caught up in the moment, but the bark seemed to grow warm beneath her palms and tingle pleasantly. She silently thanked the tree, and they all went inside.

* * *

The children had hung stockings up on the mantel over the fireplace, and last night Cilla had added some candy on top of what was already in there when she went to bed. Her first thought upon opening her eyes was how dark it still was and whether the kids had gotten up to check if Santa Claus had visited in the night. Lucky was already awake, watching Cilla get her bearings. She smiled and reached for Cilla beneath the bed covers.

"Do you hear that?" Lucky asked.

Cilla listened but couldn't hear anything. "No?"

Lucky scrunched her nose up and grinned. "Exactly. And you know what that means?"

Cilla shook her head. "No."

"Come on, up. Just for a moment."

Cilla pulled tighter into the shape she was curled up in. "It's freezing."

Lucky ruthlessly peeled the covers back. "Come."

Cilla let herself be led to the window, and the dogs looked up from where they lay curled together on a bed in the corner, Benson's lip smooshed into the side like a goofball. Cilla couldn't wait to put him in his elf costume.

Lucky drew back the curtains to let in the watery dawn light. Cilla looked beyond the frosted edges of glass to the day outside, leaning one shoulder into Lucky as they watched delicate snowflakes flutter down.

They took the scene in for a moment and then made their way back to bed where they wrapped themselves around each other to get warm again. Lucky didn't have to say anything, but Cilla knew how excited the kids would be. She pictured Georgina's face too, looking outside her townhouse window. Cilla kissed Lucky and then they lay there, talking in whispers until the footfalls of the children racing down the stairs rang out, signaling the day was underway.

"Lucky," Cilla said. "I'm pretty sure right now, in this very moment, someone's Christmas wish is coming true."

"And I'm pretty sure it's not just one wish coming true today." Lucky leaned forward and kissed Cilla.

As Cilla felt Lucky's lips on hers, she was happy to know that Lucky was, and always would be, the last woman she kissed.

Bella Books, Inc.
Happy Endings Live Here
P.O. Box 10543
Tallahassee, FL 32302
Phone: (850) 576-2370
www.BellaBooks.com

More Titles from Bella Books

Hunter's Revenge – Gerri Hill
978-1-64247-447-3 | 276 pgs | paperback: $18.95 | eBook: $9.99
Tori Hunter is back! Don't miss this final chapter in the acclaimed
Tori Hunter series.

Integrity – E. J. Noyes
978-1-64247-465-7 | 28 pgs | paperback: $19.95 | eBook: $9.99
It was supposed to be an ordinary workday...

The Order – TJ O'Shea
978-1-64247-378-0 | 396 pgs | paperback: $19.95 | eBook: $9.99
For two women the battle between new love and old loyalty may prove
more dangerous than the war they're trying to survive.

Under the Stars with You – Jaime Clevenger
978-1-64247-439-8 | 302 pgs | paperback: $19.95 | eBook: $9.99
Sometimes believing in love is the first step. And sometimes it's all
about trusting the stars.

The Missing Piece – Kat Jackson
978-1-64247-445-9 | 250 pgs | paperback: $18.95 | eBook: $9.99
Renee's world collides with possibility and the past, setting off a tidal
wave of changes she could have never predicted.

An Acquired Taste – Cheri Ritz
978-1-64247-462-6 | 206 pgs | paperback: $17.95 | eBook: $9.99
Can Elle and Ashley stand the heat in the *Celebrity Cook Off* kitchen?

9 781642 475852